Whistler wipes his eyes, then reaches for his bag. We move from the center of the sidewalk, and lean against the brick building, just feet from Zenovia's storefront window. He produces his tablet, and clicks on the photos app.

He calls up a high-quality image of Zenovia, entering an office building.

"How'd you get this?"

"I followed her," he says, with the glint of a smile.

"Whistler," I say, careful not to scold him with too much force. Had I not just acted like the mortified, exposed junkie that I am, I'd be much harder on him now. "I told you. No field-work without me. I haven't trained you yet. You're not ready. But let me see."

ACKNOWLEDGEMENTS

This book is dedicated to all the first responders and medical professionals doing all they can to help ensure our health and safety during the COVID-19 crisis.

Special thanks to John French, Don Philbrick, and Raphael Sutton, who gave me critical feedback on the manuscript, and to Aaron Rosenberg, for being the layout master.

— AN ANGELA HARDWICKE MYSTERY —

CRACKLE AND FIRE

RUSS COLCHAMIRO

CRAZY 8 PRESS

OTHER WORKS BY RUSS COLCHAMIRO:

NOVELS:
The Finders Keepers Trilogy:
Finders Keepers
Genius de Milo
Astropalooza

Crossline

ANTHOLOGIES:
Love, Murder & Mayhem
Murder in Montague Falls

AUTHOR'S NOTE

Although I started it long before, *Crackle and Fire* was completed while on lockdown due to the COVID-19 pandemic. It's a strange time to be an author and, of course, an even stranger time to be a resident of this planet. During the earliest days of the crisis I was, like so many of us, filled with fear, anger, frustration, confusion, and the stunning sense of overwhelm about just how quickly all of our lives changed, and how dramatically it all happened.

Unsure what to do with those jumbled emotions, I did what writers do. I wrote something new. So in the back of this book you'll find a bonus Angela Hardwicke Sci-Fi mystery, "The Case of Jarlo's Buried Treasure." It takes place after the events of *Crackle and Fire.*

Angela is out there doing the best she can, in a world that seems ever more mysterious to her with every case she takes. I know the feeling. She may not have all the answers, but she's asking the questions.

In fact, another case just landed on her desk. Which means it's time to start writing again. Because as strange as these days might be, the Angela Hardwicke mysteries aren't going to uncover themselves.

Thanks and best wishes that everyone is safe and healthy.

Russ
June 2020

PART I:
RED MOON RISING

CHAPTER 1

Friday night cases are the worst. Especially in E-town.

They never start well, go well, or end well. But I took the meeting anyway. Why?

Because withdrawal is a bitch. And withdrawing from *dRops* is a bitch with spiked heels, an axe to grind, and a fully loaded K71 plasma shell shotgun, double barrel.

Work is the best way to keep me occupied, to let the urges pass.

Only, when you're a private eye like me, taking cases in E-Town—the core city in Eternity, the cosmic realm responsible for the design, creation, and maintenance of the Universe—you never know where the investigation will take you.

On-realm… or off.

"Miss Hardwicke," Gil Habersau starts, barely above a whisper. "You're good at finding people, right?" Skittish, he looks side to side, then leans lower and closer across the table, hunching his shoulders. "And being discreet?"

"You mean, like handing me a stack of cash, literally under the table?"

He retracts the envelope he didn't think I knew about and slips it back into his breast pocket. His sad puppy dog eyes give away more than he realizes.

"Yeah, okay," he says as rock music thrums over the constant chatter. The pub is busy, a candle on each table. "I just… you know… can't take any chances."

I knock back the rest of my Scotch. I'm Jonesing for another. The fog was so thick when I walked over here I could barely see a foot in front of me. "When did he go missing?"

"About a week ago, maybe longer," he says, clearly out of his element, acting the way he thinks this is supposed to go down. "But I can't bring just anyone into this. I need to know—"

"You came to *me*, Mr. Habersau."

"Gil," he says, cutting me off. "Call me Gil." He breathes deep, exhales, then fumbles his beer. "Sorry, sorry." He wipes off the table with the side of his hand, shakes it out. "I'm a little nervous. I don't know how to do this."

"Easy, Gil. One step at a time. Tell me about your guy. What's his name?"

"Arthur. Hanson."

I gesture to the waitress to bring me another drink. "And you work where? Accounting?"

"Y-yes, yeah. Breslin, Anders & Li. We rep luxury airship companies and other hospitality corporations. We nearly tripled in size since Astropalooza."

Astropalooza. The celebration of the Universe.

Comets ripping across the sky. Constellations changing shape. Pulsing nebulas. Wormholes. Hot air balloons. Galaxy cruisers. Drinks, music. A party across the realm.

"Nobody can keep their accounts straight. I've been there about two years. They just put me in charge of the interns. Everything was fine, business as usual. Well, usual for E-Town. And then we got this new guy."

"Hanson," I say.

"Right. Hanson. He's older for an intern, but it happens all the time. People change careers. It's mostly clerical work to start. He'd only been there a month or so when we had an internal issue. All hands on deck."

"What issue?"

Gil hesitates before answering. He's young, late twenties, with grey slacks, blue blazer, and a white pocket square he's hoping looks more dapper than it does. He's only average height, maybe five-foot-eight or so, but he's thick, with arching shoulders and stubby hands. And despite having an outsized, oval head, he squints a lot, afraid to look right at me.

"A major account went sideways. Everybody had to work on it. But it was too high-level for the interns, so I gave them busy work. We have this new file-sharing system. I had them input data. Figured it would keep them out of trouble. But days turned into weeks. We were all working round-the-clock. By the time I checked back, Hanson was gone. And some of the files he worked on."

"I'm assuming they're valuable? Sensitive?"

"You have no idea."

"I'd have a better idea if you told me."

"I can't. Client confidentiality. You know how it goes."

"Everybody's got secrets. So you want me to do what, exactly?"

"Find him!" he threatens, revealing his inner bulldog. He went there fast. "Sorry. I just... need you to find him."

"I already used my supa dupa private eye powers to deduce that part. But say I find him. Then what?"

Gil's eyes get shifty again. He's trying to hide just how anxious he is. It isn't working.

"He downloaded some client files onto a star drive. I need to know what he's seen of those files and I need the files back. Including any copies he might've made. The originals are gone."

"Let me guess. You guys handle some accounts that are not quite on the up and up?"

His lip quivers.

The waitress hands us another round of drinks, then takes the order at the six-top across the aisle. The savory tang of hot wing sauce finds its way over here, making my eyes water. Damn, they smell good.

"If my boss finds out, I'm done. My life? My career? Gone."

I need to calm him down, so I sip my drink... slowly. "What else can you tell me about this guy? Is he married? Single? Hobbies? Things like that."

"No, sorry. It's been a zoo at the office. I hardly know what day it is."

"You said he's older. What's his background? He must've filled out an application of some kind. Should have some details on it. Work history, place of residence."

"Alright. Yeah. I'll check. I'll get you what I can."

"What about the other interns? They might know something."

"No! I mean"—he takes a deep breath, quieting himself—"I don't want to raise suspicion."

"He's already missing, Gil. Isn't that suspicious?"

"Interns quit all the time. You know how it goes."

I do, actually. But I need more to go on.

"Where do the interns hang out? Maybe I could pop in. Don't worry," I say, anticipating his pushback. "I'll be discreet."

"Uh… maybe. I don't know. I'm not sure. I'll try to find out."

There's so much Gils's not telling me I barely know where to start. Either he doesn't want me to know the whole story or he doesn't know it himself. You work enough cases that take you halfway across the Universe and back, you learn half the battle is extracting the real reason your clients want to hire you in the first place. They rarely want resolution. They want validation. Even if it's the last thing they need.

"Listen, Gil. I can tell you're stressed out, and I appreciate your need to handle this quietly. You're also telling me it's urgent, but you're giving me no leads."

"I'm"—he takes a huge swig of beer—"I'm not trying to be difficult. I'm not. I just really need those files back. I need you to find him."

"And how do you propose I do that?"

"I don't know. Be *persuasive*." Though he keeps his head straight, he quickly eyes me up and down, thinking I don't notice. "Isn't that what you do?"

"No, Gil. That's not what I do. I find people. Or, to be more precise, I look for people. But the thing is… some people just don't want to be found. And for good reason."

"Just get me in a room with him," Gil says. "I can do the rest."

"No offense," I say, trying, although not very hard, to hold back a chuckle, "but you don't strike me as an *I'll do the rest* kinda guy. What're you gonna do? Have Hanson arrested? Nah. If you wanted that, you'd have called the cops already."

Gil leans in closer. Sweat rolls down his temple. Mentioning the police is a great equalizer. A client's response can tell you a lot.

"Promise me," he demands through gritted teeth, "that what I'm telling you never leaves this table. No police. No way."

There it is. He's scared. He's into something he shouldn't be. Something he can't handle, no matter how much he claims otherwise.

I assure him with my best Angela Hardwicke smile. I'm told I have soothing eyes. Or scary. Eh. Whatever works. "It's in the vault."

He lets out a breath so long I almost expect his chest to invert.

"You ever heard of"—he's leaning in so close now I smell the bratwurst he ate for lunch—"the Anshani crew?"

Now it's my eyes that light up.

Seema and Boscoe Anshani. They work for their Uncle Haji. The Anshanis are small-time in the underworld, but they're unhinged in a way others are not. Vicious, vindictive. I tangled with them once a few years back. Nobody you want in your life.

"Our client... the one with the missing files? They own a hospitality chain across the realm. Moonglow Suites. They control dozens of smaller companies under the umbrella."

I immediately piece it together. Classic scam. "Let me guess. The Anshanis are 'consultants' of some kind. They hand Moonglow duffel bags of cash, Moonglow launders their money with a 'clean' payment for services rendered. Minus a fee."

"I don't know what Hanson knows," Gil says, answering without answering. "And I don't know *why* he's gone. He doesn't respond to calls, texts, holomessages, or video streams. And his phone is dead. There's no signal. So there's no way to track him. Maybe he's on the run, maybe he's been kidnapped. Maybe he's..."

"Dead?"

Gil's hands tremble. "I know he downloaded the files. I have to get them back. Immediately. Before anyone knows they're gone."

"Sorry, Gil. This one's not for me. I don't mess with the Anshanis unless I absolutely have to. And let's face it. I don't have to. I can recommend some other PIs if you want."

I stand up, tie the waist straps on my trench coat, then down my Scotch. I'm meeting the gang to shoot pool. I missed it three months in a row. Not missing it again. Not for this.

"But you do," Gil says. "It *has* to be you."

I turn up my jacket collar, smooth out the rim on my well-worn fedora. "And why's that?"

"Because"—his face betrays him—"you're in the file, too."

CHAPTER 2

A few years back I worked an arson case. A burned-out inter-dimensional travel agency. Turns out the owner's younger brother, Lonali, torched it for the insurance money. He was also an Anshani cousin, and on the payroll.

At the time I took the case, I didn't know the Anshanis were involved. They weren't too happy when I solved it. Not to mention Seema and me. It could get personal.

"It's how I found your name," Gil says. "There was a payment in the files for *Angela Hardwicke: Private Investigations*."

I sit back down, my heart beating with a slow, dense thud.

"So let me get this straight. Your intern stole files connected to the Anshani crew. You don't know why, what he's done with them, or what's happened to him. Did you consider that maybe the Anshani crew planted him to steal the files in the first place? Did Hanson steal other files, too?"

Gil stares at me. No. He stares past me, trying to avoid that deep connection you risk when your eyes meet. He can't face it.

"Gil?"

"Not here," he says, then tosses a few credits on the table. He leads us up from the basement pub and into the alley, hustling us two blocks down to a courtyard with a communal garden.

Eleven full moons tonight. Lime green. Last night they were blue. Tomorrow? Your guess is as good as mine. And the fog? Gone.

That's Eternity for you. Especially these days. Ever since Astropalooza, E-town hasn't been the same. Then again, none of us have.

Gil keeps to the shadows. "You've been around Universe business, right? You know about Jacques Abladujue?"

This case is escalating quickly. Jacques Abladujue is a serious player in the galaxy supply sector. "He owns a ton of sub-
sidiaries with connections to half the power in this town. Real
estate, too. Big portfolio."

"That's right. He leases retail and office space to Moonglow
Suites. He gets linked to the Anshani crew because of this and
I'm—"

"In a ditch next to Hanson?"

"I was going to say *fired*, but… wait, you think they'd…?"

"Kill you? In a heartbeat. Maybe quicker."

"You gotta help me, Hardwicke. Please. You gotta do this."

I may not give a camel's hump about much these days, but I
don't want any part of this case. So I reach into my jacket, adjust
my gun holster. Partly because it's digging into my side boob,
partly because I want Gil to appreciate that violence might be
headed his way.

And one other reason. "I don't have a choice, do I?"

"I-I," he stammers, the lost little boy in him screaming from
behind fretful eyes. "I didn't know. I didn't think."

"No, you didn't. Just… give me what you can on Hanson."
He power hugs me like I just pulled him out of a river. Maybe I
did. "Gil. Let go."

"Right, sorry. Like I said, I'm just a little nervous."

I pry his fingers from my jacket.

"You should be. But for now… go to work on Monday, shut
your mouth, and keep your shit together. Until then I'll do some
digging, see what I can find. Then we'll talk again. There's a lot
I need from you."

"If I hadn't found your name," he begins, but then his voice
trails off.

"Thanks, Gil. You're the gift that keeps on giving."

This isn't how I wanted my week to end. I step beneath a
street lamp, the halo shining over me. I turn back to Gil.

"The Anshanis are no joke," I warn. "Keep your phone close.
I'll be in touch."

*****

Pool balls ricochet across green felt like new solar systems exploding into existence. The six, eleven, and thirteen snap into various pockets. The cue ball is set up mid-table to take down the five in the side.

I need this. A night out.

And it's not that I might be getting pulled back in with the Anshanis. Although that certainly doesn't help.

I'm worried about Owen. My son.

He's not living with me right now. I miss him so much my cells ache. He's only four. He's been gone awhile, under someone else's care. Someone I trust. It's worse at night, when I'm alone. Nowhere to hide. That's why I've been taking so many cases, one after the other.

I have better and worse moments, wondering if Owen's happy or afraid, or if he misses me at all. I try holding onto my memories, his face covered in strained peas and plums, playing with my hair.

But I'll get Owen back, though. I know I will. At least, that's what I tell myself.

Because if I ever get to the point where I give up, if I never again get to hold my baby boy in my arms and feel his little heart beating against mine, there won't be any cases left for me to solve except for one. A missing person.

Me.

I am in the Universe business, after all.

If I want to disappear into uncharted nooks embedded within the Cosmos, there's ways of making that happen. More than you'd think.

Esteban hands me another beer. He just wrapped a ten-hour shift driving his cab, so he's flush with credits.

Nini bumps her hip into my mine, then side-kisses my cheek. Her skin is black as the night, a striking contrast to my modest white complexion. She's a tiny thing, barely four-foot ten, if I'm being generous. But she's the toughest ER nurse at E-Town General. She's sewn more stitches into my skin than Cedric has on my trench coat. And no, I'm not getting a new one.

I drape said coat and hat over the high-backed chair. McGeer's is one of the few pool halls in E-Town that's not some glorified arcade with 3-D video games, holocubes, and movie screens bleating so much noise your nerves are about to go supernova.

You can almost smell the oaky Scotch soaked into the walls. I love this place.

Buzzed, I tell my crew about Gil.

"Hardy," Esteban says, then lines up his next shot. "Did you say Breslin, Anders & Li?"

"Yeah. Why?"

Nini and Esteban look at each other, then to me. They know I have their backs. And they have mine. That includes telling me like it is, not the way I want it to be. They don't work every case with me, but they show up when I need them.

Esteban pockets the five, then with perfect draw nails the two ball off the side and then into the corner. Bank shot.

"You know that's not an accounting firm, right?"

There's a moment during certain investigations when you realize the one critical piece of information you've been over-looking, the key detail you missed, has led you down the wrong path. Into danger. You get a rush to the head, overwhelmed by rage, adrenaline, and humiliation.

This case is only twenty minutes old and I'm having that moment already.

Never take a Friday night case, I remind myself. Never ever.

"What do you mean?"

"It's a real firm," Esteban says. "I swing by a lot, all hours." He power-slams the three ball as Nini sips her cocktail through a tiny red straw. "It's a front."

I already explained about the Anshani crew, which doesn't seem to faze them. That annoys me. Yet now my friends are looking at me like I just stepped between two flaming comets. Been there, done that. So I ask: "Front for what?"

A part of me hopes they don't answer. It's not just the clients who fear the truth.

Nini digs credits from her tiny silver purse. "Let's get another round. You need to hear this."

CHAPTER 3

Ambush. I usually reserve this technique for suspects, but sometimes the client needs to be caught off guard.

Dawn is my favorite time of day, especially now, in the fall.

The soft plum of sunrise easing into the first breath of morning sapphire.

Been this way nearly half an hour, a half-moon ghosted across the sky.

There was a stretch when I was kid, when dusk lasted for hours, dawn even longer. It took some getting used to, but those long transitions between evening and night, night and morning—the end of one phase, the beginning of another—gnawed at me.

Though I couldn't decipher it then, I took those phases of anticipation as a sign. A warning? A divination of hope? That however my life was at that moment was in no way an indication of how it would someday be. A lesson I'm about to lay on Gil.

I'm over on Pearl Street, waiting across from his apartment building. He's on the sixth floor. I see a woman pass by his window and pull on her coat. Being the ace detective that I am, I surmise that she's heading out, no doubt after a night of bouncing beneath the sheets.

She's pretty. A light-skinned black woman, taller than Gil, early 30s my guess, full figured, an oversized scarf bunched around her neck. She exits the building, the door drawing closed. I wait until she's away, then from the other direction dash over and get my fingers in there before it shuts on me.

Powered by my second amaretto latte with hint of raspberry, I take the elevator, get off on Gil's floor. I press the buzzer.

Groggy-eyed, he greets me in his boxers—juggling elephants

motif—and an open robe. His hair is mussed.

"That's a good look, playa."

There's a delay before Gil realizes I'm not his lady friend already back for another go.

"Hardwicke," he says, and pulls his robe closed. He's a bit puffy around the middle, but otherwise in good shape, his hips and thighs thick as tree trunks. He needs a shave. "What are you doing here?"

"I told you I'd do some digging. I got some early results. Figured you'd want to know."

"Yeah, okay, come in." There's a framed poster mounted on the living room wall. Cordova and Belagra. They're opera singers, standing on the front steps of the Bainbridge Coliseum. "How'd you know where I live?"

"Same way I know you had company," I say, getting a faint whiff of vanilla extract. I'm guessing his lady friend dabbed some behind her ears as a perfume substitute.

"I've got coffee brewing." He's ducking me, trying to hide his awkwardness. "You want?"

I counterpunch, quick and fast. "Why'd you lie to me, Gil? Why'd you hold back?"

His jaw clenches, his nostrils expand—physiologic responses to being confronted without knowing what to do next.

"It's a good cover, the accounting firm. But that's not the division you're assigned to, is it? You work for the VCP."

The VCP—Visitor Consulting Program—is a semi-secret, but sanctioned organization that identifies beings across all dimensions, recruits them to Eternity, then trains them to observe the Cosmos.

On a rolling basis they assess how well (or poorly) we Eternitarians are doing in the design, creation, and maintenance of the Universe. Off-realmers live in that Universe, so it stands to reason they might have some useful insight.

VCP executives compile their reports and send them up to the Minders of the Universe. The Minders take that information and, if they find it useful, make adjustments accordingly.

"I don't"—he shakes his head, feigning confusion—"the VC what? I don't know..."

"I don't know," I parrot. "Deny 'til you die, right Gil? Good luck with the Anshanis. Peace out."

"*Okay*," he says abruptly, like I threatened to expose his stash of porn. I feel his resentment, but he relaxes his posture, accepting that's he's busted. Gil leans back against the kitchen counter. "Okay." His eyes shift back and forth, as if he's debating how much to tell me. It takes a minute. "I didn't lie. I just... didn't tell you everything."

"I can't help you, if you don't help me."

"What was I supposed to say? That I work for a secret agency that recruits off-realm beings? I'm not allowed to do that! Besides, when I first went to work there, it really was as an accountant. I'm terrible at it, I know. But they hired me anyway."

"Why?"

"Because people *like* me, Hardwicke. Making friends isn't a bad way to live. You should try it."

I flick my jaw. I hate it when the clients are right.

"You know what's funny? I never wanted to be an accountant. I wanted to work in the hotel business. But my parents were relentless. 'Hotels are tricky,' they said. 'One day they're full, next day they're empty. No guarantees. But every company in Eternity, no matter what their line of business, always needs an accountant. In good times and bad. It's recession proof. You always have a job.'"

"They had a point."

Gil grazes a flyer for Razorback Reef, a thrash metal/techno band. Not exactly operatic. He's got eclectic tastes.

"Which is why I gave in. I got tired of fighting them. So I became an accountant."

"But how does that lead to Hanson?"

"After a few months, my boss on the accounting side came to me about a special project. More people-focused, she said. More my speed. Which is exactly what I wanted. And then she told me about the VCP, and what they really do."

"And you were interested."

"Of course! When you recruit an ORB—Off-Realm Being—it's a big shock for them. Huge shock. It's a voluntary program, but hearing about Eternity is a lot to unpack. Seeing a friendly face helps ease them into it."

"And this is how you met Hanson?"

"He was my first solo ORB. He was a middle-aged history teacher from Earth."

My heart flutters. "Earth?"

"You know it?"

I know more about Earth than I can stomach. "I'm familiar with it."

He explains that Hanson is from North Tonawanda, a struggling town outside Buffalo, New York. Early twenty-first century America. Gil made the initial outreach. Hanson had the usual panic attack before settling down.

I've seen that movie. I know how it ends.

Beings throughout the Cosmos have ideas about how and why the Universe exists, and how they fit into it. Most of them are wrong.

Just... so wrong.

Yet, regardless of the planet of origin, there's often some belief in an all-powerful being or energy that created the Universe. Earthers call that being *God*. Some believe in several gods, or claim their god is *the* god. They even go to war over it. A lot. So fucking stupid.

But it's a helluva thing.

To be confronted with the reality that you personally—and the planet you live on—exists in a Universe that is designed, created, and maintained by the three Minders of the Universe.

Gods, if you will.

And that the Minders created a realm, as a practical matter, dedicated to the mechanics of how the Universe operates.

That realm, that industry town—Eternity—is our town. And its core city is my town.

E-Town.

"Hanson came around," Gil says. "Following protocol, I brought him up here, from Earth, and checked him in as an ORB. I spent a few weeks showing him around, getting him up to speed. All things considered, it was going pretty well."

"But...?"

"That's when my boss called the all-hands-on-deck."

"It wasn't an accounting problem, was it?"

"Not entirely, no. But they don't tell me everything. I'm way too green. Obviously."

"That must've been some problem."

Gil eyes me, looks away. "It was. It is."

"And Hanson is still gone."

Gil shows me a photo on his phone. It's Arthur Hanson. He's got heft, about six-foot-two, two-hundred twenty pounds, round face, some permanent acne scars on his chin and cheekbones. His sandy hair is evenly cropped, his shoulders wide. He's a bit overweight, but more thick than fat.

In the photo, Hanson's staring right at me, even through me, like a brain surgeon fixated on a single nerve spiraled around my frontal lobe, detailing in his mind exactly how he'd slice it out.

"And the files? Was that a lie?"

"No. That's real. They're gone. Everyone in the VCP has an actual job in accounting. It's the only way our cover stories hold up. You have to be able to talk the talk."

There are more holes in his story than an unfinished star system. "Wait a second," I say, the residual caffeine kicking in, "you said he was an intern. In accounting. But that's obviously not true. If Hanson knew why he was here—giving feedback on the Universe, as an Earther—why'd he take financial files? He must have information by now... about the VCP... that's worth a lot more than that."

"That's the problem. I have no idea. I don't know why he did it. But he's gone, the files are gone, and if I don't get them both back, I'll be gone."

I'm used to clients getting agitated. Nasty even. But this one hits home. Gil's problem is my problem, too. I don't know what he's mixed up in, but if the Anshanis are involved, it's not just Gil who has to watch his back.

Seema and Boscoe Anshani? Something went down with them. Nasty. Diabolical. You see it in their eyes. I think they'd rather torture someone than take their money. Their Uncle Haji is about business. They're about something else.

"Sorry, Gil. This could get vicious. You might want to bring your boss into this one."

"I can't. Please. You have to help me."

I've known Gil less than a day and already I want to dump him in the nearest wormhole.

"Please, Hardwicke. I'm begging you."

I know I should walk away, but if the Anshani crew has new motivation to hate me, I need to know just how much, and what they have in mind. Damn.

"You're in some deep shit, Gil. This is Universe business. Even the simplest cases can tear you apart."

"I know! That's why I came to you. You're the best, right?"

He's working me, but I can't make it easy for him. I need to know how committed he really is. I don't do favors. This isn't just a business. It's my life.

"No more bullshit, Gil. Lie to me again, hold out on me... you're own your own. Got it?"

Gil exhales a sigh of resignation. But he doesn't appreciate yet that I have to work the case whether he pays me or not. If the Anshanis are after me, I need to get ahead of this. And if they're onto Hanson because of where he's from, what he knows about the VCP, and their manipulations throughout the Universe, things could get real complicated real fast.

"Just find him," he says. "Find the files. I might go broke in the process, but you don't find him, it won't matter anyway."

Clients are like puppies. You have to house train them early and often. If not, they'll piss on your leg with impunity. It's bad enough you have to pick up their turds.

"Okay, Gil. You got yourself an investigator. I charge a flat fee for a missing persons case, plus expenses, and hazard pay because the Anshanis are involved. But now that I know what I'm up against, I have a lot more questions." I take out my notepad. "This'll take a while."

*****

From his dining room table I gaze out the window as two copper-chested robins come soaring at us, then swoop skyward.

I wonder where they're off to, then sip my coffee. The caffeine helps fight off my urge for *dRops*. But it only goes so far. I'm looking for cracks in Gil's story. At least he's gotten dressed.

"Arthur Hanson. Forty-seven. Earther. Caucasian. Male. Unmarried. Taught history at the local high school in"—I flip through my note pad—"North Tonawanda, New York."

"Y-yes," Gil says with a quizzical look. "Didn't we go over this?"

"We did. But the key to any investigation, Gil, is reviewing what you do know until you can figure out what you don't. What you've missed."

The clients don't always get it right away, but you have to interview them almost as often, and sometimes more, than a witness or a suspect. Your clients usually know more than they think, and they almost always know more than they want to tell you. So you keep at them.

Besides, I know firsthand how cruel and unpredictable the Universe can be.

I know what it's like to feel your soul shattered into a million moonbeams that cast shadows on your fate. I know the ocean of pain. The regret.

That feeling of impotence, blaming yourself for being a victim, or for maybe even bringing that grief upon yourself. So I give my clients the benefit of the doubt.

Maybe they deserve it, maybe not.

As much as I try to do the right thing in this fustercluck of a Universe, I'm a private investigator. The clues lead where they lead. Justice is more of an aspirational notion. Even under ideal conditions, it's not so easy to come by.

But everyone needs a chance to make their situation right. It doesn't mean they'll make a good choice, even if we get there. A chance is the best I can do.

Because if I can't do that much, I might as well turn in my license. There are other ways to make a living.

"Remind me. How'd you select Hanson in the first place? How'd he take the news?"

Gil explains the process. The VCP is equipped with an

intergalactic monitoring system, which reads the frequencies of every sentient being in the Cosmos. Which means the VCP is watching everyone. Everywhere.

At least to the degree the Minders permit.

"Hanson's essence code was identified as being an ideal candidate to be an ORB," Gil says, shaking off his nervousness. "Not just a solid citizen, but one who could serve as a representative for Earth. They need the fortitude and emotional intelligence to handle their new lives in Eternity. Hanson was a seventy-three percent match. That's high."

"Take me back to that first day. You show up at his front door. Then what?"

"He was cordial, but reasonably suspicious. I told him I was with the Niagara County Board of Education. I showed him an ID card. I had it made up."

"Good idea." Based on the smile he tries to hide, the compliment lands as intended. "Then what? How'd you make the approach?"

"I learned from my previous assignment. Kathryn Evard. A nice woman from someplace called Antwerp, Belgium. I launched right into all the Universe business and the VCP. She had a nervous breakdown. She said God would never do something like this. I had to wipe her memory." Gil shakes his head. "It did not go well."

"I would imagine," I say, getting the sense Gil might be stalling. But I think he's dying to talk with an outsider about his life at the VCP. It's stressful having to conceal such a considerable part of your life from the people closest to you. I know a little something about that. Nobody knows why my son isn't with me. Well, almost no one. "I want to hear about that, Gil. But let's get back to Hanson. You're in his living room and...?"

Gil fills in the rest. He asks Hanson about his job: Does he still like teaching? The students? The curriculum? Is it a rewarding career? Then he gets into more existential questions.

Gil asks me what he had asked Hanson, "If you had the chance... if you could do something truly spectacular, something that would serve humankind in a way that would far exceed anything you could possibly imagine... would you do it?

Even if that meant giving up the life you have now?"

That's a helluva pitch. He's almost got me thinking about it.

"Then we had the talk. The Universe. The VCP. With Hanson's permission, I levitated us over the Earth itself. Of course, he didn't think it would be real. When it was—we literally soared over the planet, through space in a containment field—he sorta…"

"Lost it?"

"It took three days for him to come around. After that, I set him up with an apartment, clothes, E-Town ID. Things like that. We met at the VCP headquarters to observe Earth from a fresh perspective. We discussed standard Earther evolution, social attitudes and changes, and the direction of humankind. Perfect job for a history teacher."

"Guess you know Hanson after all," I say.

Gil also showed Hanson around E-Town, brought him to relevant supply centers and service providers for comets, asteroids, and the like, helping him acclimate to his new life.

I have Gil write down the names of everyone who's already met Hanson. I'll start on that list as soon as I'm done here. But he still won't let me interview anyone at the VCP office—he can put me on the restricted list if he wants, but that would raise questions—so I take the back way around.

"Anyone at the VCP who'd want to hurt Hanson? Kidnap for ransom?"

"No," he says, although his expression suggests he hadn't considered that someone within the VCP might have their own motivations to make Hanson disappear. "Not that I know of."

"Any bad habits? Drugs? Women? Men? Gambling?"

"Like I said, I lost track of him before we really got started at Breslin, Anders & Li."

"Uh-huh. Any chance he just took off? Cracked under the pressure? Maybe he wanted to get his freak on? E-Town's the place for it."

A lot of maybes. Gil has no answers.

"So what now?" he says. "Where do we go from here?"

"We don't go anywhere, Gil. You stay close to home, and hope to hear from Hanson. And like I said, when you get back to work, stay busy. Act like nothing's changed. And if someone asks about him or those missing files… improvise."

"What about you?"

"I've been up all night?" I say, my mind thumbing through various scenarios about how deep this story really goes and how much Gil is still holding out on me. "I'm going home."

CHAPTER 4

Gil wasn't thrilled when I left, much less that I showed up. He'll get over it. Every second a missing person goes unaccounted for, the odds of finding that person decrease. Which is why I'm barely able to function.

At least I know who Owen is with. I just don't know where they are along the time/space continuum, which dimension they're in, what they're doing, or when they're coming back.

For now, I'm going on fumes. It's a good thing I have backup to look for Hanson.

Nini's checking E-Town hospital registries for anyone matching his description. Esteban is making the rounds at the cab stations.

All in all a decent start, but our search only accounts for E-Town proper, just a fraction of Eternity. The entire realm, made up of Nine Spheres, has way too much real estate to cover on our own. For now I'll hope that Hanson is somewhere in the city—the urban core, as the snobs call it—assuming he's even alive. I have my doubts.

If Whistler, my new part-time assistant, was more seasoned, I'd have him poke around as well, but he's not ready for fieldwork on his own. He wants to join the police force someday. Homicide.

He thinks working with me now will give him a leg up as a detective, but I'm not so sure he's thought this one through. I can teach him the mechanics of investigation, and push him to think in ways the police can't or won't, but a quasi-internship with me isn't going to hold much water with the force. It might even sink him before he gets the chance to apply.

Me and the police have an… interesting relationship.

The first of three early morning suns peaks over a low-rise apartment building, catching my face. I shade my eyes, but there's no ducking the questions I need answers to.

What's Gil gotten himself into? Gotten me into?

A missing Earther. Missing files. The Anshani crew. The VCP.

Do I even believe my name was in those files? Is Gil just trying to motivate me? Harnessing my focus and attention?

It could be that Gil's as young and inexperienced as he seems at first glance. He's not the first client to accidentally wade into deep waters. You spend enough time inside all that cosmic lunacy, you're bound to get lost in the haze.

But he lied to me straight off. A big lie. And if he's a member of the VCP, there's a good chance he's a lot smarter and savvier than he's letting on.

And who was that woman coming out of his apartment? I need to follow up on her before I lose my train of...

My phone rings. Familiar number. Huh. It's been awhile.

Jamie. New CEO of the Rubicon Hotel Corporation.

"What's a girl like you doing up on a day like this?" I say. "A bit early, no? It's barely seven a.m."

The streets are usually busier than this, but it's Saturday, so most people are sleeping in. I like this time, the gentle before the chaos.

"Early. Late. It's all the same to me. You know that."

"Fair enough."

"Why are you up so early?" she asks as a guy walking a Great Dane and a Shih Tzu passes me by.

"Was on my way to bed. Long night."

"Of that I have no doubt," she offers with a hint of tease—and derision. "Regardless, I might have a job for you. Can you stop by?"

Jamie? Wants to hire me? Interesting.

"How's three o'clock?"

"Not ideal," she says, "but I'll make it work."

She hangs up.

I figured we'd cross paths again... eventually... but within seconds I'm scared, angry, and start to shake. Every fiber of my existence is begging, seething for a hit of *dRops*. Just a single glorious *dRop*.

The newest and most addictive black-market drug, *dRops* are spreading across Eternity's underbelly. They're synthesized from Cosmic Building Material—the Universe's liquid DNA. The building blocks of all Creation.

To form *dRops*, that liquid DNA is diluted to the most infinitesimal concentration possible without overtaking the user.

Just a single dose—one *dRop*—is like making love with the Universe itself.

But I gotta fight the urge. Gotta stay clean. I'll never get Owen back if I don't.

It's a hike to my apartment, but I manage to get myself home, down some Scotch, and take a hot shower. Cleansed of the top layer of grime, I pull on sweats and a T-shirt and collapse onto my bed. I play Josh Boden's last album. It soothes me.

As I stare at cracks in the ceiling I find myself thinking of my old room, so sickly sweet with enough pink and blue throw pillows on my bed it makes me want to eat my gun.

But that was me at fifteen, dreaming on my life ahead with my boyfriend—the life we were sure to have—him working away the days while I played mommy at home.

I hate that me. That stupid, silly me.

I miss her, too.

But for the time, the urges have passed. I rode it out once more.

Now... I need to sleep.

*****

In my dream there's a full moon. The Earth's moon.

It finds me almost every night. I don't know why.

Flat spots and indentations create dark patches, carving out a face, like a grinning humanoid. Earthers call it the Man in the Moon.

He seems to be winking, drawing me in. Telling me something I should know—something I should intuitively understand—but don't.

Underneath the full moon Gil is in his bathrobe and slippers running into the Infinity Cloud, and no matter how fast my legs move, I can't get traction. He slips away from me, into the ether, and vanishes. He's elusive. Out of reach.

My mind's way of telling me I don't have it. Don't know what's coming.

That the case I took isn't the case I have. That it isn't about Gil at all.

It's about me.

And then fireworks erupt all the way to the moon, like the Universe itself might just break apart.

The night sky alights with starbursts, the moon shining down on me. I could swear its mouth was starting to move, to speak. To tell me secrets I swore I'd never confess.

But a secret's only a secret if it's known by you and you alone.

Whoever he is, the man in that moon peers down from the black of night. I think about meeting its gaze, but I turn away.

I'm not ready.

*****

Five hours isn't ideal but it's the longest stretch of uninterrupted slumber I've had in months. I slip into my second skin—pinstripe pant suit, black zip boots, fedora, trench coat, switchblade, zipties, and retractable taser rod.

In my shoulder holster I carry a standard issue 9 millimeter Rothchild with custom grip, because I want something reliable. It gets the job done.

Although none of my gear will be necessary for this meeting. It just makes me feel better knowing I've got them.

Esteban meets me outside my apartment. Motor's running. So's the meter. I hop in the back. Dressed as a banker in a lightweight, charcoal tweed suit, pale blue tailored shirt, and striped tie, he gets tiny parts in TV shows and movies—mostly as an extra—but he loves being on set, talking to the crew, meeting a few stars. The pay isn't much, but the gigs validate him in a way nothing else can.

"You sure you're ready for Jamie?" Esteban flips off a kid on a plasma scooter who, by way of a particular finger, insisted he had the right of way. Banny's gold-plated knock-off watch jiggles on his wrist. "Last time…"

"Last time was a different," I say. "I'm okay. I'm good."

Through the rearview mirror I see Esteban roll his eyes. He's not wrong. I don't know if I'm actually okay to see Jamie. We've mixed it up before. Although she was an assistant manager of the Rubicon Hotel when we last met, she's now the CEO of the whole company.

She's also a Minder of the Universe.

She takes both jobs seriously.

Regardless, Jamie wants something from me. Needs something. And that's where my leverage comes in. It's also why most PIs avoid Universe business. You can't take cases dealing with the Cosmos if you're constantly terrified about screwing up on a galactic scale.

I just assume there will be problems, and adjust on the fly. The Minders know that.

Yet the timing is a red flag. I suppose it could be pure happenstance, but it seems more than a coincidence that Jamie reached out simultaneous with me being hired to investigate an Earther gone missing in E-Town.

When it comes to the Minders of the Universe, I've learned to never take what they say—or do—at face value. Their reach and vision of the Cosmos is impossible to comprehend.

Esteban takes us through Escahoe Circle just as the afternoon sky slides from sapphire to pineapple yellow to white to apricot and back to sapphire. The hues have always morphed throughout the day, but they've been changing more frequently.

The Universe, and now Eternity, has begun to short-circuit. The infrastructure of Existence seems to be breaking down, eroding before our eyes.

Whether it's a fundamental problem, or a bug in the system, remains to be seen.

Like a cathedral set apart from the masses, the Rubicon Hotel gleams on the corner of West 57th Street and Isenstadt Avenue, fronted by a tinted, glassed-in atrium. There's easy access across the street to Britton Square and Meridian Park, a triangular, tree-lined park with two modest parcels of green space, a center plaza, and a marble wishing fountain.

I lean forward. "Banny. You see that kid again? On the scooter? The one you flipped off? He's behind us three car lengths and to the left. Keep your eyes out."

"I see him. Try to be quick. I've got a late call time. Movie of the week. I'll be in a scene with Mira Indago. She's the killer in this one. I stand behind the police tape shaking my head in disgust. It's quite moving."

"Sure thing," I say with a roll of the eyes. "I'll tell the Minder to keep it moving."

The lobby of the Rubicon's been renovated yet again. Last time I was here it had a rainforest theme. It's been updated to coincide with the Lavanian Frost Festival, ice sculptures, penguin and polar bear caves, and mini glaciers. There's a nip in the circulated air. Guests seem to be getting a kick out of it.

Before I'm halfway across the marble-floored lobby Damian glides in my direction. His approach is flawless. He's been a bellhop here for years, and one of my best informants. With a large suitcase in tow to block the security cameras, in one fluid motion, and without saying a word, he slips me a keycard, I slip him a few credits.

Walking past the guests and hotel staff I take the elevator up to Jamie's private office. She's traded in the flowing gown ensemble I last saw her in for a brown pantsuit with a pink, silk blouse and small diamond stud earrings, her cherry blonde hair pulled back into a tight bun.

She's prettier than I remembered. And taller.

Her window extends the entire length of the western wall. It overlooks the backside of the property, including the pool area and, just beyond it, lush green hills and Titan Lake. The lapping blue water sparkles in the sun.

Throughout her office, miniature galaxies float like apparitions.

"Angela," Jamie says. "Nice to see you."

"I'm surprised you called me after Astropalooza. Wasn't my best week."

"It was a lot to take in. For all of us."

There's a humble lilt in her voice I hadn't anticipated. "Clean slate, then?"

She offers up her hands, tilts her head in a *why not?* manner, then makes her way behind her desk, a levitating glass countertop. On it is a tablet, a framed photograph I can't see, and a computer screen, bookended by blooming orchids...

Abstract paintings are mounted on the beige walls, matching the beige carpet.

The décor is both warm and cold. Jamie's still figuring out her style. Figuring out herself.

"Take a seat. I have a job for you."

I sit on the other side of her desk, cross one leg over my knee. "I'm all ears."

"I'm not sure if you were conscious during Astropalooza itself. I assume not."

I wasn't. I shrug.

"Firework displays went on for ten days across Eternity. It was a bit much."

Fireworks. I had the dream last night. Another coincidence. "What about 'em?"

"There were enough displays scheduled to last four Astropaloozas," she says, shaking her head, irritated. "There are thousands of unused firework caches all over Eternity that nobody can seem to find. Typical waste when there's no oversight."

"Let me guess. They were approved by your predecessor, and now that all properties and contracts have been transferred to you, you want your money back."

"Angela. We've got lawyers for that. It's the fireworks themselves I need you for. No doubt being rerouted for black market sales. I don't care so much about their use, but I can't let it be known that I can be taken for granted. I need you to track down as many of those caches as you can find, and report back to me."

There's no way she called me in for this. "Jamie. You're the Minder of the Universe. Snap your finger. It'll be done like that."

Her eyes narrow. She smiles at me.

"But that doesn't send the message I want. The legitimate and illegitimate business worlds alike need to grasp in a

profound manner that as CEO of the Rubicon Hotel Corp., I'm
not to be trifled with. They don't know I'm the Minder of the
Universe. You're one of the only civilians who do. This has to
be handled at street level. My name needs to be respected—and
feared. Without our reputations, what are we really?"

"So that's where I fit in?"

Jamie concurs. "You have to speak to people in a language
they can understand."

"I get that. But why me? Can't you hire a team for this?"

"Of course, I could, yes. But I'm sure to require someone of
your particular skill set now and again, and I want to see if I can
trust you to get the job done right. Our last meeting was a bit
tense, under fairly extreme circumstances. I'm willing to accept
that you were not your best self at the time. You were battling
certain demons you seem to have under control. For the time
being."

I was whacked out on *dRops* when we first met. If she didn't
know that then, she does now. I wonder if she can smell the
withdrawal oozing from my anima. Or maybe it's the pit stains.
They say you should never let them see you sweat, but the
Minders can pretty much see it all, so anything I hold back is a
measure of my own resolve.

Still, as much as she's testing me, I'm testing her.

Both as Jamie the CEO and Jamie the Minder of the Universe.

"You had your own stress, if I recall. Not a full Minder then.
It must have frosted your comets to watch your predecessor
implode—quite literally—and nearly take the Universe with it.
Tough to sit out the big ones. Especially," I add for emphasis,
"when you have no say in the matter."

Jaime offers me a conciliatory smile. I don't know if that was
reasoned acknowledgment or an unintentional slip, revealing
the doubts I know she has. I get up from my chair, to the center
of the room. I wave my hands through the holographic galaxies
floating before us.

As if guiding soap bubbles, the galaxies dance in my palm,
responding to my movements, but also to what I'm thinking.
What I'm feeling.

The instant connection startles me.

Following my lead, the galaxies scatter like butterflies in a sharp breeze. And then something occurs to me.

Gil hired me because an Earther under his charge has gone missing in E-Town, and with valuable intel, just as his own team is facing an internal crisis. There's a disconnect within the VCP. I turn back to Jamie.

"You're new to being a Minder. And there's no one to mentor you, show you how to be in charge of"—I extend my arms outward, at the collection of floating galaxies—"all this. There's always three of you, yet here you are, all by yourself." Jamie is surprisingly quiet. "It would drive me to drink. Or worse."

She waves her hand then, probably for my benefit, drawing all the butterfly galaxies into her palm. She rolls them into a single galaxy, the size of a marble, and *drops* it into a blue vase on her desk. A vase filled with marbles.

"I won't pretend to know what being a Minder is like for you," I say. "Or what it does to you. But I know what it does to me. There's lots of space out there, on- and off-realm, for things to go wrong. So there's no need to play games with me. You can let your hair down. Have some girl talk. Galaxy style."

"Like I said. I may require someone of your skill set."

Time to back off. Jamie hasn't whisked me off to a black hole, so I'm assuming I passed the test. "The fireworks. I'll look into it."

"Good." Jamie stands up from her desk. "Take a few days. Let me know what you find." I head for the door when she *drops* this one on me. "By the way... any luck with your son? That must be a lot to digest," she says, throwing the sass back in my face, reminding me that I'm not the only one with soul-crushing responsibilities that haven't been met.

I wondered if she'd bring him up. I'm not sure if she's genuinely concerned or still testing me. Maybe both. Either way, I nearly sink through the floor.

"I'm...keeping it together. Like they say, one day at a time."

"I forget you don't experience time the same way I do. Every moment in time, space, and dimension—past, present, and future—are all occurring simultaneously. To me, Owen's still with you. He never really left. Of all possible guardians,

Milo was an unconventional choice."

Jamie knows too much. I can't hide from her. So I redirect.

"One more thing," I say before the elevator door places a barrier between us. "Speaking of Milo, I never thought he'd be a new Minder. And now he's MIA. I'm assuming the other guy, too. What's his name? Jason Medley? The Earther? Have they found a place for themselves yet? You know. At street level? Must be tough running all of Eternity, on your own, knowing your partners have left you, by yourself, dangling from a comet."

Jaime smiles at me once more. "They've been... difficult to reach," she acknowledges as the doors finally close. "But focus where you need to, Angela. I'm counting on you."

CHAPTER 5

I'm so jangled from my meeting with Jamie all I can think about are *dRops*. If I ditch everything, I can have them in less than thirty minutes. Luckily, I have distractions.

I've got to get back to this Hanson fiasco, but Jamie's a special circumstance. She's a young woman, er... Minder... who's learning on the job, without a net, how to manage ongoing and immeasurable responsibility as it pertains to the fate of Existence.

And she's doing so while being accountable to her partners and attempting to define herself, whoever—or whatever—that might actually mean.

I'm not sure she even knows. Or maybe she knows most of all.

Esteban is waiting for me in the roundabout in front of the hotel entrance. I hop in back, then fill him in.

"You okay?" he says as he pulls out onto South Elizabeth Avenue just as rush hour traffic starts to pile up.

Across from the Rubicon Hotel, hordes of people meander in and out of the park, offsetting the long rows of low- and high-rise buildings stretching down the avenue.

The sidewalks flow with passersby, ice cream, pretzel, and off-world candy carts, curbside vendors hawking T-shirts and trinkets, as well as essence artists, hologram cubists, shape-shifters, and multi-dimensional musicians with their cases open so aficionados can toss in their credits. The scent of steaming Kraelic hot dogs and candied cashews drift in through the windows.

All this activity creates its own energy, a buzz, yet it upsets me, makes me clench, because I know what the others out there don't.

That the three Minders of the Universe, responsible for the upkeep of Existence, aren't even talking to each other. With no indication of when that might change.

And because of it, just how vulnerable the Universe has actually become.

Even in a realm like E-town, ignorance is bliss.

"You've got that look in your eyes," Esteban says and whips around the circle, taking us back toward my office. "The *dRops* look."

Years back, Esteban's sister Gia had a bad run of things, mixed up in a lot of the same shit I was. I got out. Gia didn't. Banny and I sort of adopted each other after that.

"You got the itch? You're making me nervous."

Esteban knows me too well. Without even realizing it, I've slipped into fantasy, so I don't think about Owen, or where Milo's taken him, or what they're up to.

In my mind, I see myself take an eyedropper between my fingers, tip my head back slightly, exposing my neck, and open my mouth.

I squeeze the dropper's soft rubber head. And with an erotic lust I await as a single droplet of the most euphoric, hallucinogenic substance in the Cosmos hits my tongue.

My very essence fuses with the DNA of the Universe and...

We stop short, the tires screeching on the street. My heart races, pounding in my ears. I'm sweating, the sun beaming through the windshield, blinding us. Blinding me. That's not a coincidence, either. It was orchestrated. Coordinated. Planned.

The kid we saw before, the one on the scooter, has cut us off next to a bagel delivery truck before we can take the left onto Claremont. The kid motions with his head.

In his three-piece suit, Esteban cuts the wheel, hard, to pull into reverse. A black four-door cruiser heaves itself in our direction, boxes us in. Still blinded, I hear a door open and close, the scrape of boot on asphalt. There's a tap on the window. Metallic. Gun butt.

I breathe three times fast, then pinch the underside of my

wrist and slap my face—*Wake up Hardwicke! Wake up!* I reach for my piece. But like pulling on a condom after you've already had sex, it's too damn late.

Seema Anshani smiles at me through the window, the kind of smile I imagine she smiles just before she gnashes someone's eye out with a grilling skewer. In a silver pantsuit, she motions with her blaster for me to exit the cab.

Though outgunned, Esteban is ready to brawl. His fists are small but hit like jackhammers—quick, repetitive, destructive. His uncle, an old flyweight boxer who fell into a bottle, used to beat the crap out of him. Esteban learned to hit back.

"Let it play, Banny. I'll be okay." I'm telling myself as much as him. I love Esteban, but his fists of fury, as dynamite as they are, won't always get it done. "But keep your eyes open."

"Don't outthink yourself, Hardy. I'm not letting you—"

Tall, wiry, and olive-skinned, Seema looks over the rim of her sunglasses. Her movements are controlled, deliberate, but when called to action—or worse, provoked—she's quick as lightning and hotter than the sun.

With a vice-like grip she coils her long, bony fingers around my bicep, puts us in the back of the SUV.

There are four seats, two-by-two, facing each other. The driver's up front, his window rolled down, eying the street. Hiding behind black-lensed sunglasses, he's round and bearded with thick hands like ballpark hotdogs. He must be new.

Seema's next to me, blaster in my ribs. Firing compressed plasma bolts, blasters have more range than traditional bullet throwers and do a lot more damage, particularly up close. But they're far less accurate from a distance and they lose their charge. I don't think she cares.

Dressed in black slacks and a chestnut silk sweater, Seema's cousin Boscoe sits opposite us, rolling a pair of dice between his fingers. He likes people to think he's mysterious and calculating, but I'm pretty sure it's a nervous habit he's trying to disguise.

It's not so easy being the heir apparent. Especially not in the Anshani crew. Seema is older and next in line, but she doesn't want to be in charge. She just likes to hurt people.

Cracking wise might not be the ideal approach here, but it keeps me from freezing up. If I shudder even once, they'll tear me to pieces.

"Funny seeing you guys here," I say. "I was just thinking about you."

Boscoe's dice clack and grind. "And why's that, Hardhead?"

"I was gonna have you over for tea and biscuits, but my assistant's new. Doesn't know the system."

"And yet here we are," Boscoe says, grinding his back teeth.

"And here we are. You called this meeting. What's up?"

It's barely noticeable, but Seema's inched toward me. She's been this close to me before. I'd love to forget, but it all rushes back, her breath as harsh and acidic as ever, a mix of Orelean humus, blue-leafed cigarettes, and unfettered hatred.

White dots imprinted on the green cubes, Boscoe rolls the dice on the black leather armrest. They come up two and four.

"I'm sure you remember cousin Lonali," he says. "Then again, how could you forget?"

Fuck. They really are pissed at me. But I can't back down.

"Arson's a funny business. You light the wrong match, the flame light you."

Sharp as razor wire, Seema's lips slice wide across her face, nearly halfway back into her cheeks. "You shouldn't be so glib. Do you even know what happened?"

"He joined the chess club? Lifting weights can get sooo boring. I mean... am I right?"

Boscoe squeezes the dice. "No, Hardhead. He was murdered. In prison."

Double fuck. I had no idea. I lost track of him.

"Yes," Seema hisses, whispering so that the hot, wet mist of her saliva tickles my ear in a way that makes me want to rip my own face off. "Because of *you*."

"I got hired to investigate. So I did. Besides... you must've had judges on the payroll. Prison guards? Somebody to watch his back?"

Seema expels a tiny puff of regret. "We couldn't get to him fast enough. The case you built was... thorough."

I offer a half-smile, though I'm so anxious I'd swear a rhino is trying to break through my chest plate from the inside out. "I did my best."

Boscoe's eyes constrict as if he's lost in a psychotic fantasy—me in a dubious position and very much at his mercy. Then the light behind his eyes switches back on.

"We'll settle up soon. I'll give the dice another roll. Very little chance they come up in your favor. They won't be kind."

Seema whispers again. "And neither will we."

"But for now," Boscoe interjects, as if he's annoyed Seema has taken attention away from him. That's always been their dynamic. Seema's smarter than Boscoe, but he needs to be in control. Or feel that way. I think being around her escalates his insecurities. "We hear you might be looking for firework clusters that never got used. The kind"—he cocks his head at Seema, who clicks the safety off her weapon—"that go boom. And maybe the kind that haven't gone boom. Not yet. We also hear you'd be real smart to forget all about them."

Gil says I'm in the same file as the Anshanis. They suddenly show up. They blame me for Lonali's death, but they're asking about fireworks. How did they even know to tail me? Then wait until my meeting was over, and follow me back?

Did Jamie know they'd be onto me? It happened so fast. Maybe I'm adding it up wrong, but I don't like the timing.

Whatever's going down right now it's clear I don't have enough information. About all sorts of things. But I'll need to get out of this car soon if I want to make it out at all.

"Fireworks, huh? I kinda like those white popcorn bursts," I say. "They're a bit more subtle. Like this."

Before I left Esteban's cab I slipped the retractable taser rod from my right zip boot into my jacket sleeve. When we first climbed in back I let the taser slide down into my cupped palm. And now that Boscoe's sitting across from me in classic manspread, it's showtime.

I press the taser's tip. The rod extends into his groin before Seema can react.

Boscoe stiffens, then pulls back against the seat. His eyes are white as soft-boiled eggs, open so wide I can see every bulging vein. He's pressing down on the seat, with his hands, while also lifting his pelvis, an attempt to relieve the pressure against his crotch.

A perfectly reasonable response given that the taser is positioned against the edge of both testicles.

Seema pulls me closer, digging the muzzle into my kidney with such pressure it's hard to breathe.

The key here is that Boscoe freezes.

Tight in his hand, the dice pop out like baby teeth. One and one.

Snake eyes.

"So, Boscoe," I say. "I admit, my memory goes in and out. But what you might want to remember is that unless you want to lose what little manhood you're still packing, Seema here's gonna holster her weapon while you get anything off your... chest."

I feel the momentum shift in my favor.

But just as quickly, the driver evens the odds.

He's got a barbed wire prison tattoo on the left side of his neck, below his ear, seven small coffin tattoos on the right. Each coffin is a confirmed kill. Over the backrest he's pointing, at my forehead, a Crenshaw 9-millimeter bullet thrower with pulsar-fused silencer. He's waiting for Seema to let him take the shot, sending me to the big sleep.

Unless I figure a way out of this, I'm gonna be the eighth coffin. Not my favorite number.

Adrenaline's got me fired up. But it keeps me laser-focused.

I'm about to retract the taser when a fist whips through the open driver's side window. Like the jackhammer he is, Esteban breaks the driver's jaw with one fist, and with the other hand, forces the driver's gun shoulder up.

The driver, twisted around, facing us, grunts in pain. He squeezes off two rounds through the roof of the car. The silencer mutes the noise, but a gunshot going off in close proximity is enough to get my attention.

Seema shifts her blaster from me to Esteban, but in the ruckus, Esteban grabbed the driver's pistol and has it pressed against the back of Boscoe's head.

One squeeze and I'm getting a brain matter facial.

His three-piece suit torn at the shoulder, Banny head-gestures to me. "Let's go."

"What do you say, Boscoe?" I've still got the taser in his groin. "Call it a day? Or you want to roll again?"

Although the configurations have shifted in my favor, even one wrong move will have me in the middle of a bloodbath.

Seema digs the blaster back in my ribs. "We're leaving on bad terms. Next time... I'll make them worse."

Like a diseased serpent, she sucks on my earlobe—it sends awful shivers through my entire body—then releases her hold.

Even as my fingers want to vomit, I keep the taser where it is, easing off just enough to let Boscoe speak.

"Fine, Hardhead. But when I roll again"—eyes still wide, he fumbles with the dice—"your number's up."

"That's just as well." I back out slowly. "My cab's waiting. And the meter's running."

CHAPTER 6

I'm jittery, pacing. Being pinned down at gunpoint will do that to a girl. You never get used to it.

The *dRops* were my crutch, especially after facing life-or-death situations. There've been too many to count.

But no matter how hard I try to push those cravings away, I can't resist.

And like any junkie, I want it. I need it. To feel a stream of cosmic ecstasy consume all that I am or will ever be. To float in the womb of the Cosmos.

But I can't give in. I won't.

I've made it eight months without a single *dRop*, and I want to make it another eight. At this point I'm concerned about making even it one more day. Another hour.

Because a single slip, just one *dRop*, could drag me back down into my own psychedelic hell. If it weren't for Owen, I'm not sure I could resist. Being face to face with the Anshani crew—Seema in particular, that whisper in my ear—has me completely on edge.

And of all the possible reasons that would force me into another Anshani encounter, Lonali wasn't even on my radar. But just because he'd vanished from my mind doesn't mean he'd *actually* vanished. Funny how that works.

Probably less funny for Lonali and a lot less funny for Seema and Boscoe. Which makes it not the least bit funny for me. Unless you find the irony of Lonali's murder coming back on me now even a little funny, in which case, it's fucking hilarious.

So I do the only other thing I know how to do when I'm like this.

I run.

Esteban, who deals with stress in his own way, drops me at my office. I kick him some credits to pay for the rip in his suit.

"I'll make it work," he says about his torn threads. "Gives depth to my character."

He peels off for the set. If he hurries he'll just make it.

I change into black stretch-band leggings with reflective stripes down the sides, a matching, long-sleeve top, and a black stretch headband. The running shoes are worn and broken in. They slip right on.

Rather than make my way across Celestial Avenue, a major E-Town artery, I run in and out of side streets, feeling the burn in my thighs, the tightness in my lungs. Sweat rolls down my neck, cool sweat against hot flesh. If only it could melt away my sins.

Night should be falling by now, but it's Red Moon Rising, the sky draped in a thick coat, as if painted crimson.

A single moon—a transient seasonal moon—is flush against the horizon. The contrast, ghost white ball against blood red, is striking. And massive.

I pass through Nosha Village, lined with branded coffee joints, upscale sex toy shops, pubs, restaurants, tattoo parlors, leather clothing boutiques, indie movie houses, underground holocube and VR arcades, and deep tissue and Laleri massage parlors.

My mind starts letting go of the last few days, images streaking across my consciousness like shooting stars.

Gil. Jamie. Seema. Boscoe. Owen. Fireworks. *dRops*.

There's no sequence I can latch onto, no composition to follow. All I have are individual pieces that I know fit together, but... how?

You track the clues, examine the evidence. But when that's not enough, then what? You do this job long enough, you learn facts without context can be more dangerous than lies. So you test theories, ferret out details, and follow the threads. And if that doesn't work, you need to clear your mind and listen. Because if you can wash away distractions and give yourself over to the embers of Existence, the ether talks to you in whispers and shadows, tickling the faint hiss of knowledge that lives beneath the surface of your awareness.

I know, I know. It all sounds very touchy feely and mystical wankstain, but the private eye life is as much about persistence as brains, refusing to give up when that's the easiest and most expeditious thing to do.

And if one technique is more successful than another, so be it. Forgo your process, and chances are you'll overlook critical information you probably would have noticed had you kept digging. Be too reliant on process, get lost in your algorithm, you deafen yourself to the undertones that trickle in from outside the lines.

From the sidewalk I cut through Half Moon Garden overlooking the Anaya Promenade, a large, public space separating E-Town East and E-Town West.

On tiptoes, beneath the stars, I take the long, winding path of cobblestone steps from the top of the tree-lined hill down to the promenade.

I run alongside the Anaya Reflecting Pool, a grey, marble monolith stretching more than two thousand feet end to end, a hundred and ninety feet wide, and two feet deep.

On the opposite side of the reflecting pool is another sloping, tree-lined hill, such that the promenade itself is below grade, lower than the streetscape.

At the reflecting pool's north end is the Anaya Memorial, a white, marble obelisk, perfectly smooth, standing nearly six hundred feet high. Hovering just above the pillar are three planets—also white marble—of different sizes. They perpetually rotate, slowly, within a shared, stationary orbit.

Those planets, those white marbles, instantly draw my mind to Owen's baby rattles. He used to giggle and gurgle with them. My happy little boy. He would look up at me and smile, the smile only an infant can smile, and only his mother can fully embrace. I'd take his tiny fingers in mine, and play eat-them-all-up-yum-yum-yum, just like my mom did with me, once upon a time.

And then his whole adorable face would light up and I'd know that he was my son, and I was his mother. And we loved each other.

I'm down at the promenade level now, the toxins oozing out of my system. The piney tinge of evergreen trees finds its way up my nostrils. Pierces my brain.

Like a babbling brook, the reflecting pool—an infinity pool—flows to the north end, toward the obelisk. The water rolls off the edge, recycles underneath, and reappears at the south end.

With the crimson sky above, the water appears red, like a lake of blood. The monument and milky white moon shimmers, reflecting on that bloody water. Mirror images.

As if they feed one another.

As if that river of blood is washing over the monument, over me, temping me to act upon my worst instincts.

The grief Eternity has in store for any one of us is always right there, on the edge, isn't it? Failed marriages? Broken deals? Missing sons?

To help us cope, we need someone to find answers to the insidious questions that haunt our dreams, or uncover secrets that do more harm by lurking in the shadows.

It's the big question.

I get asked all the time. How can you do the work you do? Poking around in ugly, dangerous corners of the Cosmos, where you are most unwanted?

With its alternate realities, dimensional portals, vanishing stars, toxic nebulas, and realm hoppers?

Your very existence puts you in the crosshairs of the Minders of the Universe.

I laugh whenever I hear the questions. Laugh inside, anyway. Because if you knew what I know, if you've seen what I've seen, been through what's come down my pike—and no, that's not a euphemism—you wouldn't have to ask.

But I get why they do.

Because even in a bonkers realm like Eternity, run by the Minders themselves, my line of work takes me to some truly bizarre corners of Existence now and then, leads me down dark alleys I wish I'd skipped right over and gone to the pub instead.

You play in the cosmic loony bin long enough and you're bound to completely lose your mind.

So why do I do this job?

You're thinking about it the wrong way. It's not the line of work that drives me. It's just me.

When you die... die inside... when the single most important creature in Existence to you disappears on your watch—and because of your laziness, negligence, and overwhelming self-indulgence—the option of returning to the life you had... to the person you once were... is gone. Obliterated.

Instead, you don't reinvent yourself so much as let the layers of your old life fall away and embrace what's underneath. What's been there all along.

And then you laugh at the absurdity of it all, realizing we're just tiny specs of light, often, although not always, wearing a physical form, masquerading as one kind of being or another, with some kind of purpose.

Maybe.

Laugh? In my line of work? There'd be no other way to survive. Well, no other way for me. Only, I don't have any chuckles in me right now. And I won't let myself cry. Because if I do, I have no idea when I'll be able to stop.

So I sprint through the promenade's south end and back around to the Harper District, until finally I'm out of breath.

Mid-block, I lean forward, hands on my thighs. I huff until my lungs no longer feel like the tip of a lit match.

It's only when I look up do I recognize the apartment building.

But who am I kidding? I didn't end up here by accident. I ring the buzzer for 4K.

"Hello," a voice says, crackling through the intercom.

"Hey," I say, still catching my breath. "It's me."

There's a buzz click. I let myself into the vestibule, take the elevator up to the fourth floor.

I give three gentle knocks. The door opens.

Darren greets me with a squint and a smile. He takes me into his apartment.

Into his bedroom.

Draped in the crimson light crawling through the blinds, I remove his clothes. Standing nude before me, his sinewy arms covered in tattoos, he peels off my running gear so that my own tattoos, and several scars, are visible to him.

I'm sweaty. Naked.

Exposed.

We hold each other in the darkness, then ease our way to the bed.

It's what I need right now.

*****

I awaken to a cinnamon-sweet breeze and a clear morning sky. It's actually blue today. Darren is fast asleep. Reinvigorated, I cab it over to my office and change into fresh clothes. My next stop is Hanson's apartment.

His is on the third floor of a five-story brownstone on Darcy Street near the VCP office. Gil said they want the off-worlders close, but not so close they feel like they're in captivity. I'm not sure there's any getting around that.

I use the spare key Gil gave me. The VCP has duplicates made for all off-world residencies. Standard backup. Although I assume it's also for the spot inspection. Just in case.

It's a big apartment, bigger than mine. And a helluva lot nicer. Exposed brick in the living room, hardwood floors with two armchairs, couch, coffee table, and recessed lighting.

The place feels barely lived in, painstakingly clean.

I dust for fingerprints. The unit was scrubbed top to bottom before Hanson moved in, but Gil said he's been there since, so his prints will likely be all over. They are.

There's two bedrooms, a bathroom with a standup shower and a glass door, a full kitchen, several closets, and a laundry nook.

The only thing of consequence I find in Gil's apartment is what I don't find.

An ordinary man from Earth, Hanson volunteers himself to a realm that creates, designs, and maintains the Universe, yet there's not a single scrap of paper. Not a newsletter, pamphlet, flyer, or take-out menu. No video chips, tablets, holocubes, or VR goggles. Items a person would normally accumulate, especially in a world outside his own.

Where's the curiosity? Wasn't this guy a school teacher? A history teacher?

Hanson's whole life was dedicated to investigating the past and applying those lessons to the present, passing along information from one generation to the next. I never met a teacher whose home wasn't overrun with lesson plans of every kind. They can't help it.

But there's nothing to indicate a teacher lives here.

Either someone's been here already and cleaned up, Hanson's an off-the-charts neat freak... or he's not what he claims to be. What Gil told me about him, anyway.

I rummage through his bedroom closet. The clothes are hanging perfectly straight, the shoes in order. From the right pocket of a cream-colored blazer, I pull out a receipt. Tico's Tacos. It's almost twenty blocks from here, the first sign Hanson's wandered into E-Town. It's not much, but it's a start.

And then I remember one of the storage facilities Jamie wanted me to check for firework caches. Strident Eyes. It's a festival company that also hosts bachelor and bachelorette parties, private gigs. I'll grab a quick bite, check if anyone's seen Hanson, then look into Strident Eyes.

*****

The smell of sizzling burritos makes my mouth water, spicy salsa practically oozing from the walls. Camilla's working the counter, her black hair curled beneath a burnt orange cap. She calls me over.

"Hey girl," she says, wearing a matching burnt orange top with a Tico's Tacos logo above her heart. "What's up?"

"Came to chow down. What's good today?"

"Stop over to my place and I'll show you."

Camilla's a huge flirt and loves all things tequila. She's got great curves and a killer smile.

I survey Tico's Tacos. It has a half dozen booths, and as many stools at the counter running along the front window. Lunch crowd will be shuffling in any time now. A video screen is playing on the wall. Some music talk show.

"I'll have my usual. Hey—" I show her a picture of Hanson. "You seen this guy?"

Camilla's auburn eyes light up, her black eyebrows immaculately groomed.

"Oh! Arthur! Sure. He's a real sweetie. Been here a few times. I think he's tried every kind of taco we have. He asks a lot of questions."

"Really? Like what?"

Camilla sashays out from behind the counter. We sit at a booth, sunlight beaming through the window. Across the street is Roy's Dry Cleaning, and a bar most unsubtly called Drinks!

Spray-painted on the chipped concrete wall between the two shops is a MinderNot symbol—an inverted red triangle with a line running diagonally through the center. The line extends in both directions, outside the borders, longer on the bottom, like a tail.

They've been popping up all over E-town.

The MinderNot doomsday nuts started showing up about a year ago. They claimed Astropalooza would bring an end to the Universe, and it was their obligation to save it.

The MinderNots were more right than they ever knew. Astropalooza was nearly the end of us all. It almost broke me.

While Astropalooza was underway in Eternity, two massive energy waves barreled toward one another across the Cosmos at incalculable speeds and rates of acceleration. Those waves consisted of the Universe's liquid DNA, the building blocks of all creation—the same base liquid in *dRops*.

Had those energy waves collided, they would have ignited the next Big Bang, eradicating Existence as we knew it. Every particle in the Universe—and everything in Eternity, including us—would have been gone. Complete nothingness.

Not sure how, but we dodged that bullet.

The MinderNots have since morphed into something different.

They know E-Town is starting to crack. But they don't know why it's happening or what, if anything they can do about it. They also don't know—virtually no one does—that the old Minders faded away, replaced by three new ones.

And they definitely don't know Jamie is one of the new Minders, and that she's running the Universe—and Eternity—entirely by herself. A job way too big for just one Minder.

So the MinderNots rally and shout and conflate their angst. Because for now, that's all they have.

"Artie said he grew up in Mandini," Camilla explains. "It's way out in the mountains. So he's fascinated by city living. E-Town's a trip for him. Says he missed all the fun of Astropalooza. He could see the fireworks from his house, but he'd been taking care of his parents, who were elderly. He moved here after they passed. Time to reconnect, he said. Start living again. He wants to take hot air balloon rides, book a galaxy cruise. He was asking about which were the best ones. Oh! And hotels! He wanted to know which were the most fun. He's very sweet. It's like he's not even from Eternity. Like he was asleep his whole life and he just woke up."

Not from Eternity. That's for sure.

"That helps, Camilla. Thanks. When was the last time you saw him?"

"Oh, shoot, let me think."

She's got a smudge of guacamole on her cheek. I'm tempted to wipe it off, but I'm afraid if my finger makes contact with her skin, she'll take it as a come-on. She's flirted with me way more over way less.

"About a week, maybe ten days ago. Said he booked a whale-watching cruise. Takes off from the marina. Downtown, by the Dooly."

The Dooly. Haven't been there in a while. Frankie the Brush has done a few construction jobs at the marina. As a general contractor and painter, Frankie works both sides of the street, commercial and residential. He also does galaxy renovation, and polishing. So he's got every reason to know people, in all walks of life. On-realm and off. He's helped me put down a half dozen cases easy. In return, I push business his way. I'll ask him what he knows. I think a minute. "You said fireworks before. Did he say anything else about that?"

"No, not that I can think of. Although... and it was really

just in passing, now that I think of it, but he said he used to watch the fireworks every year on the fourth of... oh, shoot, I can't remember. And then... sorry. I forget."

The fourth of... what? Is that an Earth reference? I can't think of anything here. There's a fireworks festival in D'iend'é Park, but that's E-Town. Could never see it from the mountains.

A few months back I was working the Fourth Annual Prescott Gala, but there wasn't much of a fireworks display then. Just a few sparkling pinwheels and parachutes.

"Anyway," Camilla says, "I loaded him up." She gestures to the windowsill. "There's tons of take-aways. He's got plenty to choose from. Does that help?"

His apartment was empty. I missed something. I need to go back.

"Maybe. Thanks. And wrap that burrito for me? I gotta run."

Camilla is called back to the counter. "Will do. Your order's up anyway." She smiles at me, her perfect white teeth glistening between red lips. "You want it now," she says, letting her finger drape slowly over the top of my hand, "or should I keep it warm and... deliver it myself?"

"I'll take it to go. But keep up that kinda talk, Camilla, and one of these days... I'm bound to say yes."

CHAPTER 7

I fire off a text, have Gil meet me back at Hanson's apartment. I need to get him talking again and see what shakes loose.

Until then I re-examine Hanson's place. Either he's stashed valuables in a crevice I haven't found yet, he's got another stash site, or there's nothing to find. Although I'm convinced there is. I get back down on my hands and knees, look under the couch, the bed, the dresser.

I run my fingertips along the walls, feeling for imperfections in the mortar, between bricks. I do the same along the hardwood floor, looking for a latch or hidden compartment. But all I come up with are splinters and bizarrely few dust bunnies.

I'm about to dig through the closets when suddenly the room is filled with darkness. I go to the window and it's pitch black outside despite being the middle of the day. And I'm not talking hurricane darkness—which blocks out the sun—but total, utter blackness.

Non-light.

The kind of black that drapes over the realm when the sun is simply gone.

There's a collective hush out there, all of us waiting for the lights to come back on. But when it doesn't happen, and the anxiety sets in, cars start honking and people on the street hem and haw until they're shouting at each other. And then, finally, MinderNot chants come from every which way. How the Minders have left us all. How Eternity itself is falling apart.

Minders of the Universe,
You leave us here to rot.
Minders of the Universe?
Minder... Minder Not!

Hard to fault them for thinking that way. Like a screaming child, the blackout is impossible to ignore. And then just as quickly as the void consumed us, there is light once more.

Needing a break from E-town's schizophrenia, I re-heat the burrito, then sit on the living room couch, set against the wall beneath two large windows overlooking the street. The blinds are down, but the slats are open enough to let in good light now that the sun is shining again, yet slanted to guard against prying eyes.

I set my fedora on the coffee table, take a bite—damn, that's good—then lean back on the couch.

Something digs into my spine. I reach behind me. There are two large cushions side by side, but no buttons sewn into the yellow olefin upholstery. Maybe it was the leather strap from my gun holster. It bunches sometimes.

I lean back again. Immediately I feel the nub. I lick sour cream from the side of my hand, then flip the large cushion on its side. There's a metal zipper on the corner. I pull on the slide and run it back along the teeth, exposing white foam within the pillow's casing. I contort my wrist and fingers, fishing around for whatever's in there.

It's a brown leather pouch, with a zipper along the edge. I look inside.

*****

Gil's scratching his thigh as it bounces nervously. He's seated on the edge of the matching yellow armchair. "You have any leads? Any word? I don't like being away from the office this long. The crisis. It's still going."

"Funny you should say that."

I study Gil studying me, trying to figure out what I'm after. So I switch to Gil himself. The clients always hate this part.

"Hanson's missing," I say. "But is there any chance you're the target?"

"Me? Target for what?"

"Don't know, Gil. You tell me. You have access to serious information that any number of people would kill for, on-realm and off. Maybe someone kidnapped Hanson as a way to get to you. You have enemies?"

"Um," he stutters, "if I do, I don't know about it. Nothing I can think of."

He's lying about this, of course. They always lie.

"Nobody? Really? Because the Anshanis paid me a visit. It was slightly less than ideal."

I fill him in about our chat. Not everything, but most of it.

"B-but..." Gil hops up and paces the room. "How could they know? Did you mention my name? Did they ask about me? Did they—?"

"Gil. Calm down. Breathe. Air in, air out." I demonstrate each action.

"Don't tell me to calm down," he growls, pushing back on me. I was waiting to see if he had it in him. "I'm the client here, remember? I'm paying you a shit ton of money—pretty much every last credit I have—to find Hanson before he ruins my life. And now you're telling me some crazy gangsters are already onto us! I'm not gonna calm down. You calm down!" He encroaches, pointing at me, his finger not two inches from the tip of my nose. "How could you let them get so close, Hardwicke? How could you—?"

I grab his right wrist, twist clockwise, so his palm is out. I press his wrist up, then force my weight against him, exerting pressure on the ligaments. It drops him to one knee. He's wincing in pain.

"Listen, Gil. I don't want to hurt you. But you stick your hand in my face again and I'll fuse it with a quasar."

He's hunched over, gritting his teeth. He scowls at me. If I put enough pressure on his wrist, it'll break.

Like on a spring, his head bobs silently. I let him go. Still on one knee, he recoils, then rubs his sore wrist with the other hand, and lets out a groan, a mixture of pain, indignation, and relief. He looks up at me.

"Yes, you're the client," I say. "But let's be clear. The Anshanis attacked me, not you. They held me at gunpoint, not you. And they warned me to back off, not you. Your name never came up. Which is good for you. But they're definitely onto me.

So unless you want me to drop your case and just take care of myself, I strongly suggest you get it together, and that you do it now."

There's not much more for me to say at this point. But I have more questions, and I need him to focus.

I help him up. We go to Hanson's kitchen, laid out with white-and-black checkerboard floor tiles and outfitted with stainless-steel appliances. The style clashes with the living room. I take an ice pack from the freezer. Gil places it on his wrist.

"Sorry. I just... I'm not used to this. And I'm not sure how much longer I can stall my boss."

"I get it. But seriously. Just... take a deep breath, then a few more. I know it's not easy, but try." He does. "Listen, Gil. I'm not sure the Anshanis know what I'm looking for. We've got history and it's not the kind you reminisce about. I'm gonna make a run at Hanson's neighbors, see what they know."

"The neighbors?" Gil's nervous again, making it impossible for me to believe he doesn't know more than he's saying. "W-why do you need to ask them?"

"You want to find Hanson? Then I need to talk to anyone who's seen him lately. Where he goes, who he's talked to. And since you won't let me talk to anyone at the VCP..."

"No," he pleads, dropping the icepack. "You can't! They can't know. They—"

"I know, Gil. I know. There are other ways to get what I need. I'll keep your cover."

"Okay. Good." Relieved, he sighs, picks up the ice pack, places it back on his wrist.

Normally I'd show him what I found in the couch—he's right, he is the client—but I'm not ready to share. I need to put Whistler on it first. He's got a knack for research and analysis. It's why I keep him around.

"Look, Gil. The names you gave me already, the distributors and such, is a good start. I'll keep you posted."

Gil's exhausted, unsure what to make of our exchange. He can't take the highs and lows.

"But hear me. At a certain point, if things get more dangerous,

I may have to bring in the cops. I have a friend on the Force."

Friend might be overstating things, but if I need it, Tarrish will help. At least, I think he will.

"The cops? But we agreed…" He sees by the look in my eyes that I'm not negotiating.

"He's with the ICD—Intergalactic Crime Division. He's good police. But let's not get ahead of ourselves."

"Yeah, okay," Gil says. "I'll… wait for your call."

Gil's strung out, but I'm not done. I lead him to the door, twist the knob, then stop. I turn to face him. "Who was that woman? The one who left your apartment. Before I showed up."

If Gil felt pressure before, he's sweating now. His face is red and puffy. "She's… I mean…"

"Lady friend, huh? What's her deal?"

"N-nothing. She's nobody."

"Everybody's somebody, Gil. And remember, I poke around in places people don't like. It's what I do. I know it's not fun, but I need to consider every angle. Hanson hasn't been in E-Town long enough to have many friends, yet he's missing and you've got a new woman in your life. Until I find him, I have to consider that you're the target, or there's some connection. I'm just doing my job. It's why you're paying me."

I feel him struggling to accept my logic, that he came to me, to do exactly what I'm doing. Most clients like the idea of a private investigator more than the reality of it. To some degree, they enter the relationship thinking it's a game, that we're partners in a salacious tryst, until faster than they're prepared for, they learn I'm not in it for kicks, and they can't always wall off the other dirty little secrets they're hiding, even from themselves.

Despite their initial protests, the serious clients acquiesce. "Her name's Zenovia Price," Gil says. "She runs a florist shop on Old Warnike Street, about ten blocks south of the Cobblestone District. Me and her. It's new."

"How new?"

"On and off the last few months. More on lately. You know, with this whole Hanson thing, I've just needed…"

"A little comfort?"

"Yeah."

"How'd you meet?"

"I went to a wine tasting with some friends. She was working the venue. She looked nice. I said hello."

"Uh… huh." I offer him a dubious look.

"Hey. Who I date's none of your business."

"Actually, Gil. Your entire life's my business. You want me to save your hide, I need to know who you know, who knows you, and if they have a reason to hurt you. Does Zenovia know about Hanson?"

"No! Of course not! Are you crazy? Nobody knows. Nobody but you."

"I guess she's not that important to you."

"I didn't say that! She's—"

"It's part of the drill. I told you that from the get-go."

"I know," he says, "but… I didn't think you'd be asking about me. Hanson's out there."

"Yes, Gil. He is. And every minute he's gone the tougher he'll be to find. So the more you can tell me about his life, and yours, the better my chances."

CHAPTER 8

After Gil leaves I take a run at the neighbors. No one's home. No surprise, since quitting time hasn't landed, but there's more movement at the bottom of a swamp than in this building. I'll have to come back after hours.

I check in with Esteban and Nini. I've also got Whistler looking into hospitality chains the Anshanis might be mixed up in. Unless we can narrow down the search it might be a fool's errand. So far no luck tracking down any firework caches, but they'll keep at it.

I make a few calls about Lonali Anshani. Not expecting to uncover much—prison murders are the toughest to solve. Still, it's worth trying.

In the meantime, I work my way down the list Gil gave me of the various galactic suppliers he introduced to Hanson.

The first three names all tell me slightly different versions of the same story. They only met Hanson the one time, usual ORB—cautious, a little overwhelmed. He asked a few questions about how stars get assigned to various sectors, the algorithm for deciding which planets can sustain life and which ones can't.

How many life forms are really out there? Too many to count.

What kinds are there? Everything you can imagine. Humanoids. Animals. Insects. Giants. Miniatures. Hybrids. Amoebas. Spores. Fungi. Beings of pure consciousness. AIs. And on and on.

They also said Hanson inquired about sociopolitical and religious issues across the various star systems, which makes sense, given that he's a history teacher and thinks about those kinds of things. As a practical matter, though, I haven't uncovered any new leads.

There are four more names on my list, but I'm fading. The fatigue always seems to hit me around now. Doesn't last long, maybe a half hour, yet even a jumbo coffee with extra milk and sugar won't keep me going and on point.

So I close my eyes during the cab ride to Elonque Industries, hoping I catch them before they close for the night. They handle supply chain logistics for the comet industry, with a specialty in custom delivery routes to deal with nebulas, radiation clusters, black holes, pulsars, quasars, and folds in the space/time continuum.

They're only two dozen employees, but they know their stuff, and their tech and guidance systems are incredible. They helped me out once with a case involving an old client, Renfro, and Halley's Comet. It needed to be temporarily re-routed near Earth's moon. Long story.

Elonque owns property along the outer banks waterfront at the southernmost tip off the Rubiyat Highway, running along the Chabaqua River. It's a one-story, brick building with a loading dock in back and dimensional-shifted windows in front. They provide crystal clear views from the inside looking out at the high-rise residential towers across the river and into the Sun Bay Marina, the boat slips fully docked.

Despite allowing copious amounts of natural light to beam in through that tinted glass, it's impossible to see inside. Elonque has the tightest security I know.

My contact at Elonque, Samantha Plemmons, is on vacation. Ten-year wedding anniversary. I need to catch up with her. Sam's a trip. Instead, I wait for her co-worker, Tevon Elba. I met him once before. Solid guy.

A cool breeze wafts in from the water, the dampness seeping into my skin. The pink leaves of an Ardous tree smell like my childhood—sweet, pungent, and about to die on the vine.

Tevon exits the building. Hands in pockets, I make my approach.

"Tevon," I call as he opens his car door. Brown-skinned, he's got hazel eyes, the kind with an easy depth of character. The kind that says *I'm here for you, if that's what you need. And when I listen, I hear you.* It's been a long time since anybody made me feel that way.

Then again, I haven't let anyone try. Maybe Darren, my drummer guy, could be that guy for me, if only I'd give him the chance. But unless I'm ready to talk about Owen with him—I'm not—I don't see that happening.

Another breeze washes over me. My skin draws tight. I forgot my scarf. Damn. "You got a minute?"

"Oh, hey." Tevon zips his jacket up toward his neck. "Hardwicke, right. Sam's friend?"

"That's what they tell me."

His eyes carry the magnificent fatigue only new parenthood can bring. He's got dried milk spittle on his shoulder.

I ask about Hanson.

"Hanson?" he says aloud, as if trying to recall who he is. "Oh yeah. I remember him. About a month ago, that other guy. Gil something? Yeah, that's it—Gil brought him around."

"You remember anything else?"

"Nothing special. Sam really dealt with him."

I run through my questions, but Tevon doesn't have much to offer. He needs to get home to his baby girl. She turned one last week. His wife needs a break.

Thumbing through my mental files I gaze out at the bay. An eight-teen foot sailboat drifts along, a single light flashing atop the mast. And then it occurs to me.

"Shot in the dark here, but Hanson didn't say anything about fireworks, did he?"

Tevon puckers his lips, shakes his head. "Not that I recall. Sorry." He opens his car door and slides in. "But if I think of anything, I'll let you know. You have a card?"

I hand him one. "Thanks. Go kiss your girls."

Tevon pulls the car back, leaving me in the parking lot with another dead end. I'm about to wave over my cab, when he circles back around. He stops beside me, lowers the window.

"You know, now that you mention it... yeah. Fireworks. Hanson did say something. I heard him ask Sam if there's a good place to watch them. If there are any festivals to check out. He said he liked to watch them back home. No... actually, he said *we* liked to watch them."

"We?"

"Yeah. He said *we*. I thought maybe he had a girlfriend… or something like that. But I didn't think much of it. Not sure if that's useful."

"It might be. Thanks. Anything else?"

Tevon fishes through his shoulder bag on the passenger's seat next to him. He hands me a laminated card.

"These hot-shot galaxy designers, Bindu and Barkley, have an unveiling tonight. They're obnoxious hipsters, if there's any other kind. There's usually a fireworks component to their unveilings. It's at Wazon Road, some new club downtown. Starts at eleven."

I run my finger over the invitation, which activates a hologram. Fluorescent flames draw out the designers' names. Tiny starbursts crackle around it. I have zero interest—I've suffered way too many of these things already—until I see who's sponsoring the event.

My pulse quickens. Finally, a lead.

"You gonna go?" Tevon asks.

I look back out over the Sun Bay Marina. The setting sun—there's only one now, although there were three an hour ago—sinks below one of the shiny residential towers, tangerine sunlight shimmering on the bay.

Camilla said Hanson booked a whale watching tour that left from the marina. I need to get down there, interview the crew.

"Thanks, Tevon. I think I just might."

CHAPTER 9

Whistler meets me at the office. He's so young and eager to please I practically have to sedate him. He's a good kid, but that's just it. He's a kid, barely twenty-two years old. And I think he might have a little crush on me. I have to keep an eye on that.

"Whistler," I say and shut my office door behind me. "Clear a space."

He knows what I mean. He immediately scoops up all the files, receipts, and holo-messages piled up on the circular table I keep to the side of my desk. He always wants to straighten up, but I can't find anything that way.

I produce my notepad so he can input the info digitally. He wants me to go purely tech, but I need to write things down first. It's my process. Makes the notes more real for me.

He's challenging me to get more structured. I told him not to hold his breathe. Unless he wants to pass out.

"Look at this." From inside my jacket I remove the leather pouch I fished out of Hanson's couch. Whistler grabs for it, but I pull it back. His hands are shaking, fighting the eagerness. He's an odd mix of organization and impulsivity. He loves when I put him on a case. "Tell me."

Using the calming technique we've practiced, he breathes in through his nose for the count of three, exhales. Then again. Then once more. He rolls his neck, centers himself.

"Preserve the integrity," he says, reciting one of the mantras I've been trying to instill in him. "Never grab, fold, crease, or crumble. Respect the clues, and the clues respect you."

"Good." I fight back a smile. He's learning. Then a pang hits me. I shouldn't be teaching Whistler. I should be raising my son, wrapping my arms around my baby boy and telling him stories he can dream on at night. But if I focus on all that Owen's been going through without me, because of me, I'll be incapacitated with mind-numbing remorse. So for now, I put my energy into the case—and Whistler. "Lay them out," I say. "What do you see."

With savant-like symmetry he categorizes the collection of take-out menus and flyers. His eyes widen, his mind already racing. Then I show him the invitation.

"Strident Eyes. Oh! I know them. They throw these wild parties. And they—" He stops, identifies a Strident Eyes flyer on the table. "Here. They match."

"I saw Camilla today."

"You had burritos? *Without* me?"

I give him the don't-be-a-jackass-just-focus-on-what's-important look.

"Right, okay," he says. "What about Camilla?"

"She said Hanson's a regular."

"So he's there a lot?"

I roll my eyes. "Sorry. My mistake. I didn't mean to confuse you by using the word *regular*, and saying it clearly and out loud. I'll know better for next time." Whistler looks at me, slightly wounded. He can take it. He'll have to if he wants to stick around. "But other than work connections, I can't find any place Hanson's been to even once, yet he keeps going back to Tico's Tacos. Either he really loves the food... or there's something else."

"Think he's into Camilla?" Whistler says. "She's foxy. I mean... way foxy."

"It's possible," I say, a tiny bit jealous, although I'll never admit it. "But the one connection we do have is Strident Eyes." I explain the case Jamie's got me looking into. I don't say a word about Jamie being one of the Minders—I'll never do that—but I tell him what she's hired me to do. "Strident Eyes has come up three times in as many days."

"So that's where we start," Whistler says, taking some ownership of the investigation.

"Yes. That's where we start. I'm going to this event tonight, see what I can find."

Whistler looks my way, plying his boyish charm on me. He's relentless, I'll give him that. A good quality for a private investigator, but annoying as hell in an employee.

"There's a plus one," he sing-songs, his voice rising, trying to lead me where he wants me to go. Another good tactic.

"Nice try. I'm taking Nini."

"Oh, man." He's nearly salivating now. "She's foxy, too. I *like* her."

"Down, boy. You're not her type."

"What do you mean?" he says with a wink. "She's black, I'm black… and white. A smooth-as-silk love machine. Benefits of having mixed-race parents. The best of both worlds."

"Whistler. Nini's into *men*. You're still… maturing. I hope. You wouldn't last five minutes with her. I want you to examine these flyers, see if there's a connection. It might be nothing, but Hanson hid them for a reason. Whatever it is, I'm not seeing it. But this is why I need you. This is where you shine."

CHAPTER 10

At first glance there's nothing special about Wazon Road. Just another hipster club along another hipster side street along Cobblestone Alley. The usual multi-color strobe lights and flashing orbs are in sync with the electronic music.

Yet there's an energy here. An expectancy. Heads are bobbing.

Maybe it's the booze and sweat and even the sweet peppermint being pumped into the air. Or maybe it's the drugs—I spot four dealers and five prostitutes I know—but I've been to enough of these events to know there's something else going on.

Normally I would've gone classic Hardwicke—pinstripe suit, fedora—but not tonight. My outfit needs to fit the occasion.

Lucky for me I don't give a comet's gas what these club punks think, so I busted out my black leather pants, leather boots with buckle clasp, white T-shirt, maroon lipstick, and thin-cut leather jacket. It's got enough pockets to conceal what I need, but flows easily with my movements. No gun, but I've got my taser if I need it.

And if Wazon Road is like every other hipster club, there will be enough action to keep even the most focused mind distracted.

Since it's a private galaxy unveiling, there's some deep pockets in attendance. Waylan Gir is sipping a martini by the bar. Sarna Ri'n is in the VIP section, no doubt surveying for another sucker to bilk, and Evelyn Aaer-Von-Maroo, in her royal blue crepe-knit trumpet dress with off-the-shoulder neckline, is making her way to management's private box overlooking the club.

She's worth a second look.

I hate being in nightclubs more than I hate P'linco mushrooms, but you pick up a ton of actionable intel there. When money's in the room, leeches follow.

A confection of magenta, yellow, and emerald lasers crawl along the ceiling. The music intensifies as the speakers unleash a gorgeous alto voice, nearly operatic, the woman producing a wordless song, a rolling stream of escalating and de-escalating aahs.

Nini hands me a cold beer. "Cheers." She clinks it against her pomegranate cocktail. "You look hot tonight. Nice to see you out of uniform."

She's one to talk. Whistler was right. Damn.

Nini's rocking a silver cowl sequined dress with an open back and split side. It dangles from her small, black body. If she wants a friend tonight, she's getting one. She works long shifts in the ER covered in every fluid that can come out of a person's body, but when she's off duty, she's glam all the way.

"I'm looking for Strident Eyes," I say. "I bet there's someone in the management box, but I can't get up there."

Nini raises her eyebrows, hands me her drink. She lets her hands fall along her hips, shuffles her dress, and puckers her ruby-painted lips. She's even got my motor running. She winks at me. "I saw Evie von M up there. I'll give it whirl."

Eighty or so guests undulate on the dance floor. Magenta lights flow over them. I stop a barback as he loads a black tub of discarded drink glasses, soggy napkins, chewed-up straws, and an empty prophylactic pill bottle.

"Strident Eyes," I say. "You seen?"

He broods, as if I'm overlooking the obvious. I slip him a few credits. The barback gestures with his head. "Over there. By the tables."

"I see 'em."

He pulls away into a streak of light, revealing a MinderNot tattoo on his forearm.

"Nice ink. How goes the rebellion?"

"It's not a *rebellion*," he huffs indignantly "It's a statement. The Minders need to unfuck E-Town before E-Town fucks us. If they don't, we know once and for all there are no Minders. It's the great big lie. Total con job."

"One person's lie is another person's mantra. Sometimes

the reverse. And usually... both at the same time."

"Be ignorant if you want. But this town is fucked up. Way more than usual. If the Minders are really running the place... then run it. If not, we gotta tear this muthafucka down."

Ah, youth. So much angst and nowhere to stick it. They're still too young to accept that *responsibility* isn't a dirty word, but rather one of the most critical elements of self-worth. Yet they're old enough to have learned that life is a helluva lot harder than they ever thought it would be. So they pick a new boogieman and call it a cause.

The MinderNots are pushing back against the forces of the Universe, convinced anything they can say, think, feel, or do will change the fabric of Existence.

That the MinderNots can exert control.

Who knows? Maybe they can. Wouldn't be the craziest thing I've seen.

But this guy's right about one thing. The Minders do need to get their shit together.

I'm about to make my way over to the Strident Eyes table when the club goes dark. There's a collective murmur, then silence.

Normally I'd switch on my plasma sensor contact lenses that enable me to see and identify various particles floating in the air. Another one of Bernice's little toys. But I forgot to put them in. I also forgot the scout orbs they synch to. They're damn useful when doing recon. Roll them on the floor and they give a ground-up view of any room. Always nice to know what you're walking into.

I reach for my leather jacket. With a press on the zipper, the teeth double as a fluorescent green glowstick—thanks again, Bernice.

A hiss of steam emerges from the center of the room, pushing everyone back. Outlined in purple fluorescent light, a square reveals itself on the floor. Ten feet away, another purple outline.

With an electrum hum, white panes alight within the purple-outlined squares. Platforms rise.

Standing atop the squares, one each, are a man and a woman.

Bindu and Barkley. The galaxy designers.

Form-fitting white body suits hug their bodies, the ensemble complete with white, leather jackets, white boots, and large white goggles with dark-tinted lenses.

The music starts up again.

Barkley's booming, tenor voice resonates through the sound system, his round, ebony face concealed behind a bushy, black beard. "What does it mean to create?"

Strands of purple light beam up from the edges of his platform, surrounding him like a cage.

Like a brown-skinned Nini, Bindu steps forward within her light-beam cage. Her voice is smoother than Barkley's, but just as powerful. Maybe more so.

"What does it mean to envision the stars?" The same number of pulsing purple bars beam up from her platform.

In unison they answer their own questions.

"*To conjure a vision in here*"—they grip those pulsing purple strands of light into a bunch, and pull them to their foreheads—"*and project it… out there!*"

They toss their fists, throwing the pulsing beams, which, above the crowd, swirl into the replica of a galaxy, and what it will actually look like upon its installment in the Cosmos.

Music rumbles. The crowd erupts in chants and applause.

Bindu and Barkley dance on their squares in sync to the music—flowing arms, swirling hips, all in perfect choreography.

Feeding on the crowd, the performers grab more purple beams and toss them—one, boom; it explodes into a woman's chest—two, boom; it explodes onto a man's head.

They continue tossing light beams until the crowd is worked into a frenzy.

In one motion Bindu and Barkley hop, both feet at once, then pivot, and pull their shoulders back. As if manipulating bolts of lighting, they launch purple beams into the center of the galaxy.

Planets explode before us. Moons. Stars. Nebulas.

The bars lining the white boxes shift from purple to tangerine. Bindu and Barkley grab the individual beams and roll them into their hands.

Together, Bindu and Barkley extend their arms out straight, angled up, and point their closed fists, knuckles out, engulfed by glowing balls of digitized light. Iridescent tangerine waves shoot from those fists until comets scorch into the galaxy replica. The comets penetrate the galaxy's orbit, then burst into flames.

"You asked for a galaxy!" Barkley shouts. "I bring you crackle!"

Bindu raises her arms, palms up, and heaves them toward the ceiling. Pulsing flames shoot from her fingertips, setting the air ablaze. "And fire!"

The crowd roars.

From that fiery blaze, innumerable red rose petals float in the air, against the replica of the newly formed galaxy. Caught up in the spectacle, I reach out for a petal. But then it darts away from me and into the galaxy.

The rose petals burst into glowing embers.

Hysterics follow.

I turn toward Strident Eyes when I get a familiar whiff of vanilla, then spot someone I hadn't expected to find. She's taller than I realized. Bustier, too.

"You're Zenovia, correct? Zenovia Price?"

"Do I... have we met?" Her teeth clack against her tongue stud. "Although..."

On the surface she seems lovely, but there's little chance us being here at the same time is chance. I let the moment linger.

"The flowers?" I say finally. "That's you?"

She smiles, somewhat relieved. "Yes, yes." She touches my shoulder. "Love your outfit. Great jacket."

"Thanks. Was in the mood." I see her look up to the management office. "Problem?"

Her eyes reveal an undercurrent of unease—and resentment.

"Gigs like this are good for business. But the owners try to stiff me. They make excuses. The flowers were the wrong color or not fresh enough or have the wrong scent. And between you and me"—she takes me by the arm, pulls me in closer—"there's something up with Strident Eyes. I don't know what their deal is, but I don't like them. They make me nervous."

"Nervous how?"

"They just seem"—she looks around to make sure no one's listening—"dangerous. I've got half a mind to bail. But I delivered fifteen thousand rose petals. I can't afford that kind of loss. They paid a deposit, but owe the rest. I'm afraid to go up there."

I'm feeling sympathetic toward her, but I need to push past it and see if she knows more.

"You might be right. I've heard some sketchy things about them."

Zenovia smiles at me, then her eyes fall sad. I've verified her fears.

So I ask: "How'd you get the gig?"

"I'm not sure. They called my shop, asked if I could help them out. They got my name from a mutual client. They wouldn't say who."

"That didn't seem odd?"

"It did, but it was such a big order, I jumped at it. Wish I hadn't."

"Listen," I say. "I'm a private detective."

"You are?" Her eyes light up. "No way. That's so cool."

"Frosty," I deadpan.

"Wait. You're working a case?" She's worried—and titillated. "Is it about Strident Eyes?"

"I'm used to dealing with a certain element. If you need help getting paid, I can probably step in."

"Oh, wow. You'd do that for me? I'd love that but"—she glances up at the office again, a look of inevitability falling over her eyes—"it's best if I handle it. If you get involved—"

Nini comes trundling down the staircase. How she moves like that in heels and a barely-there dress, I'll never know. I'm a disaster in them.

"Sorry, Zenovia. I'll stop by your shop. And be careful up there. You never know what they really have in mi … ohh, shit."

My pulse quickens. My eye twitches.

Seema Anshani has her blaster out. And it's pointed right at me.

*****

"Zenovia," I warn. "You need to leave."

"But—"

"Go now."

"Um… oh…okay," she says, shaky. "See ya later?"

"Later. Sure. Just go."

Seema pushes past a young couple who has absolutely no idea how close they are to one of the most insidiously violent women I've ever met.

"You remind me of a stray cat I found," Seema says in her sleek silver jacket. "It was mewling in the gutter. So I fed it, just once, and sent it away. But after that, everywhere I went… there it seemed to be. I took the cat in for almost a year. Do you know why?"

"There's an ugly joke there," I say, eyeing Boscoe across the club, near the stage. "But that would insult the cat."

"It was a test of my patience. If I could entice the animal to depend upon me, not just for its comfort, but its very survival. After it got comfortable, it liked to play games, to prance around my apartment, as if it owned the place. And then one night, while it purred it my lap, I killed it with my bare hands."

"You were always a giver," I say, trying not to shudder.

Seema laughs a wicked little laugh, the external visage of her inner, deranged psychosis.

"You're the cat," she says, blaster in her left hand, pointed at me, her right hand cupped over the weapon, concealing it. "I see you posture for clients, your friends. Even yourself. But I *know* you, Angela Hardwicke. Your lips say *no* but your eyes say *I surrender*. Revealing just how desperate you are to give up the struggle. To at long last… submit."

I despise this woman.

Because she does know me. A part of me. The worst of me. The weakest.

"These spineless fools may fawn over *Angela Hardwicke, Private Eye*," she taunts, and leans in close, her natural toxicity choking the air like dark matter. "But I watched you crawl on hands and knees, mewling for one more *dRop*. One more taste." She runs her fingers across my cheek. "You feel it right now. Like that feral cat, in no time at all you'll crawl back into my lap, and, of your own volition, give me your last... hot... breath."

I hate that she knew me back then. When *dRops* were still a river of celestial joy cascading through my essence, making everything beautiful. Perfect. But then I'd come down and need more. Only, like an estranged lover, they turned on me.

As much as I needed the *dRops*, the *dRops* needed me. They fed off the marrow of my life force, and I was happy to oblige, even as I withdrew, withering away in the process.

But I have people to watch my back. Maybe I always did. Only now... I let them. Which Seema is about to learn the hard way.

"You have your memories," I say, and with a tight grip, pull her hand away from me, "and I have mine."

A look comes over Seema's face I'd seen only once before, from a time I wish she'd let me forget.

"What I remember is cousin Lonali," she says. "He was the best of us. The sweetest and, in his way, the bravest. And you *destroyed* him."

She wants me for herself, to draw me out. I can't let her. So I shake my head with a hint of playful disappointment. "Even now, after all this time... you still don't see it."

Seema chortles as her eyes draw tight. "See what?"

"Her," I say and angle my eyes to the woman behind me.

With a crack, Nini bashes Seema across the back of the head with a beer bottle, sending her to the floor. There's so much club activity hardly anybody notices.

"Angela," Nini says. "You okay?"

I look down at Seema, pull the blaster out of her limp hand. Might come in handy. Or maybe I'll give it over to Tarrish, see if he can link the weapon to open cases. If I know Seema—and sadly, I do—she's got several bodies on her ledger.

"All things being equal, I'm feeling pretty damn good."

Nini pulls a shot glass away from some guy ready to pass

out. She knocks it back. "Yeah. I rather enjoyed that."

Across the club, I see Bosco's eyes bulge. Trembling with anger, he points at me.

"I hear you," I say. "But I think we ought to go."

CHAPTER 11

A fat, yellow moon hangs low in the night as the crowd empties out. Esteban's cab is waiting. Nini called ahead. We climb in.

"Thanks for the backup," I say. "I need a shower after that. Maybe two."

Nini nods. "And a cocktail to go with it. Banny. Head to the Scherzeron Airstrip. I got a lead."

Banny peels south from Cobblestone Alley, past Calico Terrace and toward the Infinity Cloud just outside E-Town's border. It's the fastest way.

The Infinity Cloud.

An all-encompassing fog with no dimensions, no discernible top or bottom, no beginning or end. It's an express route to anywhere. If you want to travel from one point in Eternity to another, you enter the Infinity Cloud, envision in your mind's eye where you to want to go... and whoosh... there you are. Right where you need to be.

Through the partition, Esteban hands Nini a change of clothes. He then floors the gas pedal as we zoom into the night.

I slide out of my leather jacket, strap on my gun holster, put my jacket back on. Sometimes I forget how naked I feel when I'm not wearing my gun. I don't use it much—thankfully I don't need to—but Seema reminded me yet again to never let my guard down.

"What'd you learn from Evelyn? You were up there a while."

Nini shakes out her hair and leans back. "About two years ago I was working a night shift in the ER. The EMTs come crashing through with a young girl, early twenties. She's seizing, all beat to hell. Heart rate's off the chart, her aura's fluxing in and out."

My chest draws tight. I can't bring myself to even think the word.

"It was an OD. The *dRops*. We had a whole team working on her. It didn't look good." Nini produces her phone. There's a picture saved on it, the girl from that night. "She coded for ninety seconds, but we got her back. She held on."

You'd think Nini's story would scare me straight, but all I want is to roll out of the cab, run like hell to a *dRop* house, and let that glorious liquid hit my tongue.

"But what's that got to do with Hanson?" I say.

"The girl in the photo? From that night?"

"Yeah."

"We checked her in under Liz Laney. But her real name is Yvette Aaer-Von-Maroo. She's Evelyn's baby sister."

"Whoa. So Evelyn... what? She owes you?"

"We called Yvette's emergency contact number. Evelyn was there within the hour. She said she wouldn't forget me saving her sister's life. And being discreet."

"That's why you went up there? To cash in that chit?"

"I was prepared to, yes. Evelyn's buying Strident Eyes from Darius Jones. He owns Wazon Road, but wants out of Strident Eyes. That's why she was there. To finalize the deal."

Evelyn's semi-gangster, semi-legit. There's probably more I don't know about, but she controls a few laundromats, a restaurant, and some illegal gambling. She's just big enough to have a rep, but she seems to play fair. All things considered.

"But if she's buying Strident Eyes," I say, "she's going after the Anshanis. Probably why they showed up. To kill the deal. And maybe her."

"I don't know," Nini says. "Maybe. But that's not the worst of it."

She explains that Yvette is fifteen years younger than Evelyn. Their parents were rampant alcoholics and drugstore cowboys, knocking off pharmacies to feed their habits and then selling off the rest.

They had Evelyn in their twenties, then Yvette later in life.

"Her parents were useless bottom-feeders. But she was in no position to raise her little sister. For years they passed Yvette between neighbors and cousins, whoever could help out while Evie tried to earn."

Esteban turns onto MaCaleesh Highway, toward the Infinity cloud. There's a blackness out here, a desolation. Nothing but open fields on both sides of the road, the horizon swallowed up by the night.

"It's not an empire," Nini says, "but it's something. She tried to keep Yvette out of the life, but then the parents were killed during a score. Yvette never recovered. She's been trying to kill herself slowly, while getting her big sister's attention. And now she's at it again, on a full-blown bender. Alcohol. Weed. Smack. Special K…"

"And *dRops*," I say.

"And *dRops*."

I'd heard rumors about Evelyn, that she has a soft spot for her sister. Rumor no more. "But what about Hanson?" I ask again. "How does he fit in?"

Nini leans forward, looking for the Infinity Cloud. It's up ahead.

"Evelyn says her sister's acting out, trying to sabotage the sale of Strident Eyes. Looks like Yvette stole one of their vans. To make it worse, she stole it with her new boyfriend. Want to guess his name?"

We all know without having to say, but Esteban says it anyway. "Arthur Hanson."

Nini looks at me. "It's him, Angela. I think we got 'im."

*****

Under the cover of night we come upon the Infinity Cloud.

Esteban drives us in. In less time than it takes me to bite my tongue, the great mist envelops us all. Before I can taste the blood in my mouth we're through the other side and speeding down Indigo Way, the narrow road leading to the Scherzeron Airstrip. A dense, wet fog rolls in from the Chabaqua River.

Though we're just minutes away, I'm desperately fighting the urge to *dRop*—wrestling with the deranged barracuda still thrashing about in my veins—consumed by the vision of Yvette staring up at me.

That young woman—beaten, OD'd, raped—is so much like me from my old life, back when I was Angela-the-wreck, Angela-with-a-death-wish, and not Angela Hardwicke, Private Eye. Investigator of crimes. On-realm and off.

Angela-the-mom, trying to get her son back.

That battered young woman could've been me. So easily. It nearly was. Many times.

It doesn't take long to track down Dolores, a quietly success-ful investor who nonetheless keeps her job as a baggage handler at the Scherzeron Cruise Port. Her luggage carrier is pulled to the side of the road, hazard lights blinking.

Three torpedo-shaped galaxy cruisers take off through the mist, their lights blinking against the wet blanket draped over the sky, black as ink. I get a whiff of the tangy salt and gassy, nutrient rich soil mixed in with Dolores's stank-ass cigar.

"Was about to clock out," she says, wearing a hooded yellow rain slicker. "I saw the brake lights. It's down there." She points to thick weeds, which slope toward the marsh. "I don't have extra gear. Sorry."

"Nini, Banny," I say. "Stay here. I'll check it out." My glow-ing jacket zipper illuminates a path as my feet sink into the mud with each squishy step. Another pair of ruined boots. I'll bill it to Gil. "Anybody else know we're out here?"

Dolores chews on her cigar. "Don't think so. No visibility. But come sunrise..." She steps around a thicket of weeds, using a walking stick and an industrial LED flashlight to navigate the embankment. "Watch your step. It can get deep out here."

We come upon the Strident Eyes van. It's stripped clean.

"You could've just told me about the van," I say. "This mud is up to my..."

My foot hits something. I look down.

A body.

"That's why I called." Dolores shines the flashlight on an adult male, dressed in a Strident Eyes uniform. He's got a bruise on his forehead, with some bleeding from scratches on his face. He's unconscious, but alive. "He your guy? Hanson?"

I kneel down. Water rolls across my nose. I'm soaked.

"Nini. Need you."

I hear her slush down to us as she grumbles my name—along with a few choice curse words. "You owe me, Angela. I'm talking a spa day, full pampering *with* champagne. At Reggie's."

"Fine. Let me have the light." Dolores hands it to me. I catch the side of his face. "Damn. I think it is. It's..."

Nini feels for a pulse, then opens his eyelids. His eyes are blue. Hanson's are brown. No acne scars, either. And this guy's got a snub nose with large, gaping nostrils. Hanson's nose is wider, with smaller nostrils.

"It's not him," I say. "It's a close resemblance, but it's not him."

"He's probably concussed. Assuming there's no internal bleeding, he'll have a whopper of a headache. But he'll live."

"Hanson and Yvette, assuming it was them, wanted someone to find the van," Dolores says. "And the body. They wanna make noise. They could've junked this van. Easily."

I agree. "Think they caught one of those?" I point to three galaxy cruisers blinking in the distance. "Or hop the next one?"

"Can't rule it out, but I doubt it," Dolores says, leading us back up the embankment. She points down the rain-slicked road. "There's only one access point to the nearest terminal. They would've passed right by me.".

"Why do you still haul luggage?" Nini huffs as if she's trudging through a soggy mud bank, in the rain, in the dead of night. Which, in fact, she is. "You're the big-time investor. Real estate and who knows what else. You got plenty of money. Not that you ever spend it."

Dolores chortles. "My money's none of your business."

I don't know where she invests, not exactly, but I know she's got quite the nest egg squirreled away. She tried looping me into a deal a while back, rental building converted to condos. I passed. I'm still regretting it. The units are selling like hotcakes.

"You earn your way," Dolores says, "I earn mine. Besides, the pension's unreal. Benefits, too. Dolores plans on retiring in *style*."

"I'll drink to that," Nini says with a wink and nod.

"And I'll pour." Dolores high-fives Nini "Gimme photos of Hanson and the girl. I'll have my buddy in security check 'em out. I'd help, but Jeanie's making dinner tonight. Valsarian bass with a vegetable medley. And No'ala pie á la mode for dessert. And you know Dolores doesn't pass on No'ala pie."

We huddle in the cab. Esteban has the front wipers on, raindrops cascading down the windows like a sheet of tears.

Esteban is facing Dolores up front. He hands me a blue, cotton towel. "What next?" he asks. "What's our play?"

I dry my face and chest. My hair is a fizzy debacle. "We have no choice. I'll call Tarrish. He transferred last year from Homicide to the ICD. Every case is confidential, so good chance it stays out of the press. But Hanson's involved a civilian, and they've attacked one driver. Chances are... he won't be the last."

I'll also ask Tarrish about Lonali Anshani. If there are any bodies on Seema's blaster—each weapon has a unique discharge signature—that's an instant closed case. Maybe Tarrish'll feel like he owes me one.

Wow. My sense of humor is improving. I almost believed that one for a second.

"When you look, though," Dolores says, "the driver, whoever he is, and Hanson... if you look quick, don't stare too hard... they could almost be brothers."

I'm thinking about what to tell Gil when that word hits me like one of Esteban's thunderbolt breaks. "What did you say? Say that again."

"Brothers." Dolores pulls a tobacco strand from her tongue. "If you look quick... Hanson and the driver... they could be brothers."

I'm cold, wet, and exhausted, yet electrified at the same time. My hands shake. "Yeah. They could. I'll give Tarrish a heads up. Dolores, can you handle him?"

"We're good."

"And Nini? Wait for the ambulance. The driver's gonna need medical attention. Tarrish'll bring his guys." Nini raises her muddy foot, rolls her smudged toenails at me. "I know, I know say. Full day at Reggie's. Deluxe package." I wipe a raindrop from my eye. "Banny. I need a lift. If we hurry"—I check the time; it's past 2 a.m.—"I can make last call."

*****

The King Beat is nearly empty.

Before I make it inside, I look up.

In a fraction of a second my mind splinters. One side is smiling, because I know this isn't real. How could it be? I must be hallucinating. Withdrawal from the *dRops*.

The other side is pure panic.

Five planets plummet from the sky, on a collision course with E-Town. Those celestial objects are so enormous they block out everything in sight, about to annihilate us. My heart rumbles, the entirety of my existence drawn to this single point. Because I know my life is over.

I knew this day would come, sooner or later.

We antagonize the Universe so often it was bound to happen. But I wanted Owen in my arms when it did. If we're done, I mean really done, all I want is my son, to kiss his cheek, and hold him close. I'll never forget him in my womb, this little creature forming inside me.

Before Owen, the idea of being a mother to any child was so abstract to me, too painful to even consider, because of what I'd been through already. The choices I made, the lives I ruined.

But then I found my way out of the gutter and made a new life for myself. This life. And then, of course, because I'm me, I crashed again. Badly. But I hung on. And then wham bam thank you ma'am, I'm living in Preggersville.

I lived within Owen, living for him, because of him. Owen reignited the embers in me that burned most bright.

I'm here, in this moment, because of Owen.

And all I can do now is close my eyes, waiting for it all to end.

For my life, for everything, to be obliterated.

The horror completely overtakes me that a cold, sad peace follows. Because there's nothing to do but say goodbye to it all.

The planets are upon us, filling up the sky.

I love you, Owen. My baby boy. Mommy loves you.

I'm already in that sacred place where my physical existence has become irrelevant. I'm an ethereal being now, drifting through the Cosmos. I look up again, the black of night replaced by the colossal foreground of planets.

Goodbye, baby. Goodbye.

Yet just before impact, the planets burst into powder, sprinkling like glitter.

I'm standing here, shaking so hard I nearly pass out again.

But I keep it together, blink a few times, slow, deliberate, to let my mind catch up.

Sometimes I hate this town.

The Minders really are losing their grip on the Universe. Either Jamie dissolved the planets before they took us all out, or it was dumb luck. I'm not sure which is more upsetting.

Either way, it's no wonder the MinderNots are up in arms. Hard to blame them. If I thought I needed a drink before, I need a double now.

Which works in my favor, as Camilla is at her second job, tending bar.

"Well, well, well," she teases with a hint of I-told-you-so as she pops the cap off a beer bottle and hands it to me. She's pulling empties off the bar, about to close up. No longer in her Tico's Tacos uniform, she's rocking blue jeans and a black T-shirt with a yellow lightning bolt across her front. Her black hair caresses her cheeks. "I knew you'd come my way. Just a matter of time." She lifts an eyebrow. "Damn, girl. What happened to you?"

Still damp, my T-shirt is wrinkled and bunching beneath my leather jacket, and my bra strap is chafing. I brush away strands of stringy hair from my eyes then gulp down my beer, the cold liquid harsh, yet soothing on my throat. And my nerves.

"Thanks," I say. "I needed that."

On the way over, before I could call Tarrish, I got a call of my own. Nini said the driver's awake. Has no idea what happened. Was out by the Manuela Projects, to make a stop, when he took a pounding to the head. Bat? Pipe? He's not sure. Didn't get a look.

And he won't go to a hospital. He's either too smart or too scared to open his mouth. Maybe both. Strident Eyes has their own tow service. They're picking him up.

And then Whistler sent me a text. Another clue. Which adds to my confusion.

Did Hanson and Yvette really attack the driver? Are they in this together? If so, how'd they meet? And what are they after? Do they have a plan? An end game? Or making it up as they go? Did Hanson kidnap Yvette? Did Yvette kidnap Hanson? And then there's Evie von M to think about. How's she going to handle this? She's trying to buy Strident Eyes while the Anshanis are muscling in. Are they headed for battle?

There are so many questions swirling in my head it's hard to keep them straight. But that's what it means to be a private eye. You can't get overwhelmed. You need to pull the clues apart. Compartmentalize. Take them out, one at a time, then assemble them every which way until you find the pattern.

But it's late, and I need to wrap this up. "Got a question for you. Two, actually."

Let's see if she corroborates Tevon.

"When we were talking the other day about Arthur Hanson... you said he watched fireworks back home. Did he say he watched them alone? Or with someone?"

"Huh. Not the question I was hoping for, but lemme think." Camilla collects more empties as the barback cleans up in the kitchen, dishes clanking. "You know," she says with a bit more conviction. "I think he did. He said *we*. I forgot about that. He might have mentioned a friend. Or a brother? Yeah. Yeah! He did once. He said brother, but stopped himself, like he was embarrassed, or maybe they had a falling out. I don't know. It was just the one time. He said *we always watched them on the fourth of...?*"

"July? July fourth?"

"Yes! That's it. Fourth of July. How'd you know?"

It's an Earth reference. Fourth of July is the annual celebration of America's independence. Marked the end of a long and bloody battle.

To commemorate their victory as slave owners who pretty much committed genocide by slaughtering the indigenous population in the name of their own freedom, they shoot fireworks and have barbeques. How colonial of them.

Whistler earned his money today.

"It's not important," I say. "But he said we? Okay."

Camilla sits on a stool behind the bar. She pours two shots, one for each of us. The tequila warms me up while sending a shiver down my spine. Funny how that works. The booze is a lot like life, the duality of it all. Light and dark. Pleasure and pain.

Gil's gonna hate this. I'll get to him in the morning. Well, later. Because I suspect what's coming.

"I'm about to get off," Camilla says with the dip of her head, then runs her finger around the lip of the shot glass. "Wanna come with?"

"After the night I've had"—I finish off my beer—"I really do."

CHAPTER 12

Whistler calls me at the crack of dawn. Says he's got something urgent to show me. Can't wait. I'm starving anyway, so I leave Camilla as she snores into the mattress, have him meet me at Belle's Diner. It's halfway to my office. Whistler's waiting for me as I roll in. He pulled an all-nighter. He looks it, too.

"Those are some bags under your eyes," I say, then sip the coffee already on the table. It's black. And hot. "You're too young to look this old."

"Just following your lead." I raise an eyebrow. "I mean"—he cowers slightly—"I examined the clues until the story revealed itself. You actually look pretty good. Better than usual."

There's a backhanded compliment in there, but I let it slide, seeing as he burned his retinas doing research for me. But I'm mildly offended on many levels, mostly because he already seems to know me better than I want him to. His comments hit the mark.

"Whistler. I'm meeting the client in forty minutes. Get to it."

From his shoulder bag he produces the fliers from Hanson's apartment. They're taped to a massive, fold-out map.

"Photocopies," I say. "Protect the originals. Smart."

Whistler beams a little. "I went over these every which way. And then I realized... look here. Larry Fin's Hot Air Balloons. Walter's Whale Watching. Zin Shou Family Restaurant. Sparkle Massage and Wellness. They're all over E-Town, and the other spheres of Eternity."

"I know, Whistler. I've seen them."

I smile at the waitress, who brings me an egg white omelet with broccoli and tomatoes, and a bowl of mixed berries. I'm trying to eat healthy. Adulting sucks.

"Here you go, dear," the waitress says. "I forgot your sausage links."

Well... healthier.

"Yes, but have you seen this?" Whistler's already marked various other locations with a green dot and circled them. "Within a six-block radius of each destination is a Strident Eyes outlet. This is all across the realm. The fliers Hanson picked up? It's a coded mapping system. I'm not sure if they're targets or for another strategic purpose, but whatever they are, it's a coordinated effort. They're linked. And Tico's Tacos is the drop site for the fliers. They keep the map updated. I think that's why Hanson goes back."

I'm pretty good at research. But Whistler's better. He keeps this up and I might hire him full time. That's a helluva catch.

He sees the layers between the layers. Not beneath—between. That's where you usually find the juicy stuff, right in front of you, yet... not.

He's so good it makes me angry, my insecurities jumping up and down at how old it makes me seem. I'm not even thirty-three and already I feel like I've lived multiple lifetimes. Maybe that's because I have. Story for another day.

But the more pressing issue is Hanson.

"With what I learned last night, this makes a lot more sense. Nice job. You did well."

It's possible Hanson's being extorted or threatened—or maybe he really did snap under the pressure of his new role in the Cosmos—but whichever it is, I'm convinced he's a key player in this mystery. I've got work to do.

I toss some credits on the table. "Get whatever you want, then get some sleep. I have an idea about what's going on."

*****

Gil's meeting me at my office in an hour.

That gives me time to poke around the Strident Eyes outlet on Durant Street. It's early, but as I head around back to the loading dock, a van passes me by. It's gone before I can get a good look at the driver, his face a blur.

Hard not to wonder if it's filled with Jamie's fireworks.

Dressed in Strident Eyes uniforms, three workers are taking a smoke break. Spray-painted on the dock is another MinderNot symbol.

"Hey," I say. "Which one of you is Craig?"

There is no Craig. It's an old private eye trick. Toss out a name they don't know and see how they react.

"I am," one guy says. He tosses his butt, crushes it with this foot. "Who's asking?"

Of course I pick one of their actual names. Nice going, Angela. Way to play the odds.

"I heard you were the guy to talk to if a girl wanted some party favors."

Sporting a goatee and thick-inked tats up and down his right arm, he leers at me, checks me over. "That's what you heard, huh? From who?"

I'm not the bustiest chick in E-town, but his eyes drift there, so I'm using it. I poke out my hip. "You know a girl never reveals her secrets."

"I thought that was magicians."

I bat my eyes, playing the flirt angle. "Is there a difference?"

"*Ooh-hoo-hoo,*" his two buddies taunt.

"She's feisty," says the short redhead with freckles across his nose and cheekbones. "Pretty, too."

"Yeah," Craig says. "Real pretty." He cocks his head, takes another step toward me. "But I don't know her, yet she knows me. And she's coming here, before hours, to where I work, asking about party favors. So either you're too stupid for your own good… or you're up to something. By the way you're dressed, I'd say you're up to something. You a cop?"

I laugh. "Me? I don't think so. I'm not real good at sticking to protocol."

"I can see that." Craig raises his eyebrows, licks his lips just enough to know that he's ready to tussle. "So what are you good at?"

I scan the area. There are at least two exit points I can reach quickly if I need to. And I might need to. "I'm good at relaying messages. I've got one for you. From Haji Anshani."

The guys simultaneously constrict, look at each other, concern in their eyes.

"He says the shipment of fireworks never made it," I say. "He paid half up front, and got nothing for his trouble. He isn't impressed. And now that Evie von M is taking over Strident Eyes, I'm not so sure you guys want to be caught in the middle. Evie's not big time, but she's got enough muscle to really make it hurt."

"No," Craig insists. "We made the drop. We don't know anything about Evie Von M. We've just been offloading the stock. Like we were told."

"I don't know, boys. Haji says they never showed, you say they did. Then last night one of your trucks goes missing. Made a stop in the Manuela Projects. Ended up in a ditch out by the Scherzeron Airstrip. The driver, Albert something, took a bat to the head. Doesn't know who jacked him. So how do you want to handle this? I can't go back empty handed. Because next time Haji won't send me. He'll send his niece. He'll send Seema."

Craig and his pals look at each other. Freckles tips me off without knowing it—his eyes twitch toward the warehouse—while the lankier guy with a baby face and small forehead slides his hands into his front pockets, fiddling nervously.

His fingertips were black. He might be a pipehead. It's also possible he's been lighting off fireworks. The burns looked right for it.

They don't know what to make of me, or what they should do. But I've got their attention.

"No, no. Wait," Craig says. "We don't ... look. The boss isn't here. And the stock is gone. You just missed it."

"Bad luck for you guys. Sure you don't have a little something tucked away? Maybe a little extra?"

"There's another warehouse," Freckles says.

Craig gives him the death stare.

"Ahh," I say. "Now we're getting somewhere. You give me an address, I forget I was ever here. Or you can explain it to Seema."

Craig's rolling his fingers in and out of a fist, like he wants to take a swing at me, but knows he probably shouldn't. His eyes are nearly bulging. The terror is unmistakable.

"*Swear* you leave us out of it?"

"This address is legit, you got nothing to worry about. At least… not from me."

Evie Von M, the Anshanis. Hanson's sure stepped into a dumpster fire. And dragged me with him.

Craig hands me a tab of paper. It's got the address. It's in the industrial zone out by Calvin Corner, just past the Aleena Refinery Center. A half-dozen developers who, thanks to various tax breaks, concessions, and well-placed contributions to dubious bank accounts, invested in this up-and-coming redevelopment zone. The plan is to convert abandoned industrial properties—including the Aleena Refinery—into vibrant mixed-use projects.

I'd check it out myself, but my meeting with Gil is the priority. I'll put Dolores on it. She knows that part of town better than anyone. It'll also give me a reason to check in with Jamie. I've got questions for her, too.

"Thanks, boys. Enjoy the day."

"Wait," Craig calls out as I leave them behind. "Who are you?"

I lift my head, tip my fedora at them. "Ask Seema," I say. "Tell her I said hi."

CHAPTER 13

"**Y**ou want me to do what? No. No way. Just... no." Gil's handling my request better than I thought he would. "*This* is why you called me to your office? You said it was urgent."

"It is." I fill him in on Hanson, Yvette, Strident Eyes, and the body dumped in the mud. It's a lot to process, so I give him a minute. "I don't know what Hanson's up to, whether he's a willing participant or a victim himself. But whatever it is, it's connected to Strident Eyes. And if he's caught in a turf war between Evie Von M and the Anshanis, there's not much chance this ends well for him. Or you. Or me. So if you want to track him down as badly as you say, you need to do what I ask and you need to do it now. If I'm going to find out where Hanson's headed, I need to know where he's been. I need to know what motivates him, because I haven't got a clue."

I've worked enough cases to know when a client's at that moment, when they finally accept how deep they're in.

The biggest dilemma clients face—on-realm and off—is reconciling the difference between how they *think* their situation is and how it *actually* is.

When that happens there's a look they get—solemn, frightened, lost, sad, and sometimes even a tiny bit defeated.

Gil has that look now. He's not talking. He's just sitting there on my couch, leaning forward, elbows on his knees, head in hands. I have to let him work it through, let him come to me. But I can't wait too long. We don't have the time. So I give him another nudge.

"There's something else, Gil. The event last night? I met Zenovia. She was there."

His head pops up. "What? What do you...?"

"She supplied the flowers, but was hired by Strident Eyes." I
see the recognition in his eyes. His girlfriend may be tangled up
in an ugly part of his life, and he's already lost control over it.
"She didn't know who she was dealing with. She sees it now. I
offered to help her out. She's lovely, Gil. I see why you like her."

He's blinking fast now, nearly twitching. "I... I didn't know.
She said she had an event and I ..."

And then I realize. "Oh. Gil. You don't like her. You *love* her.
You're in love."

Gil reaches to his chest. He's starting to hyperventilate.

And then I relieve a pressure that seems to weigh on him
like gravity itself, without him having to say anything. "I didn't
mention your name. She doesn't know you hired me, doesn't
know you're in trouble. But if you really care about this woman,
you might want to clue her in. She's mixed up with the same
people we are."

Gil rolls his lips. "Y-you can't let that happen. You have to
keep her away."

"Then help me, Gil. I've got people looking for Hanson, but
he could be anywhere. Yvette's behavior is escalating. She wants
to make a scene and Evie's the audience. We either wait for
Hanson to strike again, or we do something about it. It's your
case, Gil. But it's my life. So for both our sakes... you need to
get me where I need to be." I re-check my gun and lean in close.
"You gotta get me to Earth."

*****

Gil surprises me. I just assumed we were headed to the Breslin,
Anders & Li headquarters. I had an ulterior motive. I wanted to
case the joint, see how I might sneak back in later.

Instead we shoot across town, to the Nova District. Gil leads
us into Dante's Pizzeria, then flicks his eyes at the aproned guy
behind the counter.

Without a word, counter guy buzzes us through a steel door
in back, that leads down a flight of stairs, then through a hallway drenched in the aroma of hot pizza and fresh garlic knots.

Gil slides back an accordion gate, which opens into a narrow elevator with copper plates. He punches in a series of raised buttons on the wall mount and pulls on a mechanical lever. Rather than descend farther into the basement, the elevator rotates 180 degrees, then opens into a small room with chipped brown walls. We approach the door adjacent to us.

Gil holds his ID tag up to—I'm not sure where the surveillance camera is—but there's a buzzer. The door opens in.

Gil surprises me again. With all this cloak and dagger I expect a room filled with high-tech gadgetry, including buttons, lights, and a team of engineers milling about. Instead there's one guy—late-20s, plump, glasses, bowl haircut with shaggy bangs—sitting behind a drafting table with no drawers. The room is well-lit, with peach walls, various plants, a blue sofa, white coffee table with books, magazines, and 3-D tablets on top, and a window view of the sun sparkling off the ocean.

The seascape is a hologram—we're deep inside the bowels of this building—but I can't tell the view from the real thing.

If I didn't know any better, I'd think we're in the waiting room of a boutique travel agency. Maybe we are.

"Clancy," Gil says. "How's it hanging?"

"Low as my left toe," Clancy says without looking up from the screen.

"I hear ya. Listen, Clance, I gotta new recruit. Need to see if she can handle the jump. Mind if she goes? You know how it is. Newbies."

"Love to help, Gil, but I'm kinda busy."

I'm not sure watching intergalactic parkour constitutes as *busy*, although I get the appeal. It is pretty cool.

"Sure, sure," Gil says. "But Dino just pulled out a fresh pie. Pepperoni and olives."

Clancy looks up. "I'm listening."

"Now that I think about it... extra olives. Extra pepperoni. Extra mozzarella."

"Aaaand...?" Clancy leads, raising his voice. His eyes follow.

"Grape soda. Extra-large. Pie's waiting."

"You got twenty minutes. Then I need the room."

I wait until Clancy leaves. "This is the way to Earth? Come on."

"Don't be fooled. Clancy's a top-flight technician. And what you see," Gil says, "isn't always what you get."

He sits down at the keyboard, punches in a code. There's a hum, a whir, and a series of vibrations. A glass chamber unfolds from the wall.

"That's clever."

"We'll see. In you go."

"Twenty minutes isn't enough time, Gil. It might take a while."

He waves me off. "You can be there a minute, a day, a month, or a year. Doesn't matter. But whenever you come back, it'll be like you never left. You'll be back faster than I can blink."

"All right, then," I say, not convinced his timeline will play out as he's purporting. Only one way to find out. "Let's do it."

Gil approaches. He's standing close. Too close. He reaches up to my left ear, his breath hot on my neck. Instinctively, I grab his wrist. "What'cha doing there, Gil?"

"I need to place this tracker behind your ear. All you have to do is tap it once, and no matter where you are on Earth, what's happening at the time, or how long you've been gone, it'll instantly transport you back into the chamber, to this very moment. It's how it works."

The last time I had Gil in my grip, he was frightened. Now it barely fazes him. Maybe I'm losing my touch. Or maybe he's getting used to me. I release his hand. "Go ahead," I say. On the tip of his finger he presses what looks like a contact lens behind my left ear. I feel it dissolve under my skin.

"It's in," he says.

Gil sits back behind the terminal. He gestures for me to enter the chamber. I do. He punches in a series of commands.

"It's called a Cressa tab. This will send you to Earth, to Arthur's house. You'll arrive no more than one minute after I brought him to Eternity. I can't send you back before or during my recruitment of Hanson. It's VCP protocol. We can't interfere with that timeline or it initiates an automatic lockdown and pulls you right out. But when you arrive there, he will have just left."

"Got it. How will I know if"—I'm now standing in Hanson's living room—"it worked?"

*****

I've been off-realm many times, including Earth. I travel through the Infinity Cloud regularly. But interdimensional transport is a bit more jarring this way.

It takes me a minute to recalibrate, get my bearings.

Hanson's house is just as Gil described.

Three bedrooms, two bathrooms, living room, mudroom, kitchen, barely-there dining room, basement, and attached one-car garage. Small front yard, bushes lining the house exterior, a flower garden, a handful of trees, and a workman-like job on the lawn.

Each room is painted a different color, with throw rugs covering half of the hardwood floors. There's a hearth in the living room, but no chopped wood. Lining the mantle are various decorative items, including a framed picture of a tall, skinny teenager—not Arthur—and a middle-aged couple. If Hanson does have a brother, is that him? And the adults? Are those his parents?

I find another photo of the skinny teenager floating on a tube. The caption reads: *Summer fun. July 4th, 1986. Canisteo River.*

There's a library's worth of books in this house, bookcases with every shelf lined end-to-end, as well as stacks of books on the living room coffee table, and various other strays throughout the rooms. It's taking all of my considerable private eye experience, training, and powers, but being the keen observer of detail that I am, I deduce that Hanson likes to read.

I find other photos throughout the house, some of the middle-aged couple, and a few more of someone who looks like that skinny kid, only as a full-grown adult. But none of Arthur Hanson. At least, none I can find.

The kitchen is clean. Dishwasher is empty, the fridge about half-full. On the counter, by the phone, is an address book. It's blue, with the word SUPERMAN written in red letters, within a yellow circle. I'll need to go through it.

For now, though, I go floor by floor, opening the closets and drawers. The only thing that immediately stands out, other than his book fetish, are the various action figures I find on shelves and counter tops. The boy in him lives.

Everything about Hanson's house is modest. The entire place is neat and clean, but not like his E-Town apartment, which was immaculate, like nobody really lives there. The only indulgences I find here are his collectibles and books.

There's a pile on his nightstand, all from different authors in different genres. *The Catcher in the Rye. Pride and Prejudice. Zoomies. Zen and the Art of Motorcycle Maintenance. Stronger Than a Bronze Dragon. The Midnight Front. Frankenstein. The Dark Knight Returns. No Small Bills. Everyone is a Moon. Lamb. The Last Redhead.*

Maybe they were his active reading list, maybe he just hadn't gotten around to putting them away. Nothing here speaks to me. There's not a damn thing about this house that makes me feel like I'm chasing the same Arthur Hanson on the loose in E-Town.

His karmic signature, his energy, tells me a solid adult living a solid life occupies this solid house as a solid neighbor in this solid town.

The Hanson I've been tracking all over E-Town left a completely different vibe. Cold and exacting. Quiet yet unpredictable. Mysterious. Deadly.

It's been two hours now and I can't find even the slightest clue as to what Hanson's up to. Where he might be headed.

After going through his medicine cabinet—toiletries, ointments, some prescription bottles—I head back to the living room. I sit on the couch, in the corner. Two throw pillows are bunched up. There's an indentation in the cushion.

So I sit in Hanson's perch, occupying his space, his comfort zone, and lean back. I close my eyes.

I clear my mind and let the accumulation of his belongings wash over me. Then I get up and remove the couch cushions. I unzip the outer casings, fish around inside. Searching for a secret stash of... I don't know what. He did it in E-Town, maybe he's done it here. But all I pull out are pieces of foam.

Needing a fresh perspective I head outside, poke around in the bushes. Other than a handful of slugs and a dead mouse, I don't find a thing.

I enter the garage through a side door. I find the usual. Lawn mower, rake, shovel, and other gardening supplies, boxes of junk, a bicycle, empty gas can, tool box, and a stack of newspapers dating back several years.

I spot a silver key on a small chain, hanging on a rusty nail next to the door.

I fit the key into every lock I can find, in the garage and the house. No luck. I head down to the basement. There's a bridge table and chairs, ping pong table covered with a drop cloth, more books, and several hand-painted models. Mostly spaceships and robots. The kid in him again.

There are three built-in cabinets with bookshelves on top, each with a keyhole. Not a fit. On the industrial side I re-inspect the laundry. There's a storage closet, but no lock.

I'm about to give up when my jacket sleeve catches the large coiled hose attached to a stand-up vacuum cleaner. As I try to untangle myself, I accidentally pull the vacuum over. I kneel down, to pick it up. While I'm down here, I look up into the closet and, against the back wall I see a white, painted circle I'd missed before.

Old-style houses sometimes have closets within closets, to provide extra storage. I run my fingers over the circle. It's the outline of a lock. But I can see that a key has already been snapped off in the grooves. I rush back to the garage and find a pair of needle-nose pliers, and though it takes some doing, I'm able to remove the broken key.

I then try the key from Hanson's garage. It fits. It must've been a set. I twist it to the right. The door falls open and hits my shoulder.

As does the heavy, black bag inside, which is now splayed on the floor. I lean over, and unzip the bag. The smell sledgehammers me in the face.

There's a body.

It's tall and lanky and, based on the rigor mortis, at least a few days gone.

It's the skinny kid from the photo, only now a full-grown man. What the hell is going on?

I fish around in his pockets until I find his wallet. I remove his driver's license. It says what it shouldn't say, yet there it is, approved by the state of New York.

Arthur Thomas Hanson.

My breathe catches.

Now I know why the vibe I got here is so different from the one in E-Town. The guy I've been chasing must have killed the real Arthur Hanson and stolen his identity.

I don't know if he's Hanson's brother, a stranger, or someone else he knew, but whoever I've been chasing, he's not the Arthur Hanson Gil thought he was.

Which means Gil screwed this up royally, or there's an even bigger problem going on within the VCP.

In either case, it means Gil recruited the wrong man.

Which also means I've been *searching* for the wrong man.

Arthur Hanson's killer is also a thief, con artist, and who knows what else, armed with knowledge of the Universe very few off-realmers in any part of the Cosmos ever comes to learn. Which makes him all the more threatening.

And my closest, most loyal friends—who have no idea what they're walking into or who they might actually be dealing with—are trying to find him.

If anything goes down, it's all on me.

PART II:

BEAUTY AND THE BEAST

CHAPTER 14

I'd love to say this is the first time a dead body has fallen at my feet. But that would be a lie.

I'd also love to say it sends shock waves through me, because it should. But it doesn't.

Don't get me wrong, it's unpleasant, but as a PI, if you can't handle the occasional corpse, you're in the wrong business.

Yet the fact remains that Arthur Hanson, whom I was hired to find, is dead.

On Earth.

And unless I can find compelling evidence to refute it, he was murdered.

Time to assess. If I'm correct, and Hanson was in fact killed by the man in E-Town who's coopted his name, then I'm in no immediate danger. I've already searched the house. I'm alone.

I also have the rare benefit of not having to hurry, because no matter how long I take to investigate here, I'll return to E-Town at exactly the same time I left.

In that sense, the risks in E-Town won't escalate on my account. But my instinct is to warn my friends. Although it's not lost on me that I don't think of Gil right away.

He's my client, and yes, even after I learned he was mixed up in Universe business, with the VCP, I could have dropped him. But I didn't. I still have the Anshanis to deal with.

I'm not sure what I'm going to tell him, because I don't know how Gil recruited the wrong man, if Hanson actually *is* the wrong man. I'll also have no choice but to bring Tarrish into this, and Gil certainly won't like *that*.

Like a wannabe stud who gets rejected on prom night, life is filled with disappointments.

But while time may be on my side Eternity-wise, I am actually standing over a dead body—a murder victim—on Earth. The last thing I need is for the mailman or one of Hanson's neighbors to spot me through a window. That might get awkward.

And for the sake of decorum, I should alert local law enforcement, but not until I'm done. No matter how good they might be, they're never solving this one.

I pull a pair of disposable gloves from my pocket to inspect the corpse. If you've never done it, moving a dead body is extremely difficult. The existing weight is distributed unevenly, the internal fluids bunching in quadrants, so the body feels heavier, even though it isn't.

This Hanson—the real Arthur Hanson, Earth Hanson—looks nothing like E-Town Hanson.

Earth Hanson is tall and skinny, with thick black-framed glasses. And while he has the same sandy hair as E-Town Hanson, it has more of a wave to it.

There's not a single bruise I can find, except—ah, there it is—for the flat-head nail jammed into the base of his neck. That'll do it.

I'm not sure what else the body can tell me. There's also not much I can do with it. He's simply too heavy for me to lift back up into the closet.

But I need some connection to E-Town Hanson. Who are they to each other?

Lots of questions, but no answers.

Then I remember the address book. I dig it out of my pocket. There's a few dozen names in here, some written in pen, some in pencil, with a few crossed out, some with updated addresses and phone numbers, but no one else with the last name of Hanson. I'll need to rummage through the house again.

I hate to do it, but I toss Hanson's books, hoping another picture or a letter might fall out, a slip of paper, anything that'll give me a clue about what went down here. It takes me more than an hour just to get through the books in the living room, and though I'm making a mess, ironically, it helps unclutter my mind.

Was the murder an accident? Spur of the moment? Premeditated?

Come on, Angela. Think.

How could Gil recruit the wrong guy? Even it was Hanson's brother, E-Town Hanson must have been… what? Hiding in the house? Was he on the lamb? Trying to reconnect? The timing had to be precise, and there's no way to mistake these two men for each other.

And how did Gil overlook that Arthur Hanson, being recruited for a highly specialized role within the Universe, was murdered in his own home? How did the VCP? Is it possible they just didn't know? Or maybe their screening methods are flawed? I wouldn't put it past them.

With Jamie holding down E-Town—and the entire Universe—by herself, practically with duct tape and twine, the infrastructure of the Cosmos has been cracking. Maybe the VCP off-world program has been affected too?

As a private eye who's worked the Universe for as long as I have, you learn the mechanics of the Cosmos are not as tightly coiled as you'd like to believe.

Just think about your typical construction site, with all the waste, design flaws, graft, and overall shoddy work. Now extrapolate those problems across Existence, and suddenly it's easy to comprehend why the Universe has more holes than a recycled diaphragm.

In any case, whatever went down with the real Arthur Hanson, however it happened, I trust Gil even less than before. Damn. I don't know.

It's time to recharge anyhow, my back and knees throbbing, my stomach gurgling. I head into the kitchen. There's a carton of milk, a full pitcher of orange juice, and four beers.

I chug some OJ. The vitamin D will do me good. I don't get enough of it on Earth, the levels radiating from the Sun much lower than what we get in E-Town. I lean my shoulder against the fridge.

There's various magnets—a pineapple, an oval with a Buffalo Sabres logo, and another in the shape of a book that says *Book*.

But my eye goes to the magnet in the shape of an eagle. It's pinning a blue sticky note to the door. In what I assume is Hanson's handwriting, the note says:

Uncle Rich. Thursday. 4 pm. Pick up fertilizer.

I linger on the name until it hits me. I thumb through the address book. Uncle Rich. 16 Merit Road. Canisteo, N.Y.

Uncle Rich. Does that make him Richard Hanson? Only one way to find out.

On the counter, next to the refrigerator, is a brown ceramic bowl. It's filled with some loose change, a paperclip and, fortuitously, car keys.

*****

Uncle Rich. A lead.

A few problems, however. I'm driving a dead man's car. Having just left his house. Where he was murdered.

And the place was ransacked. By me. Not a good look.

I need to ditch this ride, find a new one.

I also jumped to Earth in my standard getup. A pinstripe suit, zip boots, fedora. In E-Town, it works. But here? I look exactly like what I am—a private eye, a long way from home, poking around in places I don't belong.

For camouflage I wear a Buffalo State College sweatshirt from Hanson's closet and a pair of white, moderately clean sneakers, which are at least four sizes too large for me.

That's me, Angela Hardwicke, supermodel.

I roll my gear into a knapsack, which I also took from Hanson's closet.

Sorry, Arthur. A girl's gotta make due.

I'm behind the wheel of his silver four-door. It's a standard-issue vehicle, as I've seen at least a half-dozen just like it in the ten minutes I've been on the road. It blends.

I don't like to drive even under normal circumstances, but doing it here, on Earth, is stranger to me than if I was zooming through an asteroid belt.

As a realm, Eternity is populated with urban centers—E-Town being my home turf—surrounded by waterfront neighborhoods, mountain ranges, villages, rivers, oceans, and various green spaces. But there's no true suburban landscape.

America is loaded with them.

For decades there was a mass exodus to the suburbs, although Americans are migrating back to the cities en masse because that's where the action is. If they're going to be broke or in debt or otherwise stressed beyond their limits, they want their kink to be easily accessible. Some things are universal.

But that's the problem with this country. This planet.

Earth has a population of more than seven billion people. Eternity doesn't even have a fraction of that number.

Yet it's amazing to me just how much Earth reminds me of E-Town. We have a twelve-month calendar. So do they. Our days are twenty-four hours long, our weeks seven days. They have four rotating seasons, as do we.

Although we live much longer—the perception of the passage of time is slower for us than for them—Earthers look and sound like Eternitarians. Their languages make absolutely no sense to me, but passing through the cosmic membrane allows me to understand them, and vice versa. No idea why. Then again, don't care.

Apparently, the Minders of the Universe—the old ones, anyway—had great plans for Earth. As the story goes, the Minders infused this planet with the embers of Eternity in a way they didn't for many others. Again, no idea why. Yet I'm told Earthers have the innate potential to evolve to the point where they themselves might one day be worthy of a place in Eternity, to help construct the very Universe they live in.

Do I believe it? Who knows? It's as plausible as any other scenario I've encountered.

Other than living in Eternity because that's where we keep our stuff, I couldn't give you a single reason, not one qualitative characteristic that favorably separates Eternitarians from anyone else in the Cosmos. I could list dozens of reasons why we're worse.

I wonder what it means sometimes, this power the Minders have over the Universe, the role we Eternitarians play in serving them. I've given up trying to figure out what the Minders are up to. Even when I think I have a clue, a glimmer of the truth, I realize their vision of the Universe is so far beyond my comprehension that it drives me to make decisions I quickly regret.

Makes me wonder if Owen isn't maybe better off without me. My boy. My baby boy.

Stop, Angela. Don't follow that thread. It leads nowhere good. Focus on the essentials.

Like on my need to change, pee, and eat. And not necessarily in that order.

Beneath a leaden sky I park Hanson's car in the lot of a multi-purpose, three-level retail outlet, where I use the restroom, wash my face, apply a light layer of lipstick, then recheck the money belt strapped around my waist.

I have more than thirty money belts in my safe back in E-Town, one each for the various realms I've encountered, and a few I'm either hoping to get to or, as is the nature of my business, where I'll eventually end up.

This one, labeled with an unbreakable code and decryption-proof algorithm that took me years to perfect so that no one other than me knows which is which, is marked EARTH. I've got my Earth-registered PI license, driver's license, passport, cash, and credit cards.

Renfro, the former client I mentioned, was a huge help securing these documents during one of my earliest cases out here.

Wandering through the superstore I pick up a pair of blue jeans, black sneakers, socks, and an arugula-colored utility jacket with inner mesh lining that's stylish and flexible enough for my needs.

I pull my hair into a ponytail, then grab a three-pack of underwear, a sports bra, and a small box of tampons, just in case. Going off-realm plays havoc with my cycle.

I'm dying for a steak, medium rare, but I make due in this crappy café with a crappy spinach salad and what they advertise as grilled chicken, also crappy. I then load up on energy bars, a brick of Cadbury Royal Dark Chocolate, and extra strength pain relievers. I have no idea how long I'll be here, so better to have supplies.

I also need to deal with the car.

As a private eye, you sometimes need to think like a criminal. The goal is to uncover their motives, track their progress, even anticipate their moves. But even though I swore an oath and am bound to my licensed code of ethics, sometimes you have to *act* like a criminal. And in a way, I am.

I did enter Arthur's Hanson's house without his consent. I did find his dead body, and left it unreported. I stole his car. And I'm doing so to avoid detection.

If that doesn't sound like a criminal, I'm not sure what does.

Nevertheless, I need to follow the leads I've got, so I leave Hanson's car in the superstore lot, then, with my supplies in a white plastic bag, walk past several run-down retailers, half of them vacant. There's a mobile phone service outlet, good-will donation center, auto parts shop, and a dollar store, when I reach a gas station, where a green and white cab is filling up.

"I need a lift to Canisteo," I say to the driver. "Know where that is?"

"Miss," says the driver, ebony-skinned, broad-shouldered with what looks like a shaving cut under his chin. "That's a good two hours, about half way between nowhere and the pimple of America's ass crack. And then two hours back. I'm not making the trip."

"I also might need you to hang out a while, and depending on how things go, take me back," I say, ignoring his protests. Part of the negotiation. "Can you handle that?"

"Gonna cost you extra, but if you can pay, I can handle."

I flash a thick billfold.

"Hop in," he says.

"One more thing. I need you to keep this off your log. You never met me. I was never here. You filled up with gas, had a stomach ache, called it a day."

"Sorry. Can't do that. It's against the rules. Could lose my license."

Through the partition I hand him a hundred-dollar bill. I've been in Esteban's cab so many times I'm practically a cab driver myself. He cuts side deals all the time.

"There's another one of these with your name on it, plus the fare. How do the rules feel about that?"

The driver eyes me through the rearview. "Show me a few more of those Benjamins … the rules will feel just fine about it."

I hand him the money.

It takes a minute for me to sink in, but I'm finally able to exhale, and close my eyes. There's that tug in me again, the pull of *dRops*—the desperate, inconsolable urge that cannot be satisfied any other way—but there's no way to get my super drug down here, no matter what I do. I get hysterical for a few seconds. Sweat oozes from every pore. And then it passes.

That's the key. I know the urges will never resolve, not permanently. I just can't give in when they come.

Leaving the greater Buffalo area, I let the engine's hum and rhythm of the wheels sooth me, when a magnificent breath leaves my body. It's the breaks I need, the in-between spaces, especially when I'm off-realm. When I'm totally alone.

I used to have Milo in my corner, to bail me out of a jam if I really needed him.

When I first met Milo, before he was a Minder of the Universe, he was the polar opposite. The Great Disruptor. The cosmic foil to the Minders. But we had a connection.

I think I got him, and I think he got me.

His job, his purpose—his reason for being—was to cause trouble throughout the Universe. Not to be destructive, but to interfere. Just enough to slow the Minders down. Forcing them to re-think their cosmic plains—a check on their ambition, power, and hubris.

Milo loved the Universe. More, he loved the beings who populated it. He was our watchdog, whether we knew it or not. He got a bad rap a lot of the time. A troublemaker. A fool.

But those of us who knew him, who really knew him, couldn't help but love him, even when he screwed up. Especially then. Because if he was fallible, it was okay for us to be fallible, too.

He even gave me a sequence. My own, personal call signal. Right hand balled into a fist—three squeezes. Then the same pattern again with my left hand, followed by one more squeeze, both fists at the same time. I've used it more times than I probably should have.

Milo always showed up. Usually late, but in all the jams I've gotten into, he never let me down. Never let me forget he was out there, that he was listening.

That I mattered.

I don't know what we are to each other now, if we're anything at all. And he's got my son. I've tried to make my peace with it, that Owen is out there with Milo... somewhere. That he's okay.

Because I trust, even though he's unavailable to me, that Milo is still keeping an eye out for Owen. Milo did that for me, once upon a time, when I was lost in the *dRops*, in no condition to be Owen's mother. I'm not even sure I'm ready now, but I'm working at it.

I'm fighting my addiction, getting it under control.

Milo's a lot of things, but he would never turn his back on Owen. Never ever.

Which is the reason I'm holding it together. It torments me, not knowing where Owen is or what he's doing. But I cling to the belief that as long as he's with Milo, that Owen is okay. I have to believe that. Because if I don't...

My mind drifts. I almost doze off. And then I realize.

I forgot the backpack. In Hanson's car. My suit, my fedora, my zip boots.

My second skin.

I left it all behind.

CHAPTER 15

The dirt road winds through the woods. Late afternoon.

There's a nip in the air, a cold tendril of wind, but it's fresh. Fresh for Earth.

There's so much pollution on this planet, I don't know how they breathe.

Milo told me Eternity went through its own industrial phase eons ago. The Minders figured automation would speed things up in service of the Universe, allowing for greater efficiency, but the environment became so toxic, the illness rates so high, they scrapped it completely.

The Minders supposedly blinked away all industry and replaced it with a permanent wintry environment, thinking the frigid air—plus the snow and ice—would keep everyone moving, just to stay warm. Can you imagine? Freezing my butt off year-round? No thanks.

Not sure how long the tundra lasted—Milo said it was quite a while, whatever *quite a while* means for beings at least as old as Existence itself—but as Minders do, they changed their minds again, going in the opposite direction.

They reinvented Eternity as a tropical paradise. That didn't work out, either. Too much time spent wind-surfing, fornicating, and getting drunk on the beach.

So the Minders gave Eternity yet another new look and feel. The one we have now.

As will likely happen again. And so it goes.

I have the cabbie stop about a hundred feet or so from the cabin, a one-story domicile with a wrap-around porch and a slanted roof.

Trees of various heights and thickness surround the cabin,

the leaves a mix of autumn colors. A fox scurries down to the rock-lined stream running along the cabin, and leading into a valley bounded by steep hillsides.

I'm about to make my approach when a black dog with a white snout and white paws comes bounding toward me. A mid-size dog, it barks repeatedly, but not angry. It's warning me to wait, to follow protocol.

An older man, white, with gray hair, is standing on the porch. He's wearing blue jeans, boots, a red flannel, and a brown hunting cap. His face is weathered and a little bit sad, like a man who's tired of life, but endures out of spite—or habit. Maybe both. There's a twinkle of hope in his blue-grey eyes. But not much.

"That's Paige," he says. "She inspects all visitors. You wanna come closer, you gotta clear it with her."

I kneel down, let Paige sniff the front of my hand. Her tail wags furiously, so I scratch her under the chin. The dog hurries away then, taking her place on the porch, by her owner's side.

"Sorry to come unannounced," I say, eyeing the old pick-up truck parked next to the cabin.

"No other way to come."

"It's nice out here. Quiet."

"Pretty quiet," he says.

"Mind if I come up?"

He looks at me, at Paige, then back in my direction. "All right."

Every interview requires its own approach. My play here is to stick to the truth. Pretty close, anyway. I try to sell him any nonsense, he'll discharge me right away. He might also discharge the shotgun he's got behind him. It's standing upright, leaning against the cabin.

"Are you Richard Hanson?"

"I am."

I extend my hand. "Angela Hardwicke. I'm here about your nephew."

Richard Hanson has been a still man thus far, a sentinel, his movements minimal, yet exacting. But he shifts in a way that says he's been expecting me. Or someone like me. He's got a helluva poker face. He reveals little, but the twitch above his right eye, the tiniest squint, betrays his resolve just enough to let me know he has something to say.

It's my job to get him to say it.

Paige's head darts to the side. She barks twice. A rabbit scurries through the bushes, only to be snared by the fox I'd seen.

"I'm a private investigator, Mister Hanson."

He's obviously not a trusting man. Maybe for good reason. I hand him my PI license, to prove I am who I say I am.

"I've been trying to locate your nephew. My investigation led me here."

Richard Hanson inspects my license, certified, also thanks to Renfro. "Says you're from Portland, Oregon. Long way from home."

I squint, offer him half a smile. "You have no idea."

He hands back my license.

"My employer. Gil Habersau. He's an accountant." No point trying to weave some elaborate tale. It's elaborate enough as it is. "There's a question about some missing files. Your nephew may or may not be involved. I'm trying to find Arthur. Have you seen him?"

There's a stillness, not just from Richard, but Paige, and the air around us. I've hit a nerve. I can see Richard's mind at work, his shoulder tilted back just enough to let me know he's thinking about the shotgun.

I'm a fast draw, but am I fast enough to produce my gun before he grabs his? I'd rather not find out.

He leans forward a half step. Paige responds, up on all fours. I don't know what this means. I don't want to shoot Richard. I don't want to get shot.

Before it comes to that, he drops his head.

"Arthur." His voice quivers. "Why are you really here, Miss Hardwicke? Is he in trouble?"

"Yes. I think he might be." I want to tell him his nephew is dead, but I can't. Not yet. It's a horrible thing to keep this information secret. It's one aspect of my job I hate the most. But there's so much I don't know—including how he might take the news, especially coming from me. "I've been told he might have a brother, or maybe someone close to him? I haven't been able to corroborate that. In either case, he's the one I'm trying to find. Arthur seemed the best way to do that."

Leaning slightly to the left—he must have a bad leg—Richard Hanson nearly trembles. His eyes fill up, a combination of terror and sorrow. And then his body relents. He gestures with his head, directing me into his cabin.

"Come," he says. "I need to sit down."

*****

There are more books in here than any library I've ever seen. Stacks upon stacks. The dog follows us in. "Page? I get it. You read all these?"

Richard Hanson sits in an old wood chair next to an old wood table. "Working on it."

I find an empty spot on the couch, facing the fireplace. With all the books I'd be terrified to light a fire, but the hearth looks well used. His supply of logs is running low. Same with his assortment of canned and jarred foods—peaches, beans, soup—on three shelves above the sink.

The loose sawdust nearly makes me sneeze.

There's a small radio on the table, but no TV. Exposed wood beams across the ceiling. The cabin is well constructed enough to keep out the elements, but not a luxury to be found.

Other than the dog, Richard doesn't just live alone. He lives sparse. Lonely.

"There's some tension here," I say. "Your... nephews?"

"Comstock."

"I'm sorry? I don't..."

"My nephew, who you know as Arthur Hanson. His name is actually Daryl Comstock. And his brother? The one you're looking for? That's Eddie."

"They changed their names," I say. "Right. It's why I couldn't find him."

"Not exactly."

No matter how many interviews I conduct, the one thing I can usually count on is a lack of clarity. The more someone has to say, the more they struggle to say it.

"Let's start over. Your nephew—Arthur Hanson—is actually Daryl Comstock. Correct?"

"Yes."

"And his brother is Eddie Comstock. Did he change his name, too?"

"No. He's always been Eddie Comstock. But he's not my nephew. Never was."

He's really making me work for it. "Sorry. I don—"

Richard walks over to the refrigerator, comes back with two beers. He hands me one, sits back down, then takes a drink, gripping the can like it's a tin talisman protecting him from unholy forces.

"I'm originally from Fairpoint, Missouri, near Saint Louis," he says. "Worked construction, until I wrecked my knee. The limp. Then I became a foreman. Me and Gene? Daryl and Eddie's dad? We grew up together. Gene had a hard time of it. Wanted to be a clinical researcher, but couldn't afford the degree. Became a janitor instead. Worked in the public-school system. He could've been something special, that mind 'a his. But sometimes... life gets in the way. It takes you places you never thought you'd go."

"It sure does," I say. I'm proof of that.

He's not blinking, his vacant stare making me wonder how far back he's willing to go, wading deep into those murky family waters.

"The problem for Gene? He had two boys. Loved 'em." And then the sadness drapes back over Richard's face, the wrinkle lines and ridges like road maps to his pain. "Except when you're a parent..."

He's on the verge. I push too hard, even a nudge, he might retreat. If I say nothing, he might leave it be. The mother in me and the private eye in me have very different instincts here. It's the right play to say silent. Let him come to me. And then I answer for him.

"You resent them?"

"Yes. You hate 'em for making you care as much as you do. Never knowing if they'll turn out all right. Or if any decision you make'll be the wrong one, the one that ruins their life. Gene didn't get into it with me all that much, but when he did, he talked about his boys. His boy. Daryl."

"Who goes by the name Arthur."

"Yes. Daryl's a good boy, a fine boy."

"What about Eddie? The one I'm looking for?"

Richard finishes the beer, cracks opens another. "That one. He was... difficult."

"Difficult how?"

"Could be charming as all get-out. For a minute. Maybe an hour. But he has this stare, you know? This cold, black stare that could strip the love from an angel's wings." Page slinks over to the other side of the room, then curls into a ball. "Fairpoint was a big Baptist town. But Gene wasn't much of a church-goer. That was Mary's doing. Daryl went with her every week, the dutiful son. But Eddie? He had no use for God. Said he was a sonuvabitch. A downright bastard. Said, 'what kinda god would intentionally create a world of children who can never be as holy as their own father? Only to have them suffer, and then pray they get into Heaven? Who would do that?'"

Can't say I disagree. Minders? God? Call them what you will. Because they're making it damn hard for anyone, anywhere, to believe they're invested in anything but themselves. It doesn't sound right, because Jamie at least is trying to hold things together, but the way things are going, how can you fault anyone for raging against the cosmic machine?

The MinderNots are waging the very same rebellion.

"Me?" Richard says. "I don't get hung up on these distinctions, especially after the war. Two tours. Far as I saw, their ain't no God. And if there is, he ain't interested in *if* you pray, *how* you pray, or what you pray *for*. Bullets rip your face off just the same. Eddie didn't need to love God, didn't need to believe. But who says those kinda things to his own mother? I'm not even saying he was wrong. But treating his mother that way?" Richard shakes his head. "Awful. Just awful."

"That must've been a strain."

"Wasn't the half of it. Eddie had a mean streak. But not regular mean. Scary. Sneaky, too. Folks had a habit of falling down stairs, getting into accidents when he was around. But never any witnesses. He had a way of smiling his way into a moment, then using it to strip away your soul. Gene, the poor guy, couldn't handle it. Especially when Mary started... you gotta understand. We didn't know back then what we do now. She was... what's the clinical term? Bipolar. And clinically depressed. The medications helped some, but she'd go long stretches when she wouldn't leave the house. Or get out of bed. She cried a lot. Eddie hated her for that. And hated God for giving him a mother who couldn't love 'im right. Gene worked two jobs to keep it all together. But if he worked too much, it fell apart at home. If he gave up shifts, he couldn't make rent. The whole thing... it just wore 'im down."

If I didn't know any better, and I'm not sure I do, I'd swear Richard's talking about me. About Owen. I've let him down. Failed to be the mother he deserves. Damn.

"Daryl kept on, like I said, the dutiful son. He found a way to escape with books. It's one 'a the reasons we got on so well." He gestures to the stacks surrounding us. "But as Mary got worse, so did Eddie. When he was about thirteen, fourteen ... there were fights, busted windows. Then a girl went missing from their school. She turned up a week later. Hunter found her in the woods. Cops questioned Eddie. He'd been seen with the girl the day before she was killed, but they had no proof, so the cops let it go. Gene started to think about maybe sending Eddie to military school. He was never gonna do it, you know, send his boy away. Couldn't afford it, anyhow. But he was at his wit's end. So he talked about it, because at least it felt like a plan. A solution. About two weeks after that... Gene and Mary passed on. Car accident. God rest their souls."

Richard's not saying, but I have to ask. "It wasn't an accident, was it?"

His head bobs side to side, like a tree branch in winter, hunching under the weight of a thick, wet snow. Either the branch finds a new level, or it snaps.

"I wanna tell you it ain't never crossed my mind, but the truth is... I don't know. The police asked more questions, because they had to. It was looking damn suspicious with that boy. But like before, there was no evidence to support a charge. Besides, the boys just lost their parents. They were orphans. Their lives had already been ruined."

A son who hates his mother. Enough to kill her. The thought paralyzes me. I have to force my next words out. "What happened to the boys?"

"I agreed to take Daryl. Mary's sister, Tina... she took Eddie. Her husband runs a junkyard in Seattle, by you. Thought maybe being out there would keep him occupied, give 'im some space to grieve. Figured being outside, away from the masses, would be the best thing for him."

"And keep him away from Daryl," I say. "You were trying to give him a chance."

Richard's eyes go thick with tears. He drinks the rest of his beer, as if swallowing his grief, then tells me how they needed to leave Fairpoint, for a fresh start.

First to Toledo, Ohio, then Little Creek, Delaware, until they finally settled up here. Daryl Comstock, the good egg among two yoked-up brothers. Changed his name to Arthur Hanson.

"He kept his old name, he woulda gotten looks wherever he went. Stares, whispers. Gossip. Attacks even. He'd never be free of it. Not that he's free now. But he didn't want his past to define his future. God bless that one. He found a way to get by. Went to college, became a teacher. He never married, though. Didn't date much. He coulda. Solid man, decent looking fella. But when it came to girls... no confidence. He's done 'bout as well as you could for a man in his shoes. I'm proud of that boy. Damn proud. As much as if he were my very own."

The love oozes out of him. But it's more like a leak he can't plug, a wound that won't close.

"I know this is painful. But if I could just ask a few more questions."

"I ain't spoke a word of this in decades, Miss Hardwicke. I knew it was a matter of time. Might as well keep going."

"I appreciate that."

"Nothing to appreciate. I ain't doing this for you."

"Fair enough." I look at my note pad. A single word is circled. *Fireworks*. I'd nearly forgotten. "This might seem like an odd question, but did Eddie ever mess around with fireworks? It's come up a few times."

Richard lets out a short, tight huff. "Fireworks? Oh." He shakes his head. "That boy."

"So he did?"

"That's all he did. Whenever he could. Em-eighties, Roman candles."

"Roman candle?"

"It's a stick about yay long"—he stretches his hands out a foot apart—"that shoots different colored balls in the sky."

Back in E-Town we call them Tarusian candles. Same difference.

"But he had a knack for shooting at people. Nearly blinded some poor girl. Eddie bought 'em when he could scrape together a few dollars, or would steal 'em. But what he was really trying to do, was get the attention 'a God. He wanted to shoot those flares into the eyes of the Lord. One night he snuck into the Lady of the Righteous Light and set off enough firecrackers to wake Jesus Himself."

Fireworks. Getting the attention of God. My heart speeds up. "It's starting to make sense," I say, not meaning to say that out loud.

"Any 'a this makes sense to you? More'n I can say."

"Yes. I mean, no. I mean"—*slow down Angela, slow... down*— "I'm starting to understand the family dynamics."

"A damn shame," Richard says. "A damn, damn shame."

"What happened with Eddie?"

"Funny enough, he seemed to take to Seattle. Maybe he really did need a change. Then Tina and Doug had a baby 'a their own. And from what they said, I think Eddie loved being a big brother again. They had a bond."

I'm skeptical, but keep listening.

"It didn't last, though. Once the baby, Chet, got to be five or so, he was becoming his own person. He worshipped Eddie, but the age difference. Eddie was about nineteen at the time. So they got a babysitter. Used to come around a few times a week, to help out. And then..."

"She went missing?"

"Never found the body. Could be it's buried in that junkyard somewhere, but good luck with that. Between this girl an' the suspicion about their parents, cops brought in Eddie for questioning. Couldn't get a confession, but he finally lost it. Started wailing again about how God was a cruel and vindictive beast and the Universe was the great void. The cosmic graveyard. No choice after that. They put him in a hospital. Hillside Psychiatric Center. Been there ever since. Ain't seen or heard from that boy in more'n twenty-five years."

As if sensing what Richard needs, Page walks over to him, lays at his feet.

"Until recently," I say.

"Hospital released him. Said his lawyer got him out. Don't know how. Eddie was here yesterday. He saw a picture on the wall—that one right there—of me an' Daryl... Arthur. Seemed no point in lying about it."

"How'd that go?"

"That shotgun on the porch? Only reason I'm still here. That boy's got a corroded soul. It's got more rust on it than the back 'a my truck."

I roll my shoulder, feel the holster against my side. To make sure my gun's where it's supposed to be. "You tell Arthur?"

"Called him right away. Told him to watch his back. Wanted to go to his place myself, but my truck's busted and the part ain't due in for a few days."

I already know the answer, but I ask anyway. "What happened then?"

Richard's face scrunches in on itself. Tears refill his eyes. Page lifts her head, whimpers, then rests her chin on her paws.

"I ain't heard from him since."

CHAPTER 16

There's not much more I can get from Richard. He's done. I'm still struggling with what to tell him, if I should say anything about his adopted son. Then we hear a car horn. The cabbie. Page scurries to the door, let's out two ruffs. I ease up from the couch.

"Richard," I say, barely above a whisper. "I should let him know I'm all right. I'm gonna step outside."

Night is falling, the bitter scent of pine needles singeing my sinuses, like I just did a line of blow. If only.

I didn't realize how long we'd been at it. I eat a power bar. Holy crap, these are bad.

"Sorry," I say to the cabbie, whose window is lowered half way. Piano jazz music plinks through the radio. "It's taking longer than I thought. You can take off."

"You sure? It's a long way from town."

I feel for the Cressa tab behind my ear. "I'll get back okay. Just remember," I continue, and hand him another two hundred dollars.

"You were never here. I was never here. We've never met. I've never seen you."

I take my bag of supplies and leave them in the bottom nook of a tree trunk, then give the driver a nod. He shifts into drive, about to turn away, then pulls up next to me. Through the window he hands me a business card with his number on it.

"I still don't like you being out there like this. It's late and I'm hungry. Gonna grab a bite at the diner up the way. You get stuck, give me a call. I'll come back and getcha."

I regard the tires, which crackle on the dirt road between the valley of trees. As he comes to the turn, his rear lights thicken like two red eyes. It's like they're searching the night for predators until, finally, they shrink, disappearing from sight.

I head back toward the cabin, when Richard appears on the porch. Page is by his side.

"Miss Hardwicke," he says, his eyes red and swollen. The porch light shines watchfully. "I didn't think of it until now, but … how exactly *did* you find me? I'm not so easy to find."

Careful, Angela. Don't get defensive.

"You turned up in my investigation."

"Yes. You said." He rubs his hands together, the night air getting chilly. "But how?"

I realize he's taken hold of his shotgun. He's got it by the stock, the barrel facing down. The last thing I want is a confrontation, but now he's had a minute to think, he's piecing things together. If I were him, I'd be leery, too.

"Richard," I say, and let my jacket fall open in case I need to reach for my sidearm. "You're a good man. You've been through a lot. And I'm sorry to say, I really am, but you should prepare yourself."

"He's dead, ain't he? Arthur is dead."

I knew it might come to this. I walked into a shit storm that is this poor man's life. Maybe I even caused it. "Yes. I'm afraid, he is."

In a single motion he flips up the shotgun so it's pointing right at me. He pumps the barrel, keeping one hand on the stock, the other on the trigger. "Where is he? Where's my boy?"

With night encroaching, the porch light gleams in my eyes. "At his house. In the basement."

"You were there. You saw him."

"I'm sorry I didn't tell you, Richard. I had to be careful. I was only trying to find him. I was afraid he was in trouble. I got there too late."

"You're sorry?" he says. "You're *sorry*? That's my boy!"

He raises the gun so that the butt is propped against his shoulder. His finger grips the trigger. He's centered on his target, right between my eyes. He's a man with nothing left to live for, and I've given him no reason to take mercy. Maybe I have none coming. I have to hope his decency is stronger than his grief.

I pivot quickly and draw my gun. He shifts on the porch, keeping his weapon locked on me. He's wheezing, starting to unravel.

"Richard. I'm deeply, truly sorry. I wanted to tell you. I did. But please, believe me. Eddie is still out there. I want to find him. I want to bring him in."

"I don't believe you," he says, his hands trembling, eyes filling with water. "Tell me how he died. I want to see him."

"That's not a good idea. Let the police handle it. We'll call it in."

"*How'd he die?*" he repeats, his forefinger this close to pulling the trigger. "Tell me how it happened, Miss Hardwicke, or you're going to die in these woods. I'll let the coyotes do the rest."

I believe him. "It was a nail. To the base of the neck. Painless." I have no idea if that's true. I hope it is.

Richard's eyes enlarge—a passageway into his heart—allowing Arthur's final moments to become a permanent part of him, too. His breaths are short and tight.

"The girl who died when the boys were teens?" he starts. "Nail to the back of the neck."

I don't know if that realization helps me or hurts. He's emotional and desperate. He's in shock. And pointing a loaded weapon at me.

"What do you really want, Miss Hardwicke? And don't tell me it's to find Eddie. It's something else."

It's only as he's saying it out loud that I realize where I am. I'm listless, stuck between worlds—not just E-Town and Earth—but between the Angela Hardwicke I think I am and the Angela Hardwicke I need to be.

I'm also wondering if sending the cabbie away was such a good idea. Then again, had he still been here, it could've made things worse.

Maybe I can't tell Richard everything. But I can tell him enough. It's time to speak the truth. More truth. My truth.

"You're right, Richard. I do want something else. But you're also wrong." He's pumping his hand on the rifle, as if debating whether to believe me. "I want to find Eddie. And I want him to answer for what he's done. I have a son, too. He's missing. I don't know where he is, if he's all right, or if I'll ever get him back. I hate everything and everyone, all the time, including myself. Especially myself. I want my son back so badly I can barely stand up. But what I also want, Richard"—my eyes draw tight—"I want Eddie to *pay*. I want him to feel the pain and anguish and grief and horror that keeps me up at night, screaming into my pillow. I know I'm not supposed to feel that way about a case. As a private eye, I'm not even supposed to care. But I do. And you know why? Because he's playing me for a fool. He's desecrating the bond between parent and child. Between you and your son. And that, Richard... *that* is something I cannot forgive. I can't. I won't. And I don't care where it takes me or how far I have to go. If it comes down to it, I'm putting Eddie down."

There's a silence between us as dusk fades to night. An animal rustles in the bushes. Richard looks at me, really looks, until his eyes soften just enough. And then he lets his gun hand fall to his side. Blood rushes to my ears.

"You should go, Miss Hardwicke. There's nothing left for you here." He reaches into his jacket pocket. He tosses me a flashlight. I pick it up. "Road's about a mile up the way, then take a left. You'll find your way from there."

"I'm not sure I should leave you here. You've been through a lot."

"I have. But you still need to go."

I open my mouth, to convince him to let me stay, but he's made a decision. There's no point trying to fight. It'll come up with the police, sooner than later, so I tell him about Arthur's car, that I left it in the lot, and that I can't go back for it. To the house either. Anyone could've seen me. It's a consequence I'll have to live with.

"I'm sorry," I say as Richard and Page turn from me. "I wish I'd gotten there sooner."

Richard's up on the porch, standing in the corona of the overhead light. His hand is on the edge of the open door. He looks back at me. "So do I."

We both know how this is going to end between us, but I say

it anyway. "Please, Richard. I can't leave you like this. Why don't I stay. Put up some coffee and you can tell me about Arthur."

He glowers at me, a man with nothing left but agony.

"You can walk away or I put you in the ground, Miss Hardwicke. Either way, we won't be talking again. Goodbye."

Richard disappears into the cabin, leaving me alone in the pitch-dark woods. I turn on the flashlight, and take one last look, hoping that maybe he'll change his mind. He won't.

So I walk down the road, the dirt crunching beneath my feet. I turn the collar up on my jacket, the cool night air pinching my ears, sending a chill right through me. I look up into the starry sky, beyond the trees, and consider Eddie Comstock's words about God. About the creators of the Universe. About the Minders.

If they really created an existence of kiss-asses and groupies just to satisfy their ego. To worship their existence and idolize their power.

Or if their plan all along was just a glorified version of the carrot and the stick. Dangle the ultimate prize—become one with the Creators—obtainable in the next life, only through subservience in this one.

Or maybe that's my withdrawal talking, my insatiable need to reconnect with that Universe. Maybe the *dRops* are my pathway. To the Minders. To Comstock's God.

Or maybe I'm just a junkie, desperate for a fix.

That could also be the mother in me, pining for my son.

Maybe I'm all those things. Or none at all.

At the end of the road, I look back at the woods, toward Richard's cabin.

I think about the dead man in the basement and the brother who killed him and, of all things, about Milo. The second Minder. About how much I need him.

About how accustomed I'd become to knowing he was out there, and that he'd come to my aid, if I asked. And how he's out there somewhere, with Owen, maybe closer than I think, yet still so far away.

I think about being out on this dirt road. About being off-realm. About being alone.

I think about Owen. About how much I love him.

But then I close my eyes, exhale the weariness within me, and open my eyes again. I can't face the future if I'm stuck in the past.

"Goodbye, Richard," I say, even though he can't hear me. "I hope you—"

Facing the woods, a white flash emerges in the darkness. I hear a distant pop.

Page howls.

My heart sinks.

I stop on the road, my foot dragging on the pebbled dirt. Lost in a stare to nowhere, I finally turn and walk back to the cabin, dreading every step. Page is standing on the porch. I approach, to take her with me. I can't leave her out here. Not like this.

Gently, I extend my hand. She growls. I take another step. She's snarling now, showing me her teeth. A hellhound, she's warning me to stay away. That I'm not wanted here.

That I should go.

Introduced to me as Arthur Hanson, Eddie Comstock has claimed another life. Destroyed another soul.

Did he get the Minders' attention with that one? Did they notice?

Clouds drift, revealing the moon. A full moon.

I feel it again, as if the face in that satellite is watching me, judging me, reminding me just how much, and how badly, I've failed.

I turn away, and walk along the road, a pebble in my left sneaker. It's digging into my heel, but I can't let myself stop and dig it out. I need to keep moving. I don't want to, but I look once more into the night sky, and wonder if I'm doing any good at all.

I'm afraid to know the answer.

CHAPTER 17

What I do think about is what to do next.

I reach behind my ear. I press the Cresa tab beneath my skin.

Faster than a current passing between atoms I'm back where I started, in the transpo room with peach walls and plants and the sofa and holographic image of the sun sparkling on the ocean.

"I never get used to how fast this is," Gil says. "New clothes. What happened?"

"Where's Clancy? The tech."

Gil furrows his brow. "Getting pizza. Remember?"

"I need to get out of this room. Take me up."

"Okay, but—?"

"Upstairs."

Gil tries to engage, but I'm not having it. He leads us back to the pizza joint, where Clancy is noshing an entire pie.

"Gimme a slice," I say to the counter clerk. "Meat supreme."

He offers to heat it up—it's been sitting behind the counter, congealed cheese and all. I take it as is. I've never being this hungry. I devour half the slice in a single bite, chewing as we walk.

I fire off a quick text to my crew to back of Hanson, then shove Gil into an alley. I ditch the rest of my slice in an open dumpster, wipe my mouth with my palm.

"Hardwicke," Gil says as I force him against the brick wall, the narrow back alley leading us to a maze of back alleys. A single sun shines down on us. "W-what are you doing?"

"Don't give me any bullshit, Gil. Who are you? Who are you really?" I extend the taser, arm at my side. Usually it's just for show. Not this time. "Did you set me up? Is this a con? What are you up to?" I lean him tighter against the wall. I raise up the taser. "Tell me, Gil. Tell me now."

I depress the taser, blue sparks crackling inches from his face.

Gil shakes his head nervously. His eyes widen. "Angela. I swear. I-I don't…"

"Gil," I repeat, my own eyes locked on his. Over the years I've confronted numerous clients over information they've held back, distorted, or just lied about. Nature of the business. Especially some of the cases I take. I'm not in the habit of physically threatening my clients, but sometimes it has to be done. "Don't. Just don't."

He holds out for another minute, trying to win me over with his eager-to-please, confused puppy-dog whimper. I see him about to protest again, the corner of his mouth initiating the proper contortion to form words.

And then it happens.

His startled eyes relax and refocus, for the first time showing me a Gil Habersau I've never met before. His posture changes, standing more upright. His face is still young, yet he seems years older now.

"All right," he says, no longer nervous, slouching, and begging for my approval, but a confident man who has accepted that field conditions have changed.

I ease him off the brick wall, give him some space in the tight alley. I tell him about the real Arthur Hanson—born Daryl Comstock—his murder, and my standoff with Richard Hanson.

And that Eddie Comstock, an unpredictable psychopath masquerading as his brother, under the name Arthur Hanson, is loose in E-Town.

"I was afraid of this." Gil produces a pack of cigarettes. He lights one. "This was bound to happen."

"What was bound to happen? Gil. Who are you?"

He takes a drag, exhales through his nose, then leads me deeper into the alley. A white cat with red eyes sneaks in behind us, then, as if it senses what's coming, scurries away.

"Miss Hardwicke," he begins.

"Miss Hardwicke?"

He takes another drag, exhales, then tosses the butt. He stamps it out with the bottom of his shoe. "Miss Hardwicke... yes, my name is Gil Habersau. And yes, I do work for the VCP. But you are also correct, I am not an off-world liaison. I'm not a liaison at all."

I'm studying him, looking for cracks in his story. I don't see any. And he's fooled me before.

"Have you noticed" he begins, "that ever since Astropalooza, the infrastructure of the Universe, and even Eternity itself, has been a little bit...?"

"Off?"

"I was going to say *inconsistent*, but yes, things have been off. The temperature's been fluctuating, the sky rotating through color gradations much faster and at different frequencies than normal." He's right. When we first left the pizzeria the sky was light blue. Now it's cotton candy pink. "Torrential rains fall, and within seconds, not a drop of moisture. The sequence of moons and suns no longer follow their previous cycles. Just yesterday a half dozen planets nearly pummeled this realm, only to vaporize before impact."

"Yeah, that was a delight. The MinderNots are up in arms, waging a revolution. And their numbers are growing."

"Yes," he says. "They are. The infrastructure of the Universe, and even Eternity itself, has been an issue. At first we thought the disruptions were a natural side effect of Astropalooza. The celebration is quite the indulgence. There's always an adjustment. A need to re-set."

"A hangover."

Gil hmphs with a close-mouthed smile. "I've never heard it that way, but a hangover. That's the gist of it. The system implemented by the Minders to secure the structural integrity of Existence isn't functioning according to specifications. More misfires than normal. We figured it would pass. It's only gotten worse."

He's leading me somewhere. He's good. He's controlling the narrative.

"Maybe that's true, Gil. But this is E-Town. What does *normal* even look like? Regardless, what's this got to do with you? Why are you involved? And more to the point... why am I?"

Gil slides his hands into his suit pockets, gives a half-shoulder turn away from me, as if he's still deciding how much to tell me. He faces me again. He removes his hands.

"We've been tracking defects all across the Cosmos. At first they were minor and, given the scope of the Universe, infrequent. An asteroid melted. A moon vanished. A quasar replicated itself. That sort of thing. But the malfunctions escalated. Galaxies collided, space/time tore open, parallel universes merged."

"Couldn't that be the Great Disruptor? Isn't that what he does? Cause trouble? Upset the Universe?"

I say *he* because I'm not sure Gil knows who the new Disruptor really is. And if he doesn't, I'm not going to be the one to tell him.

"It's possible. Yes. We've considered that. But we've never seen this level and intensity of system-wide malfunctions and at this escalating rate of occurrence. There are too many incidents too close together. Most significant, however, is these malfunctions have never infiltrated the VCP. Never. Not once. And certainly... not like this."

"What kind of infiltration?"

Gil rolls his tongue over his front teeth, then loops his thumbs into the beltline on his slacks. "Miss Hardwicke. If I tell you, it extends far beyond whatever standard client nondisclosures are in our agreement. You cannot repeat, to anyone... anywhere... ever... what I'm about to say."

"It's in the vault."

"No, Miss Hardwicke." He steps closer. With his eyes, he gestures upward. He speaks again, his mouth drawn tight, gritting his teeth. *"Do you understand?"*

I nod. I do understand.

He nods back at me in recognition of his recognition. We should start our own club.

"We've had problems with security," he says, stepping back. "We've had issues saving data. And we've had false identifications."

"False how?"

"A few months ago, the system identified a woman from

Antwerp. On Earth. I told you about her. She was in no way prepared to work with the VCP. Third misfire in as many months. And now with this Hanson fiasco—the system misidentified him, swapping out the brothers—we have a crisis we've never seen before. The VCP system approved by the Minders? It's breaking down."

"Not to bust out the hits, but again, couldn't this be the Great Disruptor?"

"It's possible, although these issues are more insidious than we've seen before. A different M.O. But as I said, we've never had an infiltration of this magnitude. We've rebooted, reprogrammed, done system checks of every kind. We've rotated personnel. There are no technical reasons we can identify that would cause these disruptions. Which leads us to believe..."

"You have a saboteur," I conclude. "A mole. The crisis you were dealing with."

Gil stands still. "Yes. I think we do. And it's my job to find him."

"Or her."

"Correct. Or her."

I wonder if Zenovia is more than meets the eye, and if he's considered it, too.

I'm already overloaded from my time on Earth, but if I've learned anything as a private eye, what I expect to find and what is finally revealed will rarely be the same. The best way to keep my focus, to prevent the scope of an investigation from devouring me, is to keep things as simple as possible. It's one of the qualities I most admire about Tarrish. No matter what's going on around him, he can almost always push it aside.

Don't assume, Hardwicke. Work the case. Ask your questions. Follow the clues. And trust your gut. If something doesn't feel right, it probably isn't.

I bring Gil back to center. Where I want him.

"If your system malfunctions are so extensive, why do you need *me*? Why don't you send a squad to find Hanson? You could..." I stop, scrutinizing the edginess that's seeped back into his face, my inner gears tumbling into place. "You don't trust anyone, do you? You really don't know who it is."

My mouth is hanging open. I close it. I look up from our narrow alley, hidden in this urban maze. The sky is no longer pink, but a confectionary swirl of burgundy, white, and lavender—massive free-forming bubbles that roll and transmogrify like oily pockets in a lava lamp.

My attention back on Gil, his shoulder tips against the wall. His secrets are pulling on him, like the orbit of a distant sun. It's as if he simply can't lift his head to face me. His eyes fall away.

"It's even more than that," I say. "It's personal for you."

"I've been with the VCP almost ten years. I started young. I've devoted my life to the Minders. What a gift we have, we Eternitarians. We are entrusted by the Creators of All to help them, in our own way, guide the Cosmos. We are advocates, executors, and stewards. We are devotees, at the ready. And when the moments arise, when even the Minders themselves cannot bring themselves to ask, we activate ourselves."

"This isn't just a job for you, is it?" I hadn't seen it until now. "It's a calling."

"I feel it in places I can't describe. Do you know what that's like?"

More than he knows.

"I'd gotten away from handling ORBs," Gil says. "So when the malfunctions cropped up, I took the next case in rotation. Hanson. It took three days to get him on board, which is well within normal range. But typical with ORBs, there's down time. He paced the house. He hid in his room. He went up and down to the basement, a dozen times at least, muttering to himself. And there was so much I needed to keep an eye on back here that I..."

"Didn't see how big the problem really was," I say as thunder rumbles close by. "The system didn't only miss that Hanson had a brother with a violent, unstable past, but that Eddie Comstock may have murdered his own brother... then took his place. That's why he was in the basement so long. He was covering his tracks."

Lighting crackles against the sky, now ashen as pummeled asphalt.

"Wait," I say. "Eddie and Arthur. They look nothing alike.

There's no way you could make that mistake unless... the system switched them up. And you never double checked."

"Like I said, Miss Hardwicke. It's not something I want my boss to know. But it may be too late for that. I need you to find Hanson. Eddie Comstock. Because I have to find the mole. And as my performance clearly shows, I can't do both at the same time."

I'm about to agree, when another thought pierces my mind. "My name in the files. Was that a lie? To manipulate me?"

"Mmm," he says. "Yes and no."

"Swing and a miss, Gil. Do better."

I'm already tweaked from my time on Earth. Now I'm seeing red. By the way he shifts his weight, subtly, ready to counterstrike, I think he realizes that.

"Your name's really in there," he says. "Just... different files."

"*What* files?"

"While at the VCP, Comstock became obsessed with Earth. He found RFTs—Red Flag Transports—between Eternity and Earth. We keep tabs on questionable off-realm jumps. Your name came up several times. So even before I put you onto him..."

"He was already onto me."

"Yes."

"And you thought mixing my name with the Anshanis would give me extra incentive."

My worst suspicions about Gil have been confirmed. He's in deep. So am I. With the life I lead, the cases I take, I shouldn't be surprised. But now that I know, I see why Gil was so desperate for my help. And I also know the VCP is keeping tabs on me. Peachy.

"You have to find the mole," I say. "If you don't, you're petrified the Minders will blame your whole division. Or worse... you."

Gil looks as if he's about to say something, but doesn't.

There's more to this, Angela. Work the case. Ask your questions. Trust your gut.

And then it hits me.

"You *want* to find the mole. Not to be rewarded, or even

exonerated. You want a mole to actually exist." With a final scorch of thunder and lighting, the sky is once again a childhood blue. Bulbous white clouds drift on the breeze. "Because if it doesn't, if there's no saboteur, then the glitches in the system have nothing to do with the VCP. It would mean the Minders caused the problem, are responsible for the problem or, at the very least... have failed to solve it. Which would mean they're failing everything, and everyone, all across the Cosmos, just like the MinderNots claim. And if that's true, then maybe the greatest powers in Existence aren't so powerful after all. And nobody, not even you, wants to be the messenger."

CHAPTER 18

Explaining the scope of this investigation to the team is going to take a while. And I need to bring in Tarrish. It's a manhunt now, and Tarrish has the ICD to help.

Gil didn't fight me on it. He knows we have no choice. And now that I know who my client really is, and why he's been cagey with me, I have more clarity about a path forward.

But after my time in the woods I'm strung out, and there's something I need to do.

I know I shouldn't, but I'm doing it anyway, because I'm the only one who can.

I guzzle two extra-large lattes during the cab ride over. Three different cabs, to be exact. I'm not taking chances. Not after last time. For all I know the Anshanis are still following me. Or trying to.

Jamie's in her private residence, lying face down on a massage table. The masseuse, dressed in a light-blue jumpsuit with white sneakers and a white braided belt, digs a knuckle into the back of her right shoulder.

Lavender-scented candles illuminate the otherwise lightless room. Those, and the wall-size window facing the Universe, innumerable stars twinkling in the expanse.

Galaxies swirl. Comets streak.

"I'm next," I say, announcing myself.

Jaime rolls her cheek on the side, facing me. "Angela. How did you get in here?"

"It's why you hired me. I have my sources."

"Indeed you do," she says beneath the white satin sheet. "Ah." She winces. "Lawrence. Too much. Can you do my neck, please?"

"Of course. But you should really use the M'nela salt rub on your shoulder. You hold that tablet so tight sometimes it's no wonder you can move your arm at all." The masseuse addresses me. "Hello, Miss Hardwicke. You look better than the last time I saw you."

"Lawrence. I guess I shouldn't be surprised."

"No," he says, and with his fingers, digs into the knots in Jaime's neck. "You shouldn't. As I've told you before, I have served the Minders of the Universe since long before the beginning of time. And yet my shift has only just begun."

"I assumed Jaime would select her own assistant. You were with her predecessor for... actually, I don't know how long. An eon or two, I would think."

"I'm far more than a personal assistant, Miss Hardwicke. Surely you know that. Miss Jamie chose to retain me because she knows what the previous Minder forgot. That ultimately I am in service of the Universe. The best way for me to fulfill that obligation is to serve the Minders. Now... why have you intruded?"

"I need a minute with Jamie. I have an update on her case."

Lawrence stops kneading her neck. He tilts his head. "You need? Your audaciousness may have its occasional charm, but you are far from charming. You do not summon Miss Jamie. Miss Jamie summons you. I suggest you go."

He's right. Jamie is a Minder. But cow-towing to my clients, no matter who they might be, doesn't earn their respect. They want to know I'm willing and able to walk in and out of the shadows on their behalf so they don't have to.

Sometimes the way to establish that presence is to step over lines no one else would even think of coming near.

"Your suggestion is noted. I'll even write it on a sticky pad, with a rainbow. And a starburst. Maybe a unicorn. But I still need a word."

"Excuse me?" Lawrence strides toward me. Slow, deliberate. On the viewing wall, an oval-shaped galaxy twists into a braid matching his belt. "You very much do not want to—"

"It's all right, Lawrence," Jamie says. "I was going to call upon Angela anyhow. Would you hand me my robe?" Like the loyal centurion he is, Lawrence locks his glare on me. "Lawrence," Jamie repeats, naked beneath her white sheet. "My robe."

Lawrence may be in service of Jamie, but he's no butler. Finally, after a time, he breaks eye contact, relaxes his posture. "Yes, yes of course, Miss Jamie. My apologies." He helps her into her robe. "Would you like me to stay?"

Jamie offers him an appreciative smile. "That won't be necessary. But thank you for the massage. Representing myself in this physical form—while simultaneously doing so as numerous other forms throughout time, space, and dimension and across the Universe—sometimes takes more concentration than I'd like to expend. My muscles bunch up once I exceed twelve hundred forms. I'm in the tens of thousands at the moment, no thanks to my supposed partners, who are nowhere to be found. So you can understand why the knots are so tight. You are truly the magic man, Lawrence. Your hands are a gift."

"Very good. I'll prepare this evening's agenda." Lawrence steeples his fingers, angled in my direction. "Miss Hardwicke. You will not show up here unannounced. All meetings are to be scheduled through me, and only me."

I've provoked him long enough. Time to play nice. Well... nicer. "You the boss, Big L. Whatever buttons your collar."

As much as he wants to be offended, the corners of his mouth betray the inkling of a smile. He prides himself on his dedication to service, but like all servants, he secretly, and sometimes not so secretly, clamors for the occasional recognition. Acknowledgment of stature. Like he said, he's far more than Jamie's personal assistant.

The Universe owes him a debt of gratitude. I know I do. I should probably tell him that. But not today.

It's just the two of now. In her robe and slippers, Jamie eases toward the view screen. She rolls her neck.

"I remember working the registration desk downstairs, in this very hotel," Jamie says as the braided galaxy is now so knotted up it's choking the stars. Two have already extinguished. "And how lucky I felt to even have that job. And when I say *remember*, it's as clear to me now as it was then, as if I'm in that very moment as we're talking here. Which, of course, I am. It's the nature of being a Minder."

"It must be overwhelming. To oversee the Universe."

"I would gladly settle for *overwhelming*, Angela. Whatever you have to tell me, let's get to it."

Her face stern, Jamie listens noiselessly as I explain about Strident Eyes, that Evie Von M is buying them out, and my run-ins with the Anshanis.

"I have a lead on the caches, but I haven't pinned them down."

"What's the hold-up, Angela? I accept these things take time, but I expected more progress by now."

I debate telling her about Hanson, but assume she already knows, and is waiting for me to fess up. Truth is, I never know what she does or doesn't know. That's the problem with having a Minder for a client. And yet she asked for my help.

"I was working another case when you hired me. Missing person. I think it's connected to yours. The investigation took me off-realm." The galaxy up on the view screen seizes. Like a love affair gone bad, its life force is gone. "To Earth."

Jamie pinches her nose, near the corner of her almond-shaped eyes. "Go on."

I'm not prepared to tell her everything, but I explain that Eddie Comstock is a lethal man, who may very well be out to get her attention, and use her missing fireworks to do it.

"No matter how hard I try," Jamie says, "I simply cannot escape the dramas of Earth. I spent some time there myself. Who's your other client? And how did this Comstock get on realm?"

"It's… complicated. But I'm worried…" I need to be careful here. She's allowing me a lot of leeway, more than expected. But she hired me to investigate. She wants to know what I've found. "… the reason that galaxy just extinguished, right in front of us, is extending here. On realm. Comstock is a problem, but I think he's also a symptom. The Universe might be…"

Jamie clenches her fists. She squeezes her eyes shut. I'm not sure if she's forcing the issue or if she's trying to contain it, but the room starts to vibrate.

"I know exactly what the Universe is going through. It's tearing me apart."

I can't breathe. Blood pounds in my ears. Jamie has me hovering off the floor, against the view screen. I feel the immensity of the Universe pulling me toward the center of that expired galaxy.

"My partners have abandoned me, Angela. They've *abandoned* me! They're supposed to shoulder an equal load. We're supposed to figure this out together. But instead they're out in the Universe trying to find themselves, off on some existential quest, like a bunch of entitled brats who think Mommy will make their beds for them while they're out with their friends. I don't have time for this. Do you have any idea how big the Universe really is? I'm trying to hold it together—by myself. And keep Eternity from falling apart at the same time. And now here you are, whining to me about some family squabble that's spilled onto the streets? Do you think I care about this guy? That's why I hired *you*."

She's thrust me now into the vacuum of space. Toxic fumes from the extinguished galaxy wash over me. I'm just a rag doll, hanging on a hook, an infinitesimal spec, as dozens of moons encircle me. I'm an eyelash in the vastness of space, a powerless fop cast into a cosmic netherworld from which there is no return.

Unless Jamie allows it.

My heart thrums to the beat of my inevitable death, lost to myself, my friends… my baby boy… just as I'm rediscovering my desire to really live.

I'm dizzy. I can barely see.

The forces of space should kill me instantly, freezing me, crushing me. Yet the celestial objects spin and swirl, whipping around me in a white and grey blur, until finally I force my eyes to remain open just enough I can see they're all the same moon.

Earth's moon.

Like in my dreams.

With that same judgmental face staring at me. Eroding my resolve.

Maybe this is what I deserve.

Restitution for the sins of my past, for taking case after case, to keep my demons at bay. Thinking they'll buy me time until I can find the only person who really matters.

My son's out there, somewhere, with Milo. And I don't know where to look.

Milo is the only one who can help me. As much as Jamie feels like he's abandoned her... selfishly, greedily... all I care about is that Milo's abandoned *me*.

But it's Jamie's show.

"You're here because you want my help," she says. "You want to talk it through. But get this through your head." Jamie's out in space with me now, face-to-face with me, her nose flush against mine. "I know Milo's your buddy. Was your buddy. Whatever. But that's when he was the Great Disruptor. When he looked to you for guidance. And you looked to him. But he's a Minder now, and he's gone. And I know there's some deal with him and your son. I get that it's an issue for you—I'm sorry to hear it, I really am—but I'm not here to fill the void. You want to take on Universe business? You want to work my cases? Then don't come to me with problems. Come to me with progress. Or solutions. And if not solutions... suggestions. Otherwise"—she thrusts me back into the Zen room, next to her once more—"I have no use for you. You and I will be done."

I'm trembling. Jamie offers me a glass of water. I take it from her, but spill more than I can get down my throat.

"Lawrence," Jamie says through an intercom I don't see. "I think Angela will require a ride home. Would you have a car waiting?"

"Of course, Miss Jamie. Gloria will be out front."

Jamie takes the glass back from me. "I realize you took a risk coming here, Angela. I admire your fortitude. But as you clearly see for yourself... I am not Milo. He is not me. You became a private investigator at the end of my predecessor's run. When he was the last Minder, conditions on his watch were... looser. Undisciplined. You'll need to decide for yourself if I'm the right client for you. Based on your progress, you're not the right PI for me. I'd say you owe it to the both of us to decide if you're in this for real."

Jamie leads me to the door, brushes her hand against my shoulder. "Speaking of change, I like the new outfit."

I nearly forgot. The jeans and utility jacket fit so easily I haven't thought about them since I left the woods. Now I can barely think at all.

"Your pinstripe suit never felt right to me. Like you were trying too hard. I appreciate appearances as much as anyone, Angela. Now more than ever. But my suggestion to you? Embrace these changes. Take a page from the MinderNots. They insist I don't exist, or that I'm failing at my job, and need to get my house in order. It doesn't please me to be publicly ridiculed so early in my tenure, but I can't disagree with their conclusions. Until I can get my partners back, where they belong, and likely, for quite some time after, our roles as Minders of the Universe are going to be a work in progress. We have much to figure out—and certainly to answer for. Now go work my case. And let's hope our next meeting is far more pleasant than this one."

CHAPTER 19

Jamie's driver, Gloria, asks me where I want to go. Slumped in the back seat, I mumble something incomprehensible. She asks again, but I don't answer, so she says she's taking me to my office. I don't care, because I know I'm not going there. Let her think what she wants.

We're cruising along Escahoe Circle when I tell her to turn off instead, and head through the Harper District.

Dark-skinned with tight poodle curls, Gloria eyes me through the rearview. We're stopped at a red light. "That's probably unwise. I'll take you to your..."

In the middle of traffic I hop out of the car, leaving the door open. In short order I'm at the bar of Mercury's Last Dream, a little bistro with a white and burgundy canopy out front. There's calls I need to make and Hanson is still out there, but I club those notions over the head with an iron mallet and shove them in the dungeon of my mind. Instead I wedge between the other drinkers and order a shot of tequila and a pint of Sandomier dark.

Following protocol, the bartender turns up the music filtering through the sound system, and returns with my shot. He says it'll be a minute for the beer. He has to change the keg. I take my tequila in one go, then leave, making my way back to the alley.

"Thought you were off it," Alessandro says, wearing his burgundy cook's uniform.

"You have it or not?"

Nearly anorexic, with a pencil-thin mustache, Alessandro hands me the *dRops*. I hand him the credits.

"You don't look so good," he says. "You should—"

But I'm already off.

Night shouldn't fall for another two hours, yet darkness abounds. Not thinking about it, I wander the streets, across E-Town, until I'm back at the top of Half Moon Park, then down by the Anaya Reflecting Pool.

Hidden within the trees, safety lights illuminate the promenade.

I come here to see if it will happen.

As if sensing my curiosity, the three marble planets hovering above the great obelisk begin to spin in place, in opposing gyroscopic patterns.

They rotate, in synchronicity, until finally the marble casings dissolve, revealing—like the chocolate center of a lollipop—the living planets within.

The largest planet is now orange-and-white gas swirls. The smallest planet is purple ice with a glowing crown irradiating the edges. The third, a blue and green planet, is land and water, with white cloud patterns.

And now, in the nexus of those three living planets, in the shared space between them, a nebula emerges.

A red mist with a yellow center.

A glowing eye.

That eye, which seems to look right through me, lets me know I'm not alone, yet completely isolated.

Dozens of pedestrians—professionals, joggers, musicians, junkies, artists, homeless, lovers, strangers—are milling about. It's their right to be here, but I want them gone. To die or disappear or fall victim to the gyrating planets as they fall from their funneled perch, roll about the plaza, and crush them all.

This is my space. My place.

Where I come to be alone.

But of course, that's not true because I knew there'd be people here. Maybe even a crowd.

What I should do is toss this bottle of *dRops* into the reflecting pool and go to a meeting or a hospital. Or have Nini sedate me and then ziptie my wrists and ankles to the bedposts and hook me up to a vitamin stardust drip and keep me from mauling myself, her, or anyone else while I fight off the urges.

But I don't do any of that.

Because being an addict is to crave what kills you. To be enslaved by a diseased parasite that whispers to you from a mouth with no lips, a voice with no face. It speaks to you in a dialect understood only by junkies.

In my earliest days as an investigator, I was hired to find the CEO of a small bank who'd left her office early one afternoon and never came back. The trail led me into one of E-Town's sordid neighborhoods, the kind even the rats avoid.

I found her in a hovel of an apartment, chained to a metal hook bolted to the floor.

She'd been raped and sodomized, covered in her own filth, a twitching, squirrely creature starved and beaten within in an inch of her life.

As I tried to cut her loose, she gnawed a chunk of flesh from my left arm and nearly gouged my eyes out, all because her captor was on his way back with another hit off the pipe.

To her, threatening to take away what she lusted more than life itself... *I* was the monster.

What I learned then, and, to my horror, what I know now, is that when you're a junkie, when you're a slave to your next fix, even as the shame and tears spill out of you, there is no punishment too great, no humiliation you won't endure.

If anything, outlasting the degradation makes you want it all the more.

Your need is all that matters.

So instead I remove the dropper from the tiny bottle and before I can talk myself out of it I let that cosmically charged drug hit my tongue and...

I can lift you up...or will the sky fall down? Do you know the way... or are you the mystery I've been chasing? The planets glow and pulse... or is that me? Or are we just the same?

The planets and nebula mirror in the reflecting pool, two sets of orbs touching the edges—their illusory twins.

Nini once told me nebulas are like floaters in the eye. They fill your vision with wild flecks and color, but they're symptoms that there's separation between the vitreous gel that fills the eye and the light-sensing retina. There's a problem.

I close my eyes anyway, and like a whimsical child, reach my arms out and spin three times, then in the opposite direction. So that when I open my eyes again and cross them, I guess which set of planets are real and which are the reflections, glowing bright against the raven backdrop of night.

I toggle between my eyes, back and forth and back again, to further confuse myself so I can no longer tell which way is up and which is down, or if the edges... boundaries... have any real meaning or if they're also just reflections in my mind.

"Hi, Mommy," a boy says to me, as if he knows me. "Come play."

Slowly, like wading in a pool of honey, I turn, because I can't move any faster. As my shoulder spins, the promenade spins with me. The people here are elongated and morphing, their faces stretched out like a comet's tail, but I force my eyes to focus, looking for the boy.

He's nowhere.

A young couple laughs. I assume it's at me. I don't know why.

"Mommy," he says again. "Come play. It's fun."

"What's fun?" I say, although I'm not certain I'm speaking the words I intend, or if it's pure gibberish. "Where are you?"

"I'm right here, Mom," says another boy, older. His voice is deeper. "I'm with you."

"No," I say, my eyes barely open. I smack my lips, thick and pasty and sticking together. "I don't see you. Where—?"

"Mother," a new boy says. But not a boy. A man. "You can stop looking. Everything's fine. I've been here all along."

I know he can't be who he says he is, who they all say they are. But I know. They're my son. He's my son. All of them.

It's Owen.

"Sit with me, Mommy," Owen says, at least five, older than when I last saw him. "Can you hold my hand?"

We sit on the edge of the reflecting pool. My heart is gyrating like those glowing planets, yet I'm calmer than I should be, as if I know this isn't real. Or is it? His face is as smooth and round and perfect as I remembered. His fingers are small in mine.

"Of course, baby. Here."

He squeezes my hand, his now larger than mine. I look to him again. He's a grown man.

"Mother," he says. "Look."

"I am. I'm looking right at you, my sweet, sweet boy. I... I can't believe that you're..."

"No, Mother," he repeats, then tugs my arm. "Look up."

Together we're staring up as the planets glow before us. But just like in my dreams, the moon hovers. Many moons. Earth moons. They're white, radiant.

Yet the men in the moons stare at me, like when I was deep in the woods, when I left Richard Hanson alone in his worst moment. His final moment.

They won't look away. I can't, either.

"Mom," says Owen, a teen now, "I know you're sad. But I'm happy. It wasn't Milo's fault. He was only trying to help. Life is good."

I'm crying now, though not in pain. It's confusion. And I don't know why.

"Milo? What do you mean? What did he do?"

"Mommy," little Owen says. "I'll be home soon. You'll see. Milo's coming."

"When, baby? When are you coming home?"

"You act like we've been apart, Mother," Owen says, only his voice is hoarse now, shaky. He's wrinkled and pats my hand, an old man carrying the wisdom of his lifetime. "I've been with you. Just as you've been with me. It's all right. You'll see. I'll be home soon. Until then"—he's a teen again—"just follow the moon, Mom. It'll let you know I'm close. That I'm near. But you need to sleep. And you need to throw these away."

He's tugging on my bottle of *dRops*. Only I can't let go.

An unseen hand takes a red felt marker and draws the MinderNot symbol on each moon. The inverted red triangles and their red tails streak out the moons' faces, the stains stabbing me like jagged meteorites. The symbols are not just a reflection of the Minders' absence, but a rebellion.

Against me. Staining the love of my son.

And maybe the MinderNots are right.

Maybe my love is stained, corrupted by my own abdication.

Maybe I'm exactly what I fear I am. Or what I fear I'm not.

Maybe that's what the MinderNots are actually all about. Maybe their dispute was never with the Minders of the Universe. Maybe it's always been with me. They lured me into their orbit, not so I could investigate a crime or uncover someone else's secrets. But to expose my own.

To draw me out.

They gave me a taste, enough that I couldn't resist. I was so eager to follow the clues that I ignored the mystery I was actually investigating. They led me exactly where they wanted me to go. To expose my most vulnerable self, the parts of me I bury, away from prying eyes.

In an act of desperation, weak and crumbling and tears rolling down my face, I reach up to take those moons, and accept my fate.

But then a brush washes across the sky, highlighting the moons with a fresh coat. Thick, wet paint drips from them, white against black. Erasing the MinderNot symbols. The bristles sweep against the midnight canvas, leaving their mark.

And then orange starbursts erupt across the canvas of space, like bursting into flame. Like fire.

No, not fire.

Fire*works*.

Hanson's out there. He's at it again.

The fireworks erupt from a distant part of the city. I don't know where.

The throng of pedestrians look up. They kiss and hold hands. They hug. The spectacle brings them joy. But I know better. Or do I?

"No," I say, and clutch the bottle of *dRops*. "I need them. It's the only way I can see you. The way to feel close."

"Mother," my grown Owen says. A wizened man, he's looking at me like I'm his child now. He raises his eyebrows, and holds his stare, patiently waiting, until finally I ease my grip. "They keep us apart."

The obelisk planets gyrate. Their mirror images dance on the reflecting pool. The promenade starts to thin out. I don't see Owen anymore. But I know he's still here. The white moons are dancing like fairies from another realm. And don't get me started on fairies.

"Goodbye, Mommy," my little Owen says, as if he's scampering off to play. "See ya soon. Love ya!"

My heart should be broken. Only... it isn't. My boy isn't sad or lonely. He's happy. My son is happy. And he's coming home.

There is only one moon above me now. It's white. It glows. Letting me know Owen is close. That he's never really left me. I wonder if that's Milo up there, in disguise.

Yet the Man in the Moon is still up there. Still looking down. Watching. Judging. The ghost of the real Arthur Hanson circles it like a midnight cloud.

There's only one way to get him off my back.

I'm going to find you, Eddie Comstock. I'm going to track you down, no matter where you hide. You know why?

Because it's me. Angela Hardwicke.

And I'm on the case.

CHAPTER 20

I gasp.

"Where am I? Where's Owen? Where's...?"

"Angela." Nini presses gently on my shoulder, holding me steady. My eyes are open, my vision blurry, but I can make out the frosted glass on the door, my name stenciled in black letters. I'm on the couch in my office. "You had us worried. Lie back." She hands me a glass of water. "Drink this. Slowly." Despite her directions I guzzle the water, which goes down the wrong pipe. I cough up most of it, spitting up on a shirt I don't recall changing into. Nini takes the glass. "Sip, Angela. Slowly. You're okay. You're dehydrated, but okay."

"Whadaya say, Hardy?" someone else says.

I know that voice. "What...?" I start, then reach for my neck, which is tight and sore. I sit up. "What are you doing here?"

Frankie the Brush chuckles. "You don't remember?"

"No," I mumble, but feel like I should.

"You called me last night. You kept saying the moon man was watching you. And it was all your fault."

"Moon man?"

"I had no idea what you were talking about. So I came and got you."

"You're lucky," Nini says, and wipes my brow with a cloth. "It was cold last night. If you had slept out there, in your condition, we might be in the morgue right now."

The night's coming back to me. I take the water back and, as instructed, sip until finally I'm drinking normally. I feel the color returning to my face. I look to Frankie.

"How'd you find me?"

Frankie pulls up a chair. "The promenade's your place. It's where you go."

He knows me well. "I guess I owe you. Again. Put it on my tab."

Short, trim, and balding, Frankie smiles, his complexion surprisingly light for a man who spends as much time in the sun as he does. "We'll worry about that later. Why'd you call me in the first place? Why not Nini or Esteban or—?"

I answer without thinking. "Because you have kids. They don't."

"True," Frankie says. "Five times over."

"Five? I thought you had *four* girls."

"Had another girl six months ago." He smiles at me again. "We named her Angela."

I don't know why, but I cry a little. And then last night flickers in my mind. It gets me thinking. "You worked on that Strident Eyes outlet out by Calico Terrace about, what... a year ago?"

Frankie looks at Nini, then at me. "Uh... yeah. Now that you mention it. Why?"

It takes a while, but I catch him up on my investigation.

"They wanted me to renovate five more facilities," Frankie says. "I was gonna take the gig, but one of the Anshani crew showed up at a job site last month. You know I'm agnostic when it comes to clients, but I don't want any part of them. I don't know the extent of it, but they've got their hands in Strident Eyes. And if they don't, they're trying to muscle in. It's a good business. Lots of parties, lots of cash. But the Anshanis are bad news. I need to be anywhere they're not."

Whistler barges in with a full head of steam. He's got coffee.

"Miss Hardwicke. You're awake." He hands me a cup. Lots of cream lots of sugar. "You tell her about the pattern?" he says to Nini and Frankie. "You tell her?"

The coffee goes down just right. It warms my chest. "What pattern? About Tico's Tacos? We did that already."

"No, not that one. This one." Whistler pulls the table over, then opens a map. Not just E-Town—but the entire realm. "Here. Look." Whistler's already circled a half dozen locations.

He runs his finger along the contours of the map. "I started here, by the Scherzeron Airstrip, where Dolores found the van."

I want to buy what he's selling, but I'm not seeing it yet. "Okaaay?"

"Fireworks went off last night. Nothing official."

"Yeah," I say, my memories of last night still hazy, but I remember the orange burst. "I saw them. I couldn't tell from where. Seemed a ways off."

"It was by the marina. It was on our checklist, remember? From the fliers." Whistler rotates the map a quarter revolution. "Look here. There's a Strident Eyes facility in Lancy Grove, that resort town outside the Baldamere Mountains, on the other side of the Chabaqua River. It's a small facility, warehouse only. It's near the locations where—"

"Fireworks have gone off," Frankie says. "I put a new roof on a client's house in Pinewood last week. The fireworks drew a crowd."

"So what's the connection?" I say. "I'm still not seeing it."

"There's an airstrip near each one," Nini says. We all look at her, impressed. "What? I can't figure things out? You should try doing my job."

Whistler straightens up. "You can take my pulse any time you want."

Frankie slaps him on the back of the head. "Respect, junior. That's no way to talk to a woman. And a worse way to flirt. Apologize."

"Sorry," Whistler says. "I can't help it. She's so fox..." But he thinks better of it. "Nini's right. I don't know what Hanson's up to, but it's the airstrips. That's the connection."

My energy improved, I stand up, holding the map. "Whistler. Can you upload this to my phone. With the 3-D hologram?"

"Already done."

"You just might make a junior detective yet," Frankie says. "Now get outta here. I need a minute." Whistler waits, hoping that directive wasn't meant for him. "Kid," Frankie says. "Seriously. You need to leave. It's grown-up time."

"Go," I instruct Whistler. "I'll be in touch." He grabs his shoulder bag and heads out. But he's hovering outside the door, eavesdropping. "You do realize it's frosted glass, right? We can see your shadow."

I listen for his footsteps as they trundle down the hall.

"Angela," Nini says. "You okay? Are you sure?"

"I'm good. Really."

Nini looks to Frankie, who shrugs.

"Angie. You know I love you. And I'm saying this because I love you. My shift's about to start. And I'm gonna be late. Again. You realize what that means? I'm an ER nurse. Being late is not okay. I can't keep doing this for you. We don't talk about Owen much. None of us do. We know it tears you up inside, and the more you talk about it the worse it seems to get. Because you feel weak and powerless and it shines a light on whatever you think is the worst part of you. And that's a horrible way to carry yourself. I know it is. But you have a problem, Angela. You'd been off the *dRops*, what... seven months?"

"Eight," I say, with a hint of pride... and remorse.

"That's a good run. Now you're back to zero. You can't keep going this way. I know you know this, and I'm not your keeper. But if you don't get a handle on the *dRops*, get a hold off them for real, they *will* kill you. One way or another. And when Owen comes back—and yes, I feel in my bones he's coming back— what will it do it him then, knowing you gave up, when he'd been holding on? Your body? Your essence? They can't take much more." She slings her purse strap over her shoulder. "And the truth is... neither can I."

Words rise up in my throat, to push back, but they fall back down.

"You have to decide what life you want to live," Nini says. "You're a mother, a friend, and a private eye. One of the best. Especially when it comes to taking on Universe business nobody else would touch. But maybe it's time to start thinking about why... and if it's really worth it."

"Once a mystery gets hold of me, I can't let go," I say, as if there's no other response. Maybe there isn't. "It's who I am."

"Maybe that's the problem. It's the compulsive in you, the addict. The high is too low and the fall is too far. And like any fix, it's temporary."

"Could be," I say, although I don't want to hear it. "But mysteries exist... just to be solved."

"Maybe that's true, Angela. And sometimes it's even worth it. But you need to ask yourself: What's more important? That the mystery be solved? Or that it be solved by *you*?"

I want to say it doesn't matter who solves the case, but we both know I don't really believe that.

"Like I said," I say, still protesting despite the psychological sludge mooring me to my denial, "it's not just what I do. It's who I am."

Nini kisses my cheek, puts her hand on Frankie's shoulder, in gratitude. "And I love you for it. I'm just afraid that if you don't figure out how to do your job *and* be a mother, as much as that's killing you right now, it'll tear you apart for good. This time you survived the fall. But I'm worried about the crash. I'll call you later."

It's just the two us of now. Frankie and me. It's not like him to stick around. He's always got a job to get to, or a daughter who needs him. Or his wife. But he's not here to pile on. That's not his way. There's business to discuss.

"I know, Frankie. I know. You don't have to say it."

He waves me off. "You said something last night. You were on your back, on the lip of the reflecting pool, rolling your head back and forth. 'That's not the real me. That's not the real me.' Do you know what that was? You remember?"

My chest is tight again, my hands clenched. I hate Nini for bringing Owen up like that. And I love her for it, too. "No," I say shakily, sweat leaking out of me like an infected wound. "I have no idea."

"You said something else. You said, 'baby V.'" He's shaking his head, uncertainly. "Any idea?"

Another rush to my head. "Yes. Yes! Yvette! The sister!" I'm back on my feet. My legs hold steady. "She's the key, Frankie. That's how we'll find him. Comstock's on a mission." I slug down another glass of water. "But *she* knows the town. We find the beauty... we'll track the beast."

Frankie smiles at me. Not because I'm putting the pieces together, but because he sees in my eyes that I'm under control.

"I'm gonna go home, take a shower, then head back out. Thanks, Frankie. You're a prince."

I hug him. It was going to be a hey-I'm-heading-out hug, but now that I find myself in his arms, my head on his shoulder, I can't let go.

Nini was right. I need to figure out how to be a private eye *and* Owen's mom, because no matter how much I've tried to fight it... I'm both. And they're both me. I can't crumble beneath the weight of those responsibilities anymore. I have to rise up to meet them.

Still in Frankie's arms, I cry a little. Not long, but the tears flow, soaking into his shirt. His arms around my back, I breathe in, and out. He breathes with me, helping expel my stress. Frankie's my friend. And one helluva dad.

He eases me away. "I called Tarrish. He's expecting you."

I laugh, wipe my eyes. "You always have an angle, don't you? Working the next job."

He smiles back. "They don't call me Frankie the Brush for nothing."

"No," I say and sling on my utility jacket. It's already starting to feel like my second skin. "I guess they don't. Now let me find this maniac." I pull the door closed behind us. "I gotta see a man about a boat."

CHAPTER 21

Do I believe in second chances? As corny as it sounds—as clichéd and played out as it might be—yeah. I do. I'm living proof.

But not the way you might think. Visit my childhood—all the way through my teen years—and who would you find? A junior private eye? An investigator in training?

Not me. Not her. Angela Hardwicke—Little Angie, that Angela Hardwicke? All she ever wanted to be was a happy little homemaker.

A tidy little life with two children and an adoring husband in a quaint house where problems were never so big or wounds so deep.

Oh, the beautiful lies I told myself. The fantasy of it all.

My parents worried about me, that I was too naive, unprepared, that the harsh realities of life—life in E-Town—would break me.

My friends dismissed those concerns, to my face, because that's what friends do. They close ranks and rebel against parents as if it's their sworn duty.

But I know what they said about me behind my back.

Obnoxious Angela. Deluded Angela. Little Miss Princess Angela.

They didn't know I heard their whispers, their gossip. I told myself I didn't care. That's one thing nobody knew about me.

Or that I cut myself.

Look at me now—my arms and legs especially, my inner thighs—and you'll find a roadmap of scars, pain I'd self-inflicted.

Punishment for the big lie, a carnal release of guilt I carried with me for denying my true self.

Later, after I fell into a pit of darkness and then clawed my way back out... people who knew me then, and who I became... said Angela Hardwicke, Private Eye, the seeker of light and shadow, was a mask. To cover up the pain of Little Princess Angela who finally got the beatdown everyone but me saw coming.

But what they didn't know about me then... what they don't now... is that Little Princess Angela was never my true self. *She* was the mask.

Angela Hardwicke, Private Eye. She was always there. She was always me and I was always her.

I'm not wearing a mask. Not anymore.

It's only now, being this Angela Hardwicke, being me, that I can hold up one mask, the old mask, the old me, and know that she never really existed. She was the great lie I told to hide from this me.

I paid a helluva price to finally admit that. I'm still paying for it. Maybe I always will. Either way, It's good to be back on the street, doing what I do best.

Tarrish has me meet him at the Sun Bay Marina. It's a little out of my way, but he's working another case and I need his help. I get there early and interview all the shop owners on Whistler's list, from the fliers we found.

I strike out at Larry Fin's Hot Air Balloons and was propositioned by one of the customers at Moonglow Massage and Wellness. Although I did manage a complimentary desert coupon at Zin Shou's Family Restaurant, so... score. It'll get Whistler off my back.

I have better luck at Walter's Whale Watching, a mixture of wetlands, salt water, and moss drifting upwind. The gift shop girl says Walter long since retired, but at the registration desk, his nephew, Oliver, who took over the business, immediately recognizes Comstock's photo.

The Sun Bay Ferris Wheel—constructed for Astropalooza, and the only Ferris wheel in E-Town—is mounted near the arcade, a short walk behind the marina. I rode it once. I'm only a little bit ashamed to say it was fun. You can see the entire marina and the tip of the Anaya Obelisk from the top.

"He was with some drunken bimbo," says Oliver, fortyish, in good shape. He's friendly in that shop-owner kind of way. Always on. "She's probably a nice looking girl... if she'd shower and sober up."

I show him Yvette's photo from better days. "Wow. I was right. Much better."

"They say anything? Plans they were making?"

Blonde and blue-eyed, Oliver huffs a smile. "No. Sorry. I get up to a hundred passengers per cruise. I have to focus on the tour, so I only talk to a handful of..." He pauses. "Actually... the girl. Yeah. Now I remember. Because it was kinda rude. She said something about hitting whale watching tours in the other spheres because this one was so lame." He throws up his hands. "What does she want from me?"

"I'm thinking... whales?"

"We don't always see them! Usually, but not that day. I can't help it. It's not up to me. I don't know, it's like they were scared or something."

Keeping half an eye on the front door, Oliver's letting down his shop-owner persona. I ease out a look suggesting I want to take him seriously but need a little help to get there.

"The *whales* were scared? Of what?"

"I don't know," he repeats. "Just... scared. Creeped out."

"Creeped out? Like how?"

As a private eye, you learn to anticipate the rhythm of the interview. No two are exactly alike, but if the door doesn't get slammed in your face, you learn something important. Most people love to gossip, to be in on the dirty little secret you're trying to uncover, no matter how intensely they might protest otherwise.

But they're thrown off at first, because they're not used to being asked about anything that matters. It often takes them a bit to loosen up, to realize they can let go of pretense and start sharing what they know. Or think they know.

More often than not, once you get them started, they'll tell you all sorts of things. Most of it's useless, because really, they just want an audience. To talk and talk, even if they have nothing to say. But uncovering a nugget of truth, no matter how small, can make or break your case.

"Listen," Oliver says, and looks around to make sure the gift-shop girl can't hear us. There's a framed color photo over the counter of the Wonder Wheel on the day it opened. "I don't like to talk about my customers, but that guy? He was..."

"Creepy?"

"Exactly. Weird, creepy. He was friendly enough to start. He said *please* and *thank you* and was generally polite. But then something changed. Like he saw everyone as a nuisance. Like they were... I don't know... desecrating his sacred space. It's hard to explain."

"And the girl?"

"Like I said, a total train wreck. She was drunk and laughing like she was..."

"Rubbing it in? Getting revenge?"

"She was hanging all over the guy. Which he didn't like one bit. Not that she seemed to notice. And after she'd laugh—this big cackle of a laugh—she'd dip her head, her hair falling over the place, like she was having such a great time and wanted everybody to know it. But then her face changed. The smile was gone. And she looked... distant. Mean. Like she was thinking of something. Or someone. Like you said, like she wanted revenge. And then she'd snap out of it, and start up again. She was ruining the tour."

"You let drunks on the cruise?"

"Not when they're like that, no. I tried to kick them off, but the guy wasn't having it. He just gave me this cold, icy stare, and told me there wouldn't be a problem. He whispered something in the girl's ear. Her eyes froze, like she'd heard something that terrified her, then calmed right down. Well, maybe not *calm*, exactly. But she was quiet after that."

Oliver's story matches what I'd surmised. Comstock seems to have a very specific plan in mind, and Yvette knows where to take him.

I look through the storefront window, taking in the marina. The sun sparkles off the water, shimmering between several piers, a boardwalk, small green spaces, restaurants, refueling, washing, and repair facilities, and hundreds of boat slips.

Developers have been battling over the waterfront. Makes me wonder.

But I still can't figure out why Comstock came out here. Was he casing the area? Is there a connection to the case?

"Did they mention which sphere they were hitting first? The other whale tours?"

"They might have," Oliver says, his attention drawn to the soft ding of an electronic bell. "But I don't know." A family of four walks into the shop. "Customers. Sorry. I gotta go."

*****

Tall, black, with a closely trimmed salt and pepper beard, Inspector Lionel Tarrish is sitting outside on the promenade. He's wearing cranberry pants, with a white collared shirt underneath a gun metal vest and semi-formal blazer combo with a matching cranberry pocket square, as well as loafers with no socks, and sunglasses.

He's Inspector, not Detective, now that he's with the ICD.

"What?" he says, nearly snarling.

"Nothing," I say, trying to hold back a chortle. But I can't help it. One slips out. "I've just… never seen you without a suit. You know, a cop suit. You look very… yachtish."

"Don't be a dumbshit, Hardwicke. I'm undercover. Besides, who are you to talk? Where's the pinstripes?"

I glance down at my jeans. I don't want to get into it. "Touché. It was time for a change."

"Just get to it." He waves over the server, orders an iced tea. For himself.

"That's why I love you, Tarrish. You're so romantic." He gives me the stare. I don't push it. "What were you able to find? Any leads?"

To our east is the Dreamline, a new luxury hotel with a long, rectangular pool overlooking the marina. Adjacent to us are the Dooly, Sun Rise Lofts, Zen Breeze, and One Sun Bay Terrace, the shiny residential towers lining the waterfront as it curls around the cove.

I'm not a sailor—I swim about as well as a cinderblock. Yet

I love watching the sailboats as they sit tied up in the slips. Maybe it's that I know they're not going anywhere.

Without warning the sky goes an all-consuming black, like the other day, enveloping us in a non-ness, the un-light. Total nothingness. And then just as abrupt, we're draped in sunlight again.

We let the change pass without speaking of it.

From his back pocket Tarrish removes a few sheets of paper, folded lengthwise.

"Yvette's been picked up at least seven times over the last two years," he says. "Different versions of the same story. Drunk and disorderly, minor vandalism. But no violence."

"Until now."

"If she was really involved with the ditched van, then, yes, she's moved up to assault. But if the driver won't file charges, there's nothing ETPD can do."

"*You* can pick her up."

"I need a lot more to go on then what you're telling me. ICD doesn't get involved unless we have to."

Tarrish sips the iced tea, looks upon it disdainfully, then pushes it aside.

"If she's mixed up with Comstock, assault might be the least of our problems. Isn't that your beat? Off-world investigations? Can't you call her in for questioning? At the very least?"

"I can. If I can find her."

"That's why I want to check out all Strident Eyes outlets located near an airstrip."

"Three," Tarrish says.

"Three what?"

"Bodies. Including me. That's all I can spare."

"Three? There's a madman on the loose, from Earth, who wants to get the attention of the Minders of the Universe. And from what I can tell, he's planning on using airships to do it. And you can only spare three bodies? What kind of inspector are you?"

"Watch yourself, Hardwicke. You're lucky I take your calls."

I know I'm pushing it, but sometimes he needs to be pushed. He's never eager to take risks, especially when there's possible blowback. He's a career man with a wife, three kids, and a pension on the line. He guards his reputation carefully. I get it, but it's annoying. Especially when it inconveniences me.

"Like when I solve the cases you can't?"

Tarrish furrows his brow, and starts to lean in. He's giving me the Tarrish stare. But then he backs off. We've postured enough.

"You see what's going on, all across the realm," he says. "You can add your boy Comstock to the list. I've got more cases than I can handle and not enough manpower. And speaking of you being a galactic pain in my ass... here." He hands me an encrypted star drive. "I did a little digging on Lonali Anshani's murder. Looks like you stepped in it. Again."

He walks me through the details.

"Fuck. Fuckety fuck fuck fuck."

"Classy," he sighs, then looks over the marina. "When I transferred to ICD, I figured I'd never have more than a few cases at a time. That's what they told me. I was eager and tired and dumb enough to believe them. Five years ago... I would've laughed in their faces. I must be getting old."

Tarrish knows how to work a case. He's also maxed out. But Comstock is on the loose and I feel no closer to finding him than when the case started. And after what Tarrish just shared about Lonali, looks like my Anshani problem runs even deeper than I thought. No wonder they hate me. Then again, maybe I can use it to my advantage.

"I can put Dolores on two of the airstrips," I say. "If you and your guys can look into the others, that should cover them all. It leaves a lot of gaps in between—there's a lot of territory we're missing—but it's a start."

"I'll check one of the sites myself. I've got business here first."

"Infiltrating a winery?"

Tarrish rolls his eyes. "I'm trying to bring down a sex trafficker who's been galaxy hopping. He made it on realm somehow, and his trail led me here. So don't press me, Hardwicke. Besides, what's *your* plan?"

Nice one, Angela. Way to empathize.

That's one of the differences between being a cop and a private eye. I get to choose my cases. He has to take the ones that come his way, whether he likes them or not. Still, I take the iced tea from him. I drink the rest. Eesh. It's bad.

"I've got a few leads to follow," I say. "It's time to stop and smell the roses."

CHAPTER 22

The aroma overwhelms me.

Gardenview Florists is quaint, with brick walls, ceiling fans, and a stone archway leading to the back patio. Potted lemon flowers line the floor, while the center refrigerated cases display silver buckets, each filled with pink lilies, ocean breeze orchids, and bundles of blue and orange blooms, with pops of bright pink and purple.

A pretty, middle-aged white woman with flush cheeks, and gray-blonde hair pulled into a large braid is behind the counter, clipping the stems of a mixed bouquet.

"Gotta watch those thorns," I say. "Love's got sharp edges."

She chuckles, then pops her finger from her mouth. There's a droplet of blood. She shakes it out. "That's for sure. Can I help you?"

"I'm looking for Zenovia. She around?"

"No. Sorry. She's out. Anything I can help you with? We're having a special. Two for one on blue carnations."

"Blue carnations?"

She leans forward. "I know. Between you and me, they're leftovers from a wedding we did. Groom thought they'd count for the *something blue...*"

"And the bride called off the wedding?"

She laughs. "Something like that. I'm Freya."

"Angela. Nice place. I'm here for Zenovia. I ran into her at the Bindu and Barkley event. Figured I'd see the store."

I didn't like the vibe I got during the galaxy unveiling. Zenovia doing business with Strident Eyes? She seemed way out of her league. Or was she? I still haven't ruled her out as a VCP mole.

"That was a great event for us," Freya says as a few other customers mill about the shop, being attended to by a teenaged assistant with a high-pitched voice that makes my spine curdle. "We've already gotten a half dozen orders from it. I wanted to go." Freya shifts her eyes, revealing a hint of resentment. "Bindu and Barkley are so exciting, aren't they? I saw them about three years ago in this old subway station when they were just starting out. They were great even then. Oh, well. Zenovia needed me here. We had a reception the next day, and we don't have a big staff, so…"

Not quite sure if Freya is a disgruntled employee or just disappointed in missing a night out, but either way she's eager for a compliment. I oblige.

"This arrangement is beautiful. You're awfully good."

The corner of Freya's mouth curls into a smile. "That's nice of you to say. Sorry if I was a bit of a mopey Marie. Zenovia's a great boss. She really is. I'm lucky to work here. We might be"—Freya looks around —"don't say anything, but we might be expanding."

"Zenovia said she was having money issues. That she was struggling to get by."

"We're holding our own. But she got a great deal on a second store."

"Where's the new shop?"

"Promise you won't say? Zenovia told me not to share. Just for now."

"It's in the vault. Cross my fingers."

But I'm not hoping to die. No point tempting fate any more than I already do.

"On West Fifty-fifth Street," Freya says. "Near the Rubicon Hotel. You been?"

My mouth is clammy, my breaths staggered. I'm having some PTSD from being thrust into the Universe by Jamie. My hands shake, but I hide it. "A few times. Yes."

"I'm dying to stay there. Even just a night. But I could never afford a room. I keep meaning to walk into the lobby, maybe see a few celebrities. I never do."

Rubicon Hotel. Jamie. That's too close for comfort.

"How'd she learn about the space?"

Freya clips two more thorns. "I'm not sure. I think her accountant set it up." Hearing that word—*accountant*—makes me dizzy. "Zenovia said the existing tenant, a chocolate shop, I think, is also a client, but went bankrupt, so he pulled together a quick sublease for us. If Zenovia manages the new location I might to get this one. I've never been the boss before. Of anything, really. That would be amazing."

I ease my breath out so slow I can practically hold it in my hands. "Do you know the accountant's name? They always come in handy."

"Sorry. I don't. I never met him. I think he's new. You need one?"

"I'm thinking about it."

A dapper black man in a blue suit, white dress shirt, and yellow polka dot bowtie comes up to the counter with a huge bouquet—aka your classic overcompensation.

"Would you like me to wrap these?" Freya asks him.

"Yes. Please. I had a most unfortunate disagreement with my boyfriend last night. I need to make amends. I jumped to conclusions, as I am known to do, instead of asking questions. I am, through and through, the jealous type. It appears to be my undying flaw, and yet..."

Freya smiles. "We'll take good care of him. Give me a minute." Then to me: "Um, sorry, Angela. Did you want anything while you're here? I'll tell Zenovia you stopped by."

"That's all right. I'll catch up with her. Oh... while I'm thinking of it... is Zenovia seeing anyone?" I offer Freya what I hope is a coy look. "Asking for a friend."

"You know," Freya starts, then her eyes widen in recognition. "Oh. *Ohhh*. Oh. Uh..." She chuckles awkwardly. "I don't think she..."

I smile back. "Seriously. Asking for a friend. An actual friend." There is no friend. And no, I'm not asking for me. It's for the case. Although I'm sure Whistler would love a date. "I'm... sorta seeing someone myself," I confess. "A drummer."

Freya chuckles again. She touches my arm. "Zenovia's beautiful, but she's shy when it comes to men. She doesn't date much. She could if she wanted to. Although"—Freya slides into thought, asking herself for permission, then comes back with approval—"I do think she's seeing someone."

"Really? She said anything?"

"Only that she's too busy for a social life. But she's had that look, you know? That smile." I do know. "It's been a few months, far as I can tell. Maybe she doesn't want to jinx it. Or she's just not telling me. I don't know."

The timing is right. Zenovia's been with Gil a few months. And I appreciate being discreet about your love life, but it's difficult even for us secretive types to hold back a relationship from someone you work with. The truth has a funny way of slipping out.

"Thanks. And sorry you missed Bindu and Barkley. Maybe next time."

Freya's eyes light up, her pursed lips drawn into a tight smile. She produces a tablet, and scrolls down to a half-screen image of the galaxy designers from the unveiling I attended. "They just announced it," she says eagerly. "The gig you saw was so hot they've been commissioned to do a public performance. Their biggest one ever. They're only making the venue known a few hours in advance. First come, first serve. I already told Zenovia. Sorry, but I'm going! I can't wait!"

"Have fun. It's a good show."

I'm about to head out when Freya changes my mind. "Oh, hey! Angela." She reaches behind the cash register. "Here it is. Zenovia's accountant." She hands me a business card. *Breslin, Anders & Li. Gil Habersau.* And his contact information.

I'm not exactly sure how Gil and Zenovia are tied together on this, but there's more going on with them than either one is saying. "Thanks, Freya. I'll catch you later."

I make a call on my way out the door.

"Frankie. It's Angela." He always has information. I listen. "Yeah. Better. Thanks. About the case I'm working." I head back out to the street. "I need you to check something for me. Got a minute?"

*****

Not five seconds after I hang up with Frankie the Brush I'm grabbed by the shoulder, from behind.

My adrenaline spikes, blood rushes to my face. Through sheer reflex I grab the hand, rotate the knuckle, taking the wrist with it. I pivot and, as my body shifts, sling the arm around and behind my assailant's back, forcing him to his knees. A shoulder bag falls to the sidewalk.

"Miss Hardwicke! Ow! It's me."

"Whistler?"

Down on his knees, head pointed at the sidewalk, he squints, then struggles to look up. It is him. I let go. "I could've hurt you."

He stands up, rubs his shoulder. "Could have?" He smiles at me in that scampish way of his.

"What are you doing here? And how'd you find me?"

"Easy. I need to show you something. I tracked your phone."

I'm not sure if he realizes just how close I am to punching him in the face. And firing him. In no particular order. "You tracked my what now?"

"Oh. Right. After your... you know... the other night. With the *dRops*? Nini called. I was hoping it was the other thing, because she's so foxy, but... okay, never mind. She said I should track your phone. Just in case."

I want to be furious with him. But I stand down. I'll deal with Nini later.

"Alright. Fine," I say as pedestrians pass us on the sidewalk and across the street. "But listen to me. You don't answer to Nini. You answer to me and me alone. You don't track my phone, you don't trace my movements. You don't keep an eye on me. You do what I say, when I say, and how I say, or you find yourself another job."

"Yeah, yeah, of course. Totally. We were just worried about you. That's all."

"Don't *totally* me, Whistler. Don't *totally* me. And you of all people don't get to worry about me. Ever." I step closer. "I'm serious, Eric. Don't... do it... again."

Although easily a half foot taller than me, he's nodding furiously. He's scared of me. As he should be. "Yes, I—"

"Whistler. You're not hearing me. You violated my privacy. So I'll say it differently, so there's no chance for ambiguity or miscommunication. I don't care what anyone else tells you. You follow me again, you track my phone... you're done. You got that. We're not partners, we're not friends, and we're not destined for each other. I'm your boss, you're my employee. That's it. I'll cut you loose and never look back."

The anger compresses within me, an ugly, destructive force, called upon from darker times, being directed at the wrong person.

Even that's a cop-out.

I'm not the victim. I'm the aggressor. I'm choosing to punish Whistler because he's an easy target, and he'll take it. But why punish him at all? He may have stepped over the line, but I'm the one who drew it in the wrong place. He means well, and I'm rewarding *his* loyalty with *my* cruelty.

I realize now that I'm treating him the way Jamie treated me. I want to think I'm better than that. Maybe I'm not.

Back off, Angela. Apologize.

Before I can unclench my heart, relinquish the demeaning scowl I've bludgeoned him with, his face changes. Whistler's eager, infectious charm I've grown to appreciate is gone, replaced by the recognition that he's desecrated a sacred, implied covenant with me he hadn't realized he'd already entered into, and doesn't know how, or if, he can ever get it back.

Horrified by my misstep, I course correct the best way I know how. "Show me," I say, and lean toward his bag. "What've you got? Show me." Eyes wet with tears, Whistler's reluctant to act, insecure about his next move. "It's okay. Show me."

Whistler wipes his eyes, then reaches for his bag. We move from the center of the sidewalk, and lean against the brick building, just feet from Zenovia's storefront window. He produces his tablet, and clicks on the photos app.

He calls up a high-quality image of Zenovia, entering an office building.

"How'd you get this?"

"I followed her," he says, with the glint of a smile.

"Whistler," I say, careful not to scold him with too much force. Had I not just acted like the mortified, exposed junkie that I am, I'd be much harder on him now. "I told you. No fieldwork without me. I haven't trained you yet. You're not ready. But let me see."

Whistler's back to ignoring my protests, eager to show me what he's found, and on his own initiative. "Look at the time stamp. Zenovia's entering the Breslin, Anders & Li building at two fourteen p.m. yesterday afternoon. She's carrying a bag with flowers."

"How sweet." I'm trying to be playfully obnoxious, to engender myself to Whistler, to show him I'm not the total bitch I just showcased for him. I don't think I helped my cause. Truth is, I shouldn't be trying to engender myself at all. Like I told him not five minutes ago, I'm his boss and he's my employee. I should just do my job and let him do his. "She was probably seeing Gil," I say. "They're dating. Secretly, it seems, but dating nonetheless."

"Yes, but look here." Whistler scrolls to another image. "She's leaving the building at two fifty-one p.m."

"Yeah? So? It was probably a lunch stop. A pop-in."

"Right. But she doesn't have the flowers."

"Whistler. She's a florist, bringing a gift to her boyfriend. Tell me you have more."

"Look *closer*." Whistler's eyes are wide and gesturing at the screen. "I snapped a photo of her coming out the side entrance. In through the front, out the side."

I don't know where he's going, but he's got my attention. "Could be nothing. Maybe she got confused leaving the building. Happens all the time. Multiple exits. Or they directed her that way."

"But that's not just the accountant's headquarters. It's the VCP building. You don't think they have strict protocols about how to go in and out?"

"Yeah," I say, sensing he's onto something. "That *is* odd."

"And look what she's wearing. In... no overcoat. Out... overcoat. It didn't rain yesterday and it wasn't that cold."

"She could've left it there last time she stopped by," I say, testing how committed Whistler is to his theory.

"True," Whistler shoots back. "But the overcoat *and* the wrong door? At the same time? I don't know what she was doing there, but I'll tell you what. It was more than gifting flowers. They staged her exit so she wouldn't be noticed."

I'm not sure how the pieces line up, but Gil's played me more than once. He did a pretty good job of it, too. I think Zenovia's also putting on act. But to what end? I need to see her new space. Have a chat.

"Good work," I say to Whistler, who smiles proudly. But I raise a finger, though careful not to be aggressive. "Don't do it again, okay? No more fieldwork unless we discuss it first. You never know what kind of trouble you might find. And you need to know how to avoid detection and, if it comes to it, defend yourself. But... good work."

It then occurs to me. "Why didn't you just call me, or text me the image? You didn't need to follow me here? And you weren't just looking out for me."

Caught in another moment, Whistler dips his head, and shrugs. And then I realize. He didn't want to send what he found. He wanted to *show* me. He wanted to see the look on my face when he presented the clue. He wanted instant gratification, to see the approval in my eyes. I've reminded him so often he's still just a kid, the words have almost lost their meaning. So much that sometimes I forget he's *actually* still a kid, living and dying by what he perceives I think of him. That's a lot of power to have over a person.

I may not be his mother or his girlfriend, and while I didn't plan it this way, I *am* his mentor. And not a very good one. I need to take that responsibility more seriously.

"Okay, okay. You've earned yourself a cheeseburger. But I can't now. I have to make another stop."

"You going to find Zenovia?" He's smiling again, proud of his win.

"Yes," I say, though quick to raise my hand. "You're not coming with. You had a good day. Don't push it. I'm calling Esteban for a lift."

"He's actually... around the corner. He's the one who brought me here." Whistler squints mischievously. "Gimme a ride?"

I shake my head, chuckle in surrender. The kid's got moxie. I'll give him that. "All right," I say. "Come on." He follows me to meet Esteban. "We'll drop you on the way."

CHAPTER 23

Decked out in a red sequined onesie, silver platform shoes, and matching glasses, Esteban's ripping us through Midtown East.

Sitting in back, my phone rings. It's Dolores. She hates talking on the phone, so I get right to it. "What do you have?"

"Different airstrip, but same M.O. Late-night drop. Van is stripped only... dead body this time." Dolores fills in some of the gaps. G'lina Airstrip. Eastern Sphere of Eternity.

"Let me guess," I say. "Nail to the back of the neck."

"Yeah. How'd you know?"

"Lucky guess," I say, and wave off Whistler, who's pawing at me. "It's gotta be Comstock. He's escalating. Yvette probably talked him out of killing the first driver. She might be a dumpster fire, but murder's a hard line to cross. Either she's complicit now... or she wasn't there. Anything else?"

"Not a thing. But a buddy of mine working baggage gave me a call. I put out feelers after I found the first van. We've got a bit of a head start now, and it's nearly dark. Should buy a little more time. What should I do?"

"Call Tarrish. Tell him we got another one. And let me know if anything else turns up."

"Will do," Dolores says. "I gotta call Jeanie. Tell her I'll be late. What about you?"

"I need to follow another lead." I hang up. "Banny. Change of plans."

He eyes me through the rearview. "Evie von M?"

"I'm hoping she can lead me to Yvette. Whatever Comstock's planning, we're running out of time."

With a jerk of the wheel Esteban has us careening into the

far-right lane, drawing angry looks. We barely make the off-ramp that curls under the highway. It's a minor miracle we didn't cause an accident, one car crashing into another, leaving destruction in our wake.

*****

Dudley's is packed. Dinner crowd.

Esteban draws some sniggers thanks to his sparkling out-fit—his call-time got pushed back—but it's nothing he can't handle. I have him sit with Whistler at the bar.

The dining area is in the other room, but I want to keep them close, near the door, in case we have to leave in a hurry. Evie von M isn't known to be impulsive or reactionary, but when it comes to her sister, who knows? I've eaten here before, although I didn't realize at the time it was Evie's joint.

Dudley's is all stained oak, with dim lighting, and so many framed dog photos on the walls and beams it's almost impossible to find a spot without one.

A photo of Dudley, the floppy-tongued golden retriever the bistro is named for, hangs above the bar, in between two mounted flat screens. The games are on. Baseball on the left, Adrosian soccer on the right. Set at a merciful volume, folk/rock music hums in the background.

The artery-hardening aroma of bacon mac n' cheese drips off the air. But what a way to go.

"Whistler," I say. "Eat your food, shut your mouth, and stay out of trouble. I'm heading upstairs. What Banny says... goes." Whistler's about to give me some smart-ass remark, but I cut him off. "Good. Now order yourself a beer, just one, and the bacon cheddar cheeseburger with peanut butter. I know. Sounds gross, but it works. I'll be back when I'm back. Stay ready. Banny. Make sure he behaves."

The bar is three-sided—longest on the ends, shortest in the middle. Whistler and Banny are seated at the middle portion. Not tactically optimal, as their backs are to the window, but it's the only open seating at the bar, and it gives them a clear view of the staircase, only ten feet in front, leading up to Evie's office.

I serpentine through the crowd, avoiding beer spills, eying the muscled help guarding the stairs. Wearing a black leather jacket, arms folded across his chest, his stance and stern gaze tell me he's ready to protect his post at all costs.

I look him in the eye, firm but not too aggressive, and tell him who I am and why I'm here. He looks me over, scrutinizing for cracks in my intention, then sends a PopNote—texts that automatically delete thirty seconds after they've been sent.

He waits, gets a PopNote in return, then moves aside.

"Top of the stairs," he says in a low grumble. "First door on the right."

More photos, dogs of almost every breed and size, line the walls as I ascend the staircase. I come to the second-floor landing, then face the door to Evie's office. Mounted is another photo of Dudley. The large, rust-colored dog is standing on his hind legs, and with his front paws is closing a refrigerator. Neat trick. Maybe I can teach Whistler to do that.

I recheck my holster, steel myself, then knock. First dates always bring a wave of the unknown.

"Come," Evie says. I let myself in, then close the door behind me.

Her office is small, but comfortable, homier than I expected. There are no overhead lights, only desk and floor lamps. Three are on, all shaded and dimly lit. Beneath the window, overlooking the street, is a brown leather couch with a hand-sewn afghan and several throw pillows of various designs. A striped handwoven throw rug sits in the middle of the floor.

Evie's behind her desk, muffled sounds thrumming up from the bistro below. She's wearing a long-length floral infusion maxi dress with a slit along the side seams, and a crew neckline with keyhole cutout.

"Smells good," I say. "What've you got?"

Evie leans over a large ceramic bowl, rolls pasta into a spoon, and shovels a portion into her mouth. She talks as she chews. "Linguini with grilled shrimp and red sauce." She wipes her mouth with a black, cloth napkin. "Try some. It's new."

Her invitation isn't about the cuisine. She wants to see how I handle myself, if I'm confident enough to take food from her hand, or to decline. I approach the desk, lean forward, and accept the spoon without spilling, but with enough space between us to act quickly, if needed. The flavor explodes in my mouth.

"Ooh," I say, chewing a healthy portion, rolling it around so it doesn't burn the roof of my mouth. I get a large piece of shrimp twirled up in the pasta. "That's got a real kick to it. Spicy."

"Here." Evie passes me her glass of white sangria, her dress sleeve dangling like the mouth of an eel. "Take a sip."

I do, and to my surprise, the flavors crescendo. "Wow. That's good. Really good."

"We rotate new dishes, but I've got no patience for those holier-than-thou foodie snobs with their gourmet foie gras and amuse bouche. Life's hard enough without having to suffer through some unholy concoction that only exists to stroke the chef's bloviating ego. I'm all about friends and comfort food. And money. But in the kitchen as in life, sometimes you need to experiment. Wander outside your comfort zone. Just like you and me. Here. Sit."

I take the wooden armchair facing her. I'm about to start in when I notice a picture on Evie's desk. In the photo, she's a bit younger than she is now, with Yvette. They're on a porch swing, Yvette leaning on Evie's shoulder, smiling, but also a bit melancholy, unable to conceal the sadness beneath.

Without realizing it at first, I lose myself, my mind taking leaps of logic from one memory to the next, until I'm so far away I forget where I am.

Once upon a time I was Yvette. Angry, lost, and self-destructive, drowning myself with drugs, alcohol, and grungy lovers, then fighting my way back. Then beating that life force into submission. Round and round I went.

It took me five years, but I finally made it out.

The way Yvette's going, she may not.

A decade later, I'm still a work in progress.

Evie picks up the frame. Up close I see the crow's feet, the worry lines. "The years haven't been kind to my sister. And by extension, to me."

"It's actually"—my heart flickers, my face flush, but I recover—"it's why I'm here. Yvette. Maybe we can help each other."

Evie takes another bite. "I know. I've been expecting you."

"You—?" I raise a hand in recognition. "Nini."

"At Wazon Road. She said you might stop by... if things got worse. Unless my meter's busted... they're worse."

"I'm sorry," I say. "It must be hard."

"I'm more like Vetty's mother. No matter what I do... I'm wrong. If I bring her close... she hates me. If I give her space... she hates me. If I'm gentle... she hates me. Tough love..." Evie wipes her mouth one last time, tosses the napkin in the bowl. "You have any children?"

I hate this question. "I'm not so sure me and motherhood go together."

"You don't have to tell me. Yet here I am. Vetty was one of those kids, you know? She rolled out of bed, could ace any test. She could draw, sing, act. And she never rubbed it in. They were just things she did, because she could, and it was fun. But my parents took care of that." Evie turns away, then back at me. "And now she's running around E-Town with..."

"That's why I'm here. The case I'm working involves Arthur Hanson, who you might know as Eddie Comstock. The man she's with. I'm trying to find him. He's violent... and motivated. If you can help me find Yvette, give me an idea where she might go, I'm hoping it'll lead me to him. And if I find him..."

"You'll take him out."

Evie reaches into the center drawer, produces a silver-plated pistol. The gun is simply enormous. She lays it on her desk, metal on wood.

"I was thinking more like... have him arrested. That way—"

"You'll have to forgive me, Miss Hardwicke. Actually, I don't care if you forgive me. I'm not a big fan of strangers offering their help. And I'm surely not a fan of private investigators. It's your job, your very nature, to ask questions. I'm not saying you're here to cause me trouble..." She places her hand on the gun, presses her pointer finger against the tip of her tongue, then massages the gun's trigger, her head easing back and forth like a dandelion in the breeze. "But then

again"—she examines me through raised eyes—"I'm not saying you're not."

Wandering into the belly of the beast is unavoidable in my
line of work. Witnesses have seen me enter, and a gun that size
would make a helluva racket. But I take no comfort in facing a
weapon like that. One round would put a hole in me the size of
Dudley's torso.

So I ask: "That's a Spivak eight-sixteen, correct? I fired it
once. Some kick."

Evie eyes me, holds it, then extends a closed-mouth smile.

"It's more firepower than I need, but it makes a statement.
Not real convenient, I'll admit, but when you need it... it gets
the job done." The firearm thuds on her desk. "I'm extending
you a courtesy, Miss Hardwicke. I'm hearing you out because of
Nini. She said if you ever offer to help, I should take it."

I have to be careful here, resisting any instincts I have to
reach for my own weapon. Evie's giving me the lowdown—she's
in control.

"I'll take the endorsement, especially from a friend. But
you're only listening to me now because you haven't found
Yvette. If," I continue, "you want to find her at all. Especially
now that she's interfering with Strident Eyes. And you think
maybe I can find a very specific answer to an even more specific
problem."

Moment of truth. Evie looks me over, contemplating her
next move. She nibbles on a piece of food stuck in her teeth,
like a rabbit working a single pellet of habitrail.

"It's a funny thing," Evie says finally. From behind her she
produces an orange throw pillow with white ruffles along the
edges. She places it on the desk, in between the weapon and her
dinner bowl. "I love this pillow. It's for my back. Yvette made
it for me. She's a wonderful seamstress. She can do that, too.
Thought she might become a fashion designer someday. But as
you can see here"—she points to a row of stitches—"I've had
it mended several times. The stuffing can muffle almost any
sound. Be a shame to tear this pillow up again. Not sure it can
take another round."

I'd be lying if I say my heart isn't pounding, because it is.

Whistler and Banny could just as easily be sitting ducks down there as they are my backup. But there's no reason for Evie to pull that trigger. Unless I really have been poking around in places she'd rather I leave be. Which is entirely possible.

"You can relax," Evie says, sensing my unease. "I could've had Georgie take your weapons, but I saw no reason. And look at us. Your friends are enjoying a burger, we ourselves have shared a meal, and now we're talking about family. Or, to be precise... my family. My baby sister. And now... my business. So tell me, Miss Hardwicke. You claim to know the angles. Solve my specific problem. Dazzle me."

She's smart. I took the ease in which I came up here for granted. Big mistake. I won't make it again.

"You could eliminate one problem, by selling the cache of fireworks to the Anshani crew, even at a max rate. But," I realize as I'm talking it out, "that won't do because..." In my mind's eye I see the vans driving across E-Town. Up and down the avenues, along the highways, and through the Infinity cloud to the other eight spheres. I can't believe I didn't see it before. "I thought it was odd, you buying a business like that. It's not just about the cash flow, is it? It's about the vans. You want the routes."

Evie fights back a smile. "Transporting goods can be a tricky business. I have a few friends who wouldn't mind assistance here and there. Quietly. Discreetly. For a fee."

"Smuggling," I clarify.

"Smuggling? Transporting? You have your words, I have mine."

"And the Anshani crew is trying to muscle in," I deduce. "Either they had the same idea, or figured out what you were planning, and want it for themselves. It's a turf war."

Evie points to the tip of her nose. Bullseye.

"And now my sister and this lunatic are stealing the vans, stripping them down, and taking out the drivers." Gun in hand, she leans back in her chair, toward the windows, then rubs her gun hand against her forehead. "I can't tell you how many ratholes I've pulled her out of. Then a few months back she hooked up with those MinderNot dipshits. And now she's with this... what did you call him... Comstock?"

Yvette. Comstock. The MinderNots. Another connection.

"The whole thing's turning out to be more trouble than it's worth," Evie says. "I'm not sure I can take out the Anshanis. We're all just alley dogs fighting over scraps. But then I thought... as crazy as it seems... maybe Comstock's a blessing. Let him tangle with the Anshani crew for me. And then I can..."

"Take whatever's left."

"You know, Hardwicke. You'd make a half-way decent gangster. If you ever go that way."

"Thanks. I think. But I still can't figure out where Yvette and Comstock are headed. I know you're conflicted about your sister. That maybe"—I really feel this one, it hits me where I live—"there's no way you can really save her. Maybe no one can. But let me try. Tell me where she'd go. If I can neutralize Comstock, maybe you get her back."

"That's all well and good, Hardwicke. But that doesn't solve my Anshani problem."

"Actually," I say. "I have an idea about that. If you're willing to give up the fireworks."

Evie eyes me distrustfully, yet curious. "They're worth a lot to me on the street."

"I'm not a math whiz, but I'm assuming they're worth a whole lot less if you're dead."

We sit in silence, the succulent flavor of garlic-braised meatloaf gliding up from below.

"She loved to watch cruisers take off," Evie says. "Especially at night. I took her when she was young. We had no money, but we needed an escape... and a place to dream. She said the galaxy cruisers were like fireflies in the sky. She said maybe she'd get to ride a firefly someday. And if she did, she'd visit the Minders, wherever they live. And never come back."

That's the bitch of being a private eye. You look for any way in, to get people to talk to you. To reveal their secrets. And then sometimes they do.

"Which one? Which airstrip?"

"Vinosha. Out past the old soap factory in Bryer's Pike. It

was the only one we could get to."

"Vinosha. Right. I forgot about that one. I'll check it out."

I stand up and head toward the door, then turn back. "I meant to ask. What's the story with Dudley? Was he your dog?"

Evie's already fitted her reading glasses, examining a document. She looks over the frames. "Let me know when you find my sister. I have work to do."

*****

I grab the guys and head out to Banny's cab. I need to get a hold of Tarrish. The pieces are coming together. Evie von M and the Ashanis both want Strident Eyes.

Smuggling, black market transport. The firework caches are a bonus.

And now Yvette's hooked up with the MinderNots. And so is Comstock.

Like those Tarusian candles, someone's bound to light a fuse. And when that happens, all hell's gonna break loose.

I'm about to get in the back when my phone rings again. Darren.

"Start the car," I tell Banny. "I'll be there in a minute."

I wander down to the corner, outside a liquor store. Traffic buzzes past me.

"Hey," I say into my phone, doing a poor job of holding back a smile. "What's a musician like you doing on a night like this?"

"Playing the TerryTop Lounge. Was hoping to see you later."

I don't tell him now, but just like when he's behind the drum set, he has impeccable timing. He knows my rhythm, knows how to keep the beat.

"I'd like that, but it's a work night. Gonna be late."

"The later the better."

"Tempting," I say, biting my lip. "Rain check?"

"All good. After the other night... I was calling to check in. Thought you might want to stop by. Chill a bit."

Despite what I'm up against, I find myself twirling my hair. "That's sweet. Give me a few days, a week, and maybe you can show me your drumming techniques. I love how you work my bass drum…"

White, deafening panic blanches my ears. Seema Ashani comes up on me. Her gun butt fast approaches my face.

And then my world goes black.

PART III:
MINDER . . . MINDERNOT!

CHAPTER 24

My chin drops to my chest. I can't see.

But there's a sound. A voice? It's garbled, distant, and sonorous, as if coming from the belly of a whale.

"Wah-rake?"

I'm squinting now, struggling to keep my eyes open—light peeks through—then darkness again. My right temple is thudding. I'm seeing stars.

The voice returns. "Rdck. Wah-rake?"

And then lighting crackles in the wilderness of my mind, until I hear the voice once more.

"Hardwicke? You awake?"

Finally my head snaps back, bobbing like a drunk at last call. I want to shift in my seat, but I'm stuck. The exertion is too much. My head rolls again, yanking on my neck.

There's a slap across my face. Hard. It forces the inside of my cheek against my teeth. I'm bleeding in my mouth. I taste the salt and iron.

I'm re-animated. Alert.

Seema Anshani is standing in front of me. My arms, I now realize, are ziptied to the arms of a chair. My legs, too. As my vision comes back into focus, my head throbs.

Esteban's in the middle, on my right, then Whistler. They're ziptied, too.

I survey the room. We're in a dark, empty warehouse. A beady-eyed rat scurries across the floor, sniffing at the mold and dust. It stops and looks up at me, like it's debating whether I'm worth the trouble, then, with a squeak, moves on.

Large dirty windows with paint splatters and other sludge marks line the outer wall.

Through the segmented windows I can see the Darnuth Comet Paving sign across the street. That puts us in the west side industrial sector out in Calvin Corner, maybe a dozen blocks from the Strident Eyes out here.

If I had to guess we're in the old Halston Grocery warehouse that got sold four times over then left to rot. There's a lot of talk about converting properties like this to mixed-use. Restaurants and beer gardens on the ground floor, office and light industrial space on the upper floors, and a roof deck for parties and other douchey hipster events.

Which is all really useful information when you're about to get your brains blown out.

I struggle against the zipties. There's no give.

As my vision continue to sharpen, Seema is flanked by Boscoe and the driver, his jaw wired shut, no thanks to Esteban.

The floor we're on—third or fourth, based on the view through the windows—is about ten thousand square feet in a boxed lay-out with exposed overhead pipes and creaky floorboards.

Outside lights, including the glow of brilliant moonlight, are bright enough to illuminate our space, the concrete walls and support beams streaked in light and shadow.

To the side of me, closest to Boscoe, is a folding table. My switchblade, phone, and handgun are on top.

The non-private eye part of me, just regular Angela Hardwicke, is freaking out. She's shrieking like a deranged banshee to let her friends go, to leave them alone, to go away.

Yeah. Because that's how it works.

So regular Angela Hardwicke is screaming so loud her throat is ripped raw and jagged like it's glazed with shattered glass. Her ears are pounding, snot dripping down her face.

Not exactly high fashion.

But I can't indulge that Angela. In my mind I grab her shoulders and shake with all my might until she gets a hold of herself so that the here-and-now Angela, private-eye Angela, dances-in-the-shadows Angela, can take over.

She better. Because unless I do something, every version of me and my closest friends are going to die here. And horribly so. Seema steps close.

"I told you, my dear Angela, I'd be seeing you again. And the gifts you've brought me"—she runs the back of her hand against Whistler's face—"makes our reunion that much sweeter."

My right eye is twitching. There's something in the corner. Seema takes notice.

"Let me get that." She licks her thumb, presses it against the corner of my eye, then wipes it clean, the depression thrumming in my skin. "You bled more than I expected. Then again... I hit you quite hard."

"I hadn't noticed."

Seema sneers like a racoon rummaging through garbage and I'm a chunk of discarded ham smothered with raisin gravy. She grabs me by the face, digging her cold, bony fingers into my cheeks, her fingernails sharp beneath my gumline so that my lips pucker.

I can't clamp down.

Her breath as vile as a sewer pipe, Seema leans over and kisses me forcefully, then slow and wet runs her tongue along my bottom lip. She sucks on it, licking off the blood and saliva. Then she inhales deeply. She's stealing my breath.

Seema stands upright, arching her shoulders, and holds my breath in hers, as if she'd just taken a hit off a blunt. Arms out wide, she cranes her neck up at the exposed ceiling until, finally, she exhales.

"You should think about gargling," I say. "A little mint wouldn't kill you."

That sets Boscoe off. "Gargle this, Hardhead." He stomps toward me, hits me in the gut with my own taser. The electrical surge is stronger than I remember. I howl in pain as my body contorts, twitching with so much force I feel the back corner of the chair crack beneath me.

Banny and Whistler call out in my defense—at least I think so. I black out momentarily. But their cries are pointless.

I'm in trouble. We all are. I don't want to die. Not here. Not like this. But it's a risk I take. The job I do.

But Esteban? Whistler? They're here with me now because they believe in me, although I'm not always sure why. They don't deserve this. None of us do. Well, maybe me. I always want to think I have a way out, but I don't see how. Knowing my friends are hurt, badly, because of me, demonstrates how unworthy I am of them. Reveals my arrogance.

I've stayed away from Universe business this last year. Kept my distance. Because sooner or later, it leads me into situations like this one. And now my friends are in it, too.

Only... I don't have the luxury of being sentimental. Folding into despair won't get us out of this. It'll only make it worse. I can't let this be the end.

Boscoe stands over me in triumph as my body throbs and twitches. He's shaking dice within his right hand and rolling them between his fingers. Normally, I'd jab him about playing with his tiny cubes, but I'm seeing stars again.

He's about to taser me again—his eyes bulge as he lords over me—when Seema takes his arm, and eases it down to his side.

"That's why you're so much fun," Seema says. "You're feisty. Even at the end."

As a reflex, I squeeze my hands in the sequence Milo gave me. I have no expectation he'll show up. But some habits die hard. I hope our lives aren't one of them.

Maybe it's no surprise I haven't been taking Universe cases. Milo was always my escape plan. But we haven't spoken since Astropalooza, a loss I feel more than ever.

Not just because he's isn't coming, but because I realize now how cocky I'd been.

It's easy to feel like the savviest dame in the room, easier to face down death, when you've got an ace up your sleeve. Knowing I had Milo at the ready allowed me to bluff my enemies and take risks I would've had no business considering otherwise.

Milo didn't owe. He never did. But we seemed to understand each other in a way nobody else could. Milo knew what happened to me. How my life used to be, before I was a private eye. What led me down a dangerous and corruptible road. And what ultimately brought me back.

And I saw Milo for what he always was. Or, at least, how he wanted to be.

One of us.

Yes, he was the Great Disruptor. His power... his essence...

rivaled the Minders. But what he wanted most of all was to be a regular guy. Our pal.

He was.

And he wasn't.

Because his role in the Universe, his responsibilities, were far beyond any of us. Beyond me.

He was there, though, when I needed him most.

But I guess that's why Milo and I were so close. Well, as close as you can be with someone like him. He knew the Minders needed to be kept in check, obstructing their machinations of the Universe lest they get complacent and ultimately become the architects of our cosmic demise.

Milo messed with the Universe in his big, sloppy half-assed way.

I think Milo saw me as some kind of kindred spirit, doing my own sloppy, half-assed work, with my own sloppy, half-assed style. But in my private moments I only confess to my secret self, I like to think that, deep down somewhere, my fractured heart is at least marginally in the right place.

So Milo would bail me out of trouble, transport me across the Cosmos, or just sit and talk with me. Plus, and most significant, he has my son.

And now I'm paying the price—Esteban and Whistler, too—because I took for granted a power I never had. And the Anshanis have come to collect about Lonali. That bill was long overdue, and it's payday. Which, thanks to Tarrish's intel, may be the only way we get out of this shitstorm while we're still sucking air. I need to buy some time, keep them talking.

"I love what you've done with the place," I say. "It's so warehouse chic."

"It's close," Seema says. "Mersha. Perhaps you could improve the decor."

Mersha, the driver, lumbers over to Esteban. Prison tattoos prime on his thick neck, Mersha shifts his weight, then, with his fat, meaty hand made of fat, meaty fingers, unleashes a right cross into Banny's face that knocks a bloody tooth across the floor. Payback for the broken jaw Banny gave him.

"No," I bark through gritted teeth. "Banny."

I don't know if his jaw is broken, too, but Esteban's out cold, slumped to the side. Blood and spit drools from his mouth, leaking onto his silver platform shoes.

"Now it's chic," Seema says.

"Stop!" Whistler half-demands, half-whines, struggling to break loose. But he's a mouse snared in a trap. "What do you want? What's the point of all this?"

"Whistler," I say, my heart pounding. "They'll learn from their mistake. Or they won't."

Seema's nearly laughing as her torso casts twisted shadows, crawling along the floor and up the wall. Revealing her true nature. She reaches to her head, a lump where Nini clocked her with the beer bottle. She looks over her shoulder, then back at me.

"There's no one behind me this time. So what mistake is that?"

"The fireworks you're stealing from Strident Eyes? You're stepping on big toes."

Boscoe rolls the dice out on the table. He doesn't like the play. He rolls them again. "Fuck, Evie. She doesn't play along, she'll be dead within the week."

"Most certainly," Seema says. "Although she's more like *tiny bunions.*"

Despite a high-pitched whistling in my left ear, I steady my breathing. I need to concentrate or we're all dead.

"Evie's tougher than you think. But I wasn't talking about her. I'm talking about the money behind her. You stomped in it this time. It's smeared on your shoes."

Boscoe can't hide the doubt. I just have to hope he's not dumb enough to ignore my warning and kill us all.

"She's got no backing," he says, his pushback more posturing than overconfidence. "She's just trash in a long dress."

"Tell that to Jamie. CEO of the Rubicon Hotel Corp. That's who hired me to find the stolen fireworks. She's got very deep pockets with even deeper allies. She wants to make a statement."

Boscoe bristles. "What statement?"

"That you can't take advantage of her. That she won't roll over. Trust me. She won't. If you think I'm the only one she's put on this, your brain's smaller than the dice in your shorts. You want to bet against me, go ahead. I'll take that action."

"She can send the entire concierge team for all I care. The only fireworks they'll get are the ones I shove up their ass."

"Shove this!" Whistler retorts.

Damn. He'll pay for that one.

"Come on, lucky seven." Boscoe rolls the dice again with an unnerving smile. Five and two. "Perfect." With the taser, he tags Whistler in the gut, sending him into convulsions.

"Not so rough," Seema says. "Not yet. I've heard about this Jamie. She may not break so easily. Then again... I love a challenge. Let's find out."

Seema reaches into her pocket, then steps into a beam of moonlight as it streaks through the window.

Desperate to figure my next move, I stall. "You're not gonna kiss me again, are you? I prefer my foreplay a bit more delicate."

"It's better than a kiss. A bullet in the face, perhaps? Like cousin Lonali? But, no. For you... I have something special."

I'm doing all I can to suppress my temper. But that's the thing about anxiety. It preys on you, torments you.

It wraps you in chains and hooks the end to the back of a car, dragging you along a gravel road. It slows time so that every second feels like an hour, every hour like a year, every excruciating kernel of shame amplified so that you can't think about or feel anything else.

Because we all know the truth. No matter how far you run, how hard you try, or how clever you might be, there's no escaping yourself.

I fucked up. I fucked up bad.

And now it's time to face the music, as horrible as the song might be.

Like the worst of my morning sickness, my stomach is queasy, the taste of my puke gurgling in the back of my throat. But even if I purge, my number's still up. Try as I might, there may be no escape.

From her pocket Seema produces a weapon no one's used on me before, an assault against which I have no defense.

Not because of the pain, but because of how badly I want it. The *dRops*.

"I know your taste for this," Seema says. "And if you prefer to roll your tongue over mine to get some... so be it."

I'm panting now, terrified what another run of *dRops* will do. The fighter in me doesn't want the *dRops*. She rebels with the resilience of the brightest star.

But the addict in me has already crumbled to her knees, begging, praying that Seema will give me what I so desperately crave, as much as I know it'll destroy everything I care about.

I'm one *dRop* away from falling into the fissure of my own soul.

From losing Owen.

I whisper to myself.

I'm sorry, my baby boy. Mommy loves you.

Seema unscrews the eye dropper. With one hand she squeezes my face again, digging her razor-sharp fingers into my cheeks. Boscoe and Mersha stand beside her, delighting as I squirm.

"Stop it," Whistler commands, still trying to protect me, his head hanging low, drool leaking from his mouth. But I'm the one who should be protecting him. "Leave... her alone."

Boscoe tases Whislter, who pisses himself. Boscoe bristles at the smell of ammonia. "Just dose that bitch already."

I twitch, trying to resist, but my head is pinned upright.

What Seema's doing is a form of rape, forcing something into my mouth I absolutely do not want in there.

I have one card left to play, the survivor in me screaming to play it now. But it's a dangerous move and the addict in me screams even louder, squeezing the fight out of me.

But Owen.

I have to fight for Owen.

"Lonali," I mumble. "I know what he did for you. How... he saved you. From Farbod."

Seema locks up like an A.I. whose circuitry has been compromised, paralyzed by conflicting lines of code. "Farbod?" She's rattled. "How... how do you know that name?"

"Lonali wasn't killed because of me," I say, about to pull the pin on a grenade she never knew was embedded in her psyche. "He was killed because of him. It was Mersha."

"Shut the fuck up!" Boscoe points his blaster at me as Mersha starts to sweat, unsure about his next move. "He didn't..."

Moment of truth. Either Seema has enough doubt to

probe further, or she's going to kill me.

She regrips my face. Hard.

"Explain." She digs her talons into my cheeks. "How do you know about...?"

"It was a hit," I eke out. "Mersha killed Lonali. To keep him quiet."

Unblinking, Seema leans in on me, plying her full force, the back of my neck about to snap on the lip of the chair's backrest. Her black pupils search mine, falling into the long, dark passage to nowhere—not so much scanning me for the truth, but escaping it.

Her mouth hangs open, enough to reveal the little lost girl in her still hiding under the bed. She pivots to Mersha.

Clearly shaken, Mersha looks to Boscoe for... guidance? A denial?

Even cold-blooded killers have triggers. Apply the right kind of pressure... it can capsize their domination. No matter how vigorously they might protest, all the fury, disavowal, and distance in the Universe can't protect from what scares them most.

Once you've been ripped open, that breaking point... that moment of vulnerability... never fully closes, no matter how many demons you line at the gate to keep anyone, or anything, from infiltrating the portal into your innermost self.

Or letting the black, festering puss ooze out.

"I... I did what you said," Mersha says nervously, holding his gun higher. His hand shakes. "You told me..."

Boscoe points his blaster at Mersha. "Shut the fuck up! You shut up about—"

"But you *told* me to," Mersha says, his fat fingers sweaty around the grip. "You said Lonali was going to—"

Two blaster shots erupt. The noise antagonizes my ears like a heavy metal guitar with max reverb. Mersha takes both blasts to his barrel-shaped chest, then collapses with a whump.

"Why?" Seema accuses Boscoe, snapping her out of her trance. "What did you do?"

Seema's actually rattled. That's the opening I need. Time to make my move.

"Lonali wasn't cut out for prison," I offer sympathetically, careful not to antagonize her. Push too hard too fast and she might very easily turn on me.

"No," Seema whispers. "He wasn't. He was such a"—she gasps breathily—"lovely boy..."

"That's what I heard," I continue, feeling a tinge of remorse for what Seema went through so long ago. And for the grief she's experiencing now, in real time, a loss so profound and unexpected she's adrift in the netherworld of her existential aloneness. "That underneath it all, he was a gentle soul. But he struggled behind bars. So he drank. And took *dRops*. He told another inmate about a Thursday morning in a second-story apartment building when he was only twelve, and he killed a man with a hammer... leaving that dirty room in Village Square... soaked in blood. Where two other kids"—I let the implication linger—"cousins, mabye... were curled up on the floor, shaking. Lonali rescued them. He bludgeoned a monster."

"He saved us," Seema says quietly, nodding almost imperceptibly. "What Farbod did to us, the things he *made* us do... was our secret." She raises her eyes to meet mine. "All of it."

"And Lonali was going to say your name. So Boscoe had him killed. The cops never followed up because"—I'm threading the needle here, talking to two audiences simultaneously, with distinct intents—"it wasn't worth their time."

Boscoe lunges toward me. "I'm gonna fucking kill you!"

Whether responding to a truth she can't ignore, some inner fealty she still has for me, or to a calling only she can hear, Seema puts herself between me and Boscoe. A shield.

"You did this, didn't you? My sweet Lonali. I loved him."

Boscoe is leaking sweat. "Don't listen to that bitch! She's lying! She *lied!*"

"No." Seema points her blaster at Boscoe. In response, he does the same. "*You* lied. Every minute since he died. He was my hope and my love... and you took him away from me. It wasn't *your* decision to make. It was *ours*."

Seema's a victim once more, strangled by an inescapable chasm, one that lies between loyalty, betrayal... and retribution. Her face relaxes just then, enough to let me know she's accepted what needs be done, as much as she doesn't want to do it.

And as much as she does.

People like her only have one path. They only know one way.

"But more so," she whispers. "It was mine."

"He... he...," Boscoe stammers, his body trembling, knowing Seema is far more lethal with a blaster than he could ever be. "He was gonna tell *everyone*! He was gonna—!"

Seema pulls the trigger. There's a strawberry flash of light in the dark, expansive space. My ears ring as the blaster discharge burns a hole through Boscoe's chest.

My breaths seize.

Because even though Boscoe is dead, I still have Seema to contend with. I tense up when Boscoe goes face-first onto the dusty warehouse floor.

Only his trigger finger spasms, ripping off a blast.

I don't see where it goes.

I'm afraid it's hit me and I just don't feel it yet. Or worse, it's hit Whistler or Banny.

Until, next to me, Seema drops like a sack of dirt, a half-incinerated skull where her face used to be.

I'm panting. My heart throbs. I'm not sure if it's seconds or minutes—maybe longer—before I finally exhale, but my chest is on fire.

"Whistler," I finally say. "Banny. Are you okay?"

Whistler groans.

"Eric. I'm gonna get us out of here. Just hold on."

As if Milo himself had at long last responded to my S.O.S. and sent a surrogate in his place, I hear footsteps encroach.

Must be Dolores. It's dark on the far side of the warehouse so I can't quite make her out, but I smile just knowing she's here, allowing my jangled nerves to run their course.

"Dolores. You can't *believe* the night we're having. Actually," I chuckle as her dark, bulky shadow approaches, "I guess you can. Cut me loose and we'll get Banny to a hosp..."

Thanks to the desk lamp, my eyes are able to lock on the person standing before me.

Only it's not the savior I was expecting.

Because he's not a savior at all.

CHAPTER 25

Now that I'm finally face-to-face with him, Eddie Comstock is truly imposing, like he could crush a small boulder between his hands. He's also sporting a full beard and mustache, dyed jet black. Same with his hair and eyebrows.

Unless you really know what you're looking for, it's good camouflage.

Had I not been chasing him all week, I probably wouldn't have noticed had he walked right by me. Maybe he did.

The Strident Eyes uniform also helps, although I suspect he'll ditch that soon enough.

Comstock hovers with a nail gun in hand.

"Nice threads," I say, pushing him off his gait. "I assume the driver's in a hole somewhere?"

"The driver no longer requires this uniform. I do." Naturally loud and forceful, his voice has a low timbre. "It was a simple transaction."

"By *transaction*, you mean you killed him? Like you did with the Ashanis."

"They're godless, unprincipled heathens. They cherish nothing except their unquenchable lust to smother the light, lest they be alone in the dark. But they served a purposed, for the greater good. They helped themselves to a stock of fireworks I need"—Comstock gestures with his head to several cardboard boxes on a dolly, next to a metal barrel on the opposite end of the floor—"and, quite generously, led me to him. Your protégé."

He points at Whistler, then places the nail gun on the table next to my weapons and phone, which is still dead silent. From his inside uniform pocket, Comstock produces a pair of pruning shears. He pumps the grip, metal blades slicing against each other. With his outstretched hand, he leans over my assistant.

"Don't!" I beg for all the good it'll do. So I pump my fists for Milo. Over and over. But I know I'm on my own. I'm trying to think my way through. Boscoe's dice are spilled out on the floor. Six and one. The Devil. "You don't need him, Eddie. Take me. Whatever you need. He's not worth it. But I am."

Moonglow catches the side of Comstock's face—white light against black hair, the contrast intensified by the blood-red glow of a neon sign alit across the street.

In that illumination I scrutinize the contours of his jawline, above his lip, and all the way to his head, but he doesn't flinch. He's not afraid to let me read him. He welcomes it.

I've been chasing Comstock all across the Cosmos, and now that he's standing before me, him in control, me at his mercy, the last thing I want is to dig deeper into his soul.

But it has to be done. Out of need. And penance.

So I do.

And now that our eyes finally meet, that he sees me seeing him, he delights in my terror. Because it's the moment he craves most. That I finally understand what I've feared all along.

That whatever I've learned about him, whatever it is I think I know, I've only scratched the surface of his derangement. About how far he's willing to go, and what he's willing to do—to any-one—to see it through.

He knows I know. And that I can never unknow.

With that victory over me, that dominion, he smiles.

But it's more than a smile. It's a disturbing gesture, a con-veyance of horror, like a hiss of poison steam from an old factory pipe right before it spews toxic chemicals into the water supply.

"I *am* taking what I need. And what I need... is him."

Comstock cuts Whistler's legs free, curls an arm around his neck. "Behave," he commands, snipping the zipties from Whistler's arms, "and all will be well. Resist... and your friends will be next." He gestures to the dead Anshani crew.

Barely able to stand, Whistler nods in acknowledgment.

"There's no point to this," I say, knowing I can't bargain or negotiate. Comstock is single-minded, literally from a world away. So I resort to the only bargaining chip I have left. "The police are coming. They're on their way. Let us go, Eddie. We can find a place for you here. One that makes sense."

"When I was a boy, my mother told me God had a place for me, if only I would listen." He grips Whistler by the scruff. "I listened, Miss Hardwicke. I sure and truly did. I knelt before my bed, every night, and curled my fingers together. I'd rest my forehead on the blanket, then look up, through my window, past the trees, gazing at the stars, all the way up to God. I said my prayers, begging for him to assure me, that he knew my name. And even if he didn't, that he'd heard my little voice. And then I would crawl into bed, waiting for the Lord to speak to me… or make his presence known. But no matter how long I waited… I heard nothing, I felt nothing, I saw nothing. I waited so long some nights I cried myself to sleep. Until one day I realized that maybe he didn't hear my prayers. Or worse, that he dismissed them, because I was unworthy. That I had no place in his heart. He certainly didn't love me, Miss Hardwicke. I'm not sure he even liked me. All I felt from God… was rejection."

"You had parents who loved you. Wasn't that enough?" I say, even though I know all too well the perilous spasms of loneliness that can lead us down the bleakest of alleys and hopeless roads to nowhere.

"If God truly loved me, Miss Hardwicke… if he was the divine Creator my mother swore he was… he never spoke a word of it to me. And if he did, I must've been in another room when it happened. I don't think he heard me. I don't think he heard me at all. But he will now. The Minders of the Universe. All of them. Because when I'm done talking… when I've uttered my final words… they will have heard my voice. And when they do, my message will be clear."

Comstock drops Whistler to the ground, kicks him in the stomach. Like a slab of meat on the butcher's table, Whistler's bleeding from his nose, his face flush against the dirty floor.

"All throughout history—and now, I've learned, across the Cosmos—the Minders have set us on a collision course… with one another. Galaxy against galaxy, planet against planet, nation against nation. Man against man…"

"And brother against brother," grumbles Esteban, who stirs.

Comstock slides the shears into his back pocket, and takes the nail gun from the table. As he does, I lean back, forcing my weight, the chair continuing to crack in the damaged corner. I don't know if Esteban sees what I see, if he's buying time for me to snap the chair and get to my gun. But it's the only chance I have right now.

"My brother," Comstock croaks, and in one motion grabs Banny by the back of the hair, pushing the nail gun up against the base of his neck. "Daryl was a post in a fence. A flat board committed to holding his place, to keep others from falling down. And then he ripped his own nails out when I needed him most. He abandoned me. Not once, but twice. I was sent away, to live in the rain."

"Because," Whistler coughs, curled on the floor, "because you killed your own parents."

"No!" Comstock pounces, pressing the nail gun against the back of Whistler's neck. "They died for their sins. The worst sins of all. They waited for God to solve their problems, instead of solving it themselves. So I did what they wouldn't. I solved it myself."

I want to make my move. But Comstock's too close. If the chair snaps now he's likely to kill us all. So I hold still, barely breathing. I see Owen's face before me. His chubby cheeks. His smile. His tiny finger curled around mine. I tremble.

Mommy, I hear him whisper. *Be careful.*

"You're right," I say. "What choice did you have? And what did you get for being the son your parents needed?" Comstock's up on his feet again, right in front of me, his beard and mustache as black as hot tar. "But what I can't figure... is how you got out of the hospital. And how you took your brother's place. How did you get on-realm? That's remarkable."

If I've learned anything as a private eye, it's that killers want to be heard. Recognized. And praised.

Comstock grins at me. His eyes—vacuous, glossy marbles—are locked, not on a fixed point, but in the recess of his mind. As I search for any sort of meaning, I realize I'm staring into the great void. I'm about to press on his ego again when Comstock's face seems to widen.

"Gil Habberseau," he says. "Just like he recruited you. First... he recruited me."

As if I'd just gotten off one of those free-fall rollercoasters, I'm dizzy, disoriented, my head feeling like it's about to cave in on itself.

Did Gil really set Comstock free? Did he unleash a maniac... on purpose?

I refuse to believe Comstock, fighting against his lies. But the truth has an obnoxious way of ignoring my denials, crippling my defenses, demanding I subjugate my pride and bow at its feet.

Outside I hear a vehicle roll up. The engine cuts. A car door opens and closes.

Footsteps approach.

Comstock sneaks over to the windows, eying the street. The red neon light casts on his face, as if streaked with blood. I can now see a MinderNot symbol spray-painted on the interior wall just below the window.

"I should've had more time. I didn't..."

Before he can finish his thought I toss my weight to the side. The chair crashes to the floor, me with it. I land on my shoulder. An acute pain lances the socket. I have to hope the tendons didn't rip from the bone, because it hurts like hell. But I push through the pain

The chair leg is broken, although the seat is only cracked. No way I get to my switchblade in time. I dig my wrists around the sharp, broken chair leg, using the jagged edges like a saw.

My ziptie snaps loose.

I'm still on the ground as Comstock passes Banny and runs toward me. I brace myself, ready to stab him with a piece of the serrated chair leg.

Instead he grabs Whistler by the shirt and rushes him to the back. About thirty feet away, Comstock tips over the barrel, bleeding some kind of fluid. It oozes across the floor like urine from a diseased animal.

Comstock reaches for his pocket, then flicks his fingers. I can't make out exactly what he's doing. I grab my gun, about to shoot.

"I wouldn't do that. You might hit your friend." Comstock pulls on Whistler. "Or you might hit this. The barrel's full of airship fuel. Enough to destroy the building."

I'm breathing hard, to think my options through.

Fuckety fuck fuck fuck.

Ducking, I sidestep to Esteban, and cut him loose, when Dolores busts into the room.

She looks at Comstock, holding a beaten Whistler, over to me and Banny, then takes in the leaking barrel of fuel. She rolls her shoulders, plants her feet, and focuses on the target.

"Let him go, big guy. You want to get rough. Bring it here."

Comstock digs his hand into one of the boxes, removes a Tarusian Candle, and unfolds the fuse.

"And deny his destiny? I understand Eric in ways you never will. He is a lost son, a stray, clinging to Miss Hardwicke's feet, desperate for mother's attention. Even worse, for her approval. And worse than that... her love. All from a woman," Comstock says, directing his glare at me, punishing me, "who can provide them all, but chooses not to, because she prays at the altar of a god who just won't listen. I know that torment, to covet what you can never have, to seek what you can never find. It would be cruel to let this go on. No. It is my destiny to ensure that Eric fulfills his. He will be a sacrifice, a gift. His life, only in death, will finally be worth the effort."

With a flick, Comstock lights the Tarusian candle and tosses it to the ground. I can see that Dolores wants to go for him, leaning in his direction, but instead she rushes to the flaming stick and kicks it across the floor, up against the base of the windows.

Fire erupts, crawling along the floor, to the barrel. It dances on the accelerant, the blue center engulfed by a tangy, combustible orange.

A single flame jumps onto Dolores's arm. She slaps at it while I grab Banny and my gear, then run along the opposite side of the floor, away from the escalating blaze.

We head for the doorway.

Lost in the commotion, I realize Comstock and Whistler are gone.

"Dolores!" We're separated by a wall of flame, roaring like a dragon. "Follow my voice!"

With Banny's arm slung over my shoulder, we hobble down the stairs as fast as we can. His legs flail like a marionette. At the bottom landing I turn back, to look up for Dolores. But all I see is a searing inferno. I can't go up for her, and I can't leave her behind.

Maybe I won't have to.

The building about to erupt, she barrels through the flames, rushes down to me. She tosses Esteban over her shoulders, then shoves me forward.

And we run like hell.

CHAPTER 26

The explosion is incredible. The blast throws us across the street.

I crash into Dolores's car, bruising my sore shoulder, while Esteban rolls onto the sidewalk, unconscious. The blaze mushrooms over the lot as the stock of fireworks whistle across the sky.

At first there's a surreal juxtaposition of fiery chaos and deafening silence—soundless screams and delirium—followed by a high-pitched ringing in my head, like ice picks plunging in both ears.

My body is in so much pain it feels like my bones are encased in metal and being repeatedly smashed with a sledgehammer.

I look at my arm and realize I'm covered in soot and glass, the toxic smell of accelerant and ash seeped into my pores.

From around the corner I see police sirens, but I don't hear them. Then I blink—or did I pass out? Because I'm leaning against the back of an ambulance, breathing into a mask, as an EMT holds a penlight to my eyes.

I blink again and Dolores is standing next to me, a large white bandage wrapped diagonally on her head. Her luggage handler uniform is torn and charred. There's blood on it.

Esteban's on a gurney, being hoisted into an ambulance. At least two dozen firefighters are working the hoses, expelling blue dousing foam to extinguish what's left of the smoldering warehouse.

I take it all in, the inferno raging against the night sky.

Though in the distance, two nebulas seem to grow larger, drifting closer—the Dragon's Mane Nebula, a bright yellow cluster of gases, with flaming red edges; and the Torchlight Nebula, orange, with crystal blue tentacles, waving like a jellyfish.

Together the nebulas are like eyes of the Cosmos. I wonder what they see. If they know what I've done now.

And then sound comes roaring back, blistering into my ears.

My heart races, the action speeding up around me. It's only when I see Tarrish do I feel like I understand where I am. He makes it real. He centers me.

"Hardwicke," he says matter-of-factly, taking in the mayhem, as if a building just exploded. Which, of course, it did. "You okay? You with me?"

"Yes. But Whistler's gone. He's injured. Comstock took him."

"Took him where?"

"I don't know."

"Okay," Tarrish says, letting me know he's got things under control. "What else?"

"The Anshanis. They're dead."

"Seema?" he asks. "Boscoe?"

"The driver, too."

"I'll try not to lose sleep over it. From the blast?"

"No," I say, careful not to shake my head. "Family business. They killed each other."

"I guess it helped, then. The intel about Lonali."

"Yeah. Then Comstock showed up."

Tarrish nods, hands me back my phone. "Dolores called. She said, 'Follow the blaze. You'll know where we are.' She wasn't kidding."

I hold an icepack against my head. "Don't make me laugh."

Tarrish smiles at me. I smile back. But after a moment, we don't. The heat from the fire is incredible, making me nauseous.

He offers me his hand, leading me down the block, along another industrial building, away from the EMTs, firefighters, and police securing the area. The press will be here soon.

"I know it's hard, but I need you to think. Comstock's got murder, kidnapping, and arson on his watch, and who knows what else. I've taken command of the investigation, so I can keep his name quiet. For now. We'll let ETPD put out a statement. Chemical fire. Accident. Usual nonsense. But we gotta find him soon before he completely loses control."

The ICD doesn't like cases going public. Harder to control the investigation. Their galactic nature is why the division exists in the first place.

Tarrish removes a handkerchief, wipes soot and sweat from my face. "And don't tell me you told me so," he says. "Because..."

"I actually told you so?" I grin to the degree I can.

"Thanks for not telling me so."

"Any time."

It's getting crowded here and Esteban will probably need surgery. And I need to make sure there are no loose bodies rattling around in my head. No more than usual.

"It's one of ours," Tarrish says as he helps me up into the back of the ambulance. The EMT is securing an IV drip to Esteban's arm. Dolores climbs in behind us. "We have an offsite medical facility. Best if we take you there."

"I want Nini."

"She's not cleared."

"Nini," I repeat.

Knowing I won't back down, Tarrish makes a call. "Fine," he says. "She's cleared." Seated next to me, he pats the interior wall of the ambulance, signaling the driver to head out. The lights flash. The siren wails.

"Thanks," I say and move closer to him, because we have much to discuss and little time to do it.

A killer is on the loose.

CHAPTER 27

Good news—no concussion, no cranial bleeds. Bad news—Esteban is in surgery with a broken jaw, broken nose, and possibly worse. And Whistler's being held by Comstock, a deranged Earther who also has E-Town under siege.

So, you know. Tuesday.

Tarrish comes at me, leads me around the corner. The ICD medical center seems top notch. Nini gives me an injection that protects against concussion symptoms, then applies fresh bandages to Dolores's head and knee.

"I've pulled a dozen men off other cases," Tarrish says. "I can deploy them as needed at high-value locations. I've got ETPD looking for Comstock. We've circulated his photos—clean-shaven and black hair and bearded—and alerted them to ask for either Eddie Comstock or Arthur Hanson. I've also circulated Whistler's photo, in case anyone spots him, with or without Comstock."

"A dozen men can't shut down all the airstrips."

"We're not shutting them down."

"But—"

"It'll cause a realm-wide panic. I can shut down one... maybe... if we have strong intel he'll be at a specific location."

"He's got Whistler!" I say too forcefully for my head to handle. I press the ice pack against my temple. I also have two cracked ribs. "I can't wait for Comstock to wreck another building. We need to find him. Now."

"I know. But here's what we also know. Or, what we assume. Comstock knows we're after him. He's either going to hunker down, and wait until he thinks there's a window of opportunity, or he's already on the move, and will keep moving, hiding in plain sight. He's changed his look once already that we know of. He may have changed again."

He's right, of course. Comstock might not even be headed for an airstrip. The truth is, I still don't know where he's going, what he's really up to, or how he's going to do it. Which, all things considered, is a bit of a problem.

*****

"I've got something," Dolores says as we both sip on cups of ice chips, walking gingerly outside the ICD medical center, converted from an abandoned cardboard box factory. "The warehouse crew didn't notice at first, but a supply of airship fuel is missing. They're short a stock of barrels."

"How many?" I say.

"A hundred and forty-five."

"One forty-five? Damn. That's enough for a..."

"Big boom."

"Way big boom. That's what took out the building."

"We assumeed Comstock was after the galaxy cruisers," Dolores says. "He wanted the fuel. My guess... he cased the airstrips, tracked the supply chain, and looked for an opening. It's a pretty tight system. He knew what to look for."

"How'd he do it?"

"Evie was right. Best we can tell... he either staged or knew about a MinderNot rally out at the Vinosha Terminal. It drew security off their posts. I think he slipped in during the protest. I get why these MinderNot asswipes need to shit on the realm. But for all their piss and vinegar about getting the Minders back on the job, their protests are causing more problems on-realm. A self-fulfilling prophecy. Typical. The MinderNots are so belligerent about being right they can't see how it's all going wrong."

I catch my reflection in a security mirror. I look more like Yvette now than... "Oh shit. He needed another driver. *That's* why he's got Yvette. Wait. Does that mean they've been driving two Strident Eyes vans to each location?"

Dolores spits out a wad of cigar. "Don't think so. Somebody woulda noticed. But a florist's van was heading away from the

Scherzeron Airstrip the night we found the first driver. The signs are for shit. Easy to get lost if you don't know your way around. Still... mean anything to you?"

Florist. Damn.

"Maybe," I say. "But I know who to ask."

*****

Ten minutes ago the sky was a creamy blue. Now it's gloomy and raining so hard the droplets practically rip chunks from the sidewalk. It's times like this I really miss my trench coat and fedora. I miss a lot of things. Freya is pruning a bouquet of roses.

"Oh! Hi, Angela. Back again?"

"Yup. Back again."

"Wow, it's really coming down out there. I know you're soaking wet, but I love your hair like this."

"I was going for soggy love-poodle when I got dressed today. Guess I nailed it."

"Sorry," Freya says, dropping her head. "but you seem to be on opposite schedules. Zenovia's not here. She's at the new store."

"I'm not here for Zenovia. I'm here to see you."

Freya smiles, her face flush. "Really?"

"You guys deliver, correct?"

"Uh, why?" she starts, as if she thought I was going somewhere else with my question. "You have an order?"

"Not exactly. I didn't say before, but I'm a private investigator. I'm working a case."

"A private eye?" Freya steps back and clutches her shirt, near the neck. A common reaction, a covering up. "Wow. That's... I've never met a private eye before. What's that like? What are you...?" Freya stops. "Wait. Am I in trouble? Is Zenovia? Is that why...? I thought, you know... you were interested."

"I get that a lot. Zenovia's beautiful. And so are you." A middle-aged woman trapped between her fleeting youth and the inner spark that still burns bright, Freya smiles. "But I'm here on business."

"Is there a problem with the new store? Did Zenovia...?"

Freya leans in, whispers. "Is it something illegal? With the lease?"

Interesting. She went there fast. "Why do you ask?"

"Oh. I shouldn't. It's just... I know I said we're doing okay. We're not. She can barely afford to keep me. I don't know how she can open a second store when she might lose this one."

"She's fronting."

"Maybe," Freya concedes as she pulls on a loose petal. She rolls it between her fingers like a dissolving thought, then lets it fall to the floor.

"I'm not saying she did anything wrong. The second store could be exactly what she says it is. A deal too good to pass up. That's how the real estate game works sometimes. Right place, right time. And someone to pull it all together."

Like Camilla's come-ons, I let that one linger. Let's see if Freya bites.

"Do you think the accountant is involved?"

Bingo.

A critical element of being a private eye is the art of the question. Another is counterpoint. Knowing when to keep quiet, to let their question go unanswered.

Most people react poorly to silence.

It's nearly impossible to interpret accurately, so it makes them uncomfortable. Or what we in the trade call *the twitch.*

"Oh," Freya says, and then realizes something she likely knew all along but didn't know that she knew. "Oh! *That's* who she's been dating. No wonder she didn't tell me."

If Freya can put this all together, it's only a matter of time before somebody else does. Gil's been playing sneaky little games. Zenovia, too.

"You asked about deliveries," Freya says. "Why?"

"How do you handle them? Messenger? Bicycle?"

"That's the other problem. We had this great van. But then somebody..."

"Stole it?"

"Yeah. How'd you know? About a month ago. Zenovia was in tears. She fell behind on the insurance payments, so they couldn't process her claim. She lost all of her money from the van. She couldn't afford a new one."

"Let me guess. Right after that... the second store popped up."

"Actually... it did. She was so upset about the van... and then she wasn't. It was the new store. We drank to the Minders. She said they made it up to us because, you know how it's been. They haven't seemed too interested in folks lately. Only... now that we're talking about it... maybe it wasn't the Minders after all."

Normally I'd be quick to agree, but I'm actually not so sure.

"Where was the van? When it was stolen?"

"Right in back. Can you believe it?"

I produce my phone. "You recognize this guy?" It's Comstock in his black beard and mustache.

"No. Never seen him. Why? Was it him?"

An elderly couple in raincoats stop in front of the window. Their hands are thin, their faces wrinkled, but irradiating the kind of peace that comes with forgoing worries of the past, focused on the time they still have left. They turn down their umbrellas and shake them out. As cold and grim as it was just minutes ago, the rain-soaked sky is now honeydew green.

My phone rings. Frankie the Brush. I step aside and listen.

I come back to the counter, and bring up another photo of Comstock. His clean-shaven look, posing as Arthur Hanson. I show it to Freya. "What about this?"

"Oh, I remember him. He was so sweet. Such a flirt, too. He bought three dozen roses for his girlfriend. One-month anniversary, he said."

"Yeah. He's a regular romantic."

"Is it him? Did he steal the van?"

"The two photos I showed you? Same guy."

"No. Come on. They look nothing alike."

"That's the problem. He's been going by two different names. Arthur Hanson... and Eddie Comstock. Did you hear about the warehouse last night?"

"I saw it on the news," Freya says as I shoot off a text. "Why? Is he...?" Her eyes go wide.

"Yes. He's extremely dangerous. He set the fire." She stiffens, pulls the pruning shears close to her chest, the same kind Comstock had at the warehouse. He probably stole them from here. "And he's mixed up with the MinderNots some-how. Speaking of which…" Someone enters the store. "Freya. Officer Mulraney will stay with you until further notice. It's highly unlikely—possible, but unlikely—that either Comstock or a MinderNot will come looking for you. We're hoping to have him in custody any day now."

"Any day? But what about Zenovia? What about the store? What do I… do?"

"Nothing," I say and gesture to Mulraney. "She'll be with you."

"But Bindu and Barkley are on tonight! They're announc-ing the venue in a half hour. I need to get there early. It'll be packed!"

I turn again to Mulraney. "No calls, texts, or holomessages." I don't want Freya tipping off Zenovia. I check my phone again. "Sorry, Freya. I know it's unfair, but you need to sit this one out, too."

✳✳✳✳✳

Zenovia's kneeling on a drop cloth, using a soft-laser measuring beam on the floor, orange tape marks in the corners.

"I see why you took the place. Great location."

"Angela? Hi. What are you doing here?"

Drywall flakes cover the hardwood floor. Light fixtures dangle from wires, light switches need faceplates. Sticky notes are taped to the walls, denoting the color they'll be painted, and where mirrors and shelves will hang.

"Looks like you got paid after all," I say, ignoring her ques-tion. "Wazon Road."

Zenovia stands, wipes her hands on her blue overalls, leav-ing white dust marks, like the tail of a shooting star. She's look-ing at me, unsure how to answer, a light yellow T-shirt shirt beneath the overalls.

Zenovia's eyes flit toward her phone, which is sitting on an overturned paint bucket. She focuses back on me, a white smudge on her brown cheek.

"Oh, yeah, from the other night. I worked it out. But... how'd find me? Why are you—?"

"You know I'm a private investigator, Zenovia. You know why I'm here."

"A private invest...? I didn't think..."

"Your boyfriend hired me, Zenovia. You know that, too."

"B-boyfriend?" Zenovia's looking behind me, to the front door. For a way out. "I don't..."

"I saw you at Gil's apartment. I also have photos of you at his office." Zenovia swallows, stuck in a moment she can't get out of. "And I've been to your shop. Twice now. Freya's worried about you."

I take a step closer. Zenovia leans back, arching her shoulders, but then she holds in place. She can't move, her legs taking root like the ficus trees she sells.

"Retail rents along this corridor are sky high," I say. "Especially with the Rubicon nearby. But that's the benefit of dating an accountant. Right, Zenovia? They know how to move money around."

On the counter to her right is a half-eaten chicken-salad sandwich with large celery chunks, a tin watering can, and a hammer. Her eyes go there, hold a second, then back to me.

I let my jacket fall open enough so that she can see the gun in my holster. She's stuck in place, like an actress who's forgotten her lines. Her body actually shudders.

But then she squares up, sniffs, and straightens her back, the dialogue rushing into the front of her mind.

"Fine. Gil's my boyfriend. And he's also an accountant. So what? He represents the landlord of this building. The chocolatier defaulted with seven years left on his lease. Gil said if I wanted this space on a sublease, he could help. But I had to act fast. I'm a small business owner, Angela. An entrepreneur. And I'm taking a risk. But in the long run, it's a good risk. At least, I hope so."

Zenovia recovered quickly, but I don't think she'll hold up.

"What about Eddie Comstock?"

She looks at me quizzically. "Never heard of him." I believe her. "Who is he?"

"We'll come back to it. I have a friend in the construction business. He knows the contractors who built the interior for this place. He said the previous tenant was about to file an injunction against you for taking this space illegally. They also wanted to sue Gil and his firm. The chocolatier was not only solvent, but profitable. Until they were hit with a provision in their lease they'd never seen before. It triggered a rent escalation, which they couldn't pay, so they defaulted. Funny how that worked out for you. Gil's earning his keep."

"I don't... I don't know what you're talking about. Gil just told me..." Zenovia turns away, her eyes starting to water.

"Tell me about Eddie Comstock, Zenovia. Tell me about Gil." I hold up my phone with a picture of the clean-shaven Comstock. "Look, Zenovia. Look."

She wipes the tears. "I told you," she says, her voice shaky. "I don't know any Comstock. I don't..." She homes in on his photo. "Hold on. I've seen this guy. But his name isn't Comstock. It's Arthur... something. Arthur—"

"Hanson?"

"Yeah. He's Gil's..." Zenovia looks at me again. More tears.

"Gil's what, Zenovia? His what?"

She slumps. "His tenant. Gil owns a building on Darcy Street in the Historic District. Five apartments. But they're all empty. Except for one."

Empty. Right. Why I never saw the neighbors. "The third floor?"

"Gil bought the building, then renovated all the units. Arthur's from out of town. He's Gil's first tenant. But he hasn't been working out. Gil's trying to evict him."

"Like he did here?"

Zenovia's face puckers. "He cares so much. But ever since the Minders have... since they..."

"Abandoned us?"

"Gil was such a believer," she says, raising her hands, as if to shield herself, then drops them to her sides. "He loves Eternity, loves being a part of the Cosmos. Even if it's just as an accountant. But lately he's... lost his faith."

"Is Gil a MinderNot? Is he involved with them?"

She sighs. "Maybe. I don't know. But he's so sad. And angry. He says the Minders won't do their jobs. If they're going to let Eternity fall apart and take the Universe with it, then we have to look out for ourselves. And if that means using the tax code to make it happen, then better to do it now, before it's too late."

"Too late for what?"

"I don't know! I love him, but he's scaring me. Gil's been more distant lately, leaving at all hours. He says he goes for long walks, to let the stress out. But I don't know..."

"You don't believe him?"

"I knew it was wrong to take this space. And I'm sorry I lied. But he said"—she holds her hand to her face—"it would be okay."

Zenovia's not in on this. She doesn't know who Gil really is. Hell, can anybody ever really know someone else? Can you actually know what's in someone's heart and mind? And can you believe it, even if they tell you?

"This may seem extreme, Zenovia, but has Gil ever been off-realm?"

"Off-realm? Why *would* he? He's an accountant. How...?"

"Gil's in trouble, Zenovia. His tenant? Arthur Hanson? His real name is Eddie Comstock. He's wanted by the police. He's killed at least four people that we know of in the last week."

"*What?* Is Gil okay, is he—?"

"I don't know where he is, Zenovia. I can't find him. But if you were looking for Gil, where would you go?"

"He's not answering his phone. I thought he was busy at work. But now I'm..."

"Zenovia. Please." I put my hands on her shoulders. "If he went *anywhere*, where would it be?"

Zenovia's eyes are red, puffy, and full of water. "The apartment. Where Hanson lives. Gil said Hanson, I mean... Comstock... hasn't been there in weeks. Gil's been cleaning the place out so he can rent it to someone else. He's been going there a lot."

I gesture to the front window. "Zenovia. Officer Freemont is going to take you into custody."

"Custody? Why? I don't know anything about Comstock! I didn't know who he was. I never met him!"

"The police will have their own questions. And then there's your lease. The landlord won't be happy. Jacque Abladuejue's got real sway in this town. He'll probably sue you. Or worse. And he won't be gentle or forgiving, or eager to hear your side. Do yourself a favor, Zenovia. Get yourself a lawyer. And no one affiliated with Gil. But tell the truth about Comstock—the man you know as Arthur Hanson—and you should be okay. At least about that."

The officer leads Zenovia to the door.

She turns back to me. "Will I, Angela? Will I really be okay?"

The space between us is cavernous. Her life will never be the same. "Honestly... I don't know." I write a number on the back of my business card. "Ask for Coco LaRoque. Tell her I sent you. Explain what's happened, do what she says, and deal only with her. I mean it. Talk to no one."

"And what about Gil?" Zenovia says. "What's going to happen?"

Officer Freemont opens the front door.

"Honestly," I say again, "I don't know that, either."

*****

The Rubicon hotel guests gobble up most of the cabs in this area, especially now, at rush hour.

Instead I head down to the Escahoe Circle underground rail station. There's tension in the recycled air—there's always tension of some kind. It wouldn't be E-town otherwise. But it's more palpable than it used to be. A collective angst. Uncertainty.

There's chatter about the Bindu and Barkley performance tonight, which makes me think of Freya, but I'm distracted by MinderNot protestors on the platform, holding up signs, chanting:

"Minders of the Universe,
You leave us here to rot.
Minders of the Universe?
Minder... Minder Not!"

The plasma-propelled train stops, lets off passengers as we enter the car. I'm standing next to an old woman—she's standing, not sitting, as if propping herself upon ancient, aching bones—when she looks at me with eyes from long ago.

"Where have they gone?" she says, not expecting an answer. "What have they done?"

She gets off at the next stop, leaving me alone to pull the mystery together. Whatever Eddie Comstock is planning, whatever his target may be, Gil's my best chance to figure it out.

Back on the street, not many stars tonight, but the Torchlight Nebula seems closer than it's been. Brighter. To the east is the Dragon's Mane Nebula.

Lights are on in four of the units. Gil's smart, giving the impression at least some of the non-existent tenants are home. Which doesn't mean anyone's actually here. But I see a shadow move past the window in Comstock's apartment.

I re-check my weapon, feel my pockets for additional ammo, then shimmy open the lobby door open with my switchblade. I reach for the elevator, but think better of it. I don't want to get ambushed in there. I take the stairs.

I'm barely up a few steps when I see a bloody handprint on the white railing, smears on the white wall. I've got my gun out, looking up, ascending. There's more blood, and bloody shoe prints on the stairs, with smears on the silver handle to the access door leading to the third-floor hallway.

No way to know if there's someone waiting for me. I push the door open with my hip, come in low, gun pointed.

I pivot the other way. Nothing.

I creep toward Comstock's apartment—only one unit per floor—my shoulder against the wall. There's blood on the doorframe and doorknob, the door open just a crack.

Before entering, I produce one of Bernice's scout orbs. I'm already wearing the contact lens, which is synched to the orb. I roll it on the floor. Through my right eye I can see the entire apartment from the ground-up view.

There's no one there, so I ease in, pulling the door behind me, but not enough so it closes all the way. Don't want the *click* to give away my position.

The apartment is just as I left it—couch, chair, coffee table—except there's a trail of blood on the hardwood floor leading through the kitchen, to the bathroom. I hear water running, several coughs, and the porcelain rattle of the toilet bowl lid. Thud against the door. Whoever's in there is either in real bad shape, or cleaning up after inflicting one helluva slaughter. Maybe both.

Following the scout orb, I'm about to step into the kitchen, the black-and-white ceramic checkerboard tiles also smeared with blood. I hear the toilet flush. The door clicks open.

I brace myself, breathe, and prepare to fire my weapon.

A body approaches.

*****

Gil's wearing a beige suit, his white shirt almost entirely red—blood red—clustered around his belly. There's a bandage on his neck, blood soaked through. He sees me now, braces himself, then tumbles forward. I catch him in my arms.

He's too heavy for me to hold up. I pull a chair over, put him in it. He's in bad shape.

"Anj... Angela. It's Comstock. He's..."

Gil hacks up blood. I grab paper towels off the counter, wipe his mouth.

"Gil," I say, and sit next to him, my back to the refrigerator. "What happened?"

"Comstock. I got a tip he was on his way here. I rushed over to stop him. I grabbed him in the alley, around the corner. But he gut shot me. Nail gun. The nail's still in there."

I gently peel away Gil's jacket. His belly is swollen and leaking blood. I can see the head of the nail.

"He went for the kill shot when I was down. He got behind me, put the nail gun behind my neck."

"How'd you get away?"

"I," Gil huffs, struggling to catch his breath. "I..." He reaches for his ear, waves at it. His neck is bandaged below it.

"I don't understand. How did you...?"

He takes my finger. "The Cressa Tab." I reach behind my

own ear. "Yours was limited, secured to the transpo hub. Mine is free range. It's like the Infinity Cloud. I just have to"—he coughs, sneers—"think it, and I'm there. I jerked aside as he pulled the trigger. He got my neck, and I took myself here. I ended up outside."

He laughs, grimacing with each bounce. I laugh with him, never more aware of the damage we can do to ourselves. This isn't a realm for Owen. Not for anyone.

"Comstock came after me, too. Yesterday. He said you helped him. Gil... it wasn't a glitch that brought you to Comstock, was it? You looked for someone to take on the Minders. Because you're a MinderNot, too."

He looks at me, the life struggling behind his eyes. "The Minders... they failed us. They left us behind. The VCP told me to be quiet, not to cause trouble. But it was the only way to get the Minders' attention. To see what they've done."

I hold a wad of paper towels under warm water, and wipe his face.

"Then why did you hire me,? What was the point of this?"

"Zenovia," he says breathily.

"Zenovia? But what does she...?" With Gil's blood literally on my hands, I can see her face now. Her nervousness at the night club, her feelings for him today. "Because you love her. You met Zenovia after you recruited Gil. She reminded you of what's good, didn't she? What's possible. She reminded you of why you joined the agency in the first place."

"I wanted someone gentle, to lie down with and just... exhale. But when I did, feeling her skin against mine, watching our shadows on the wall... all I could see was how cynical I'd become. How desperate I was to restore my faith. Without the Minders, what else do I have? Only... we can't control them, can we? We can sacrifice or praise or even scream through the night, but ultimately, it doesn't matter what we do, does it? Love them or hate them, worship or ignore, the Minders will keep on doing what they've always done—impose their w... will... and decide our fates. So when I looked at my shadow and saw how twisted I'd become, I put a blaster in my mouth. My hand was right there, Hardwicke. Tears streamed down my face as I shook and trembled and damned myself for committing the greatest sin of all. Believing I knew beh... better than the Minders themselves. I pulled the trigger. But the blaster lost its charge. To truly repent, I needed to accept what I'd done, and do whatever I could to put it right. But I was too far down the road with Comstock. I'd already gotten him out of the hospital, told him to find his brother. That if he really wanted to speak to God, I could make it happen. I switched their IDs in the system. Arthur's details, but Comstock's face and essence code. I let him loose, Hardwicke. I set him free. So now I have to stop him. That's why I hired you. But it's just too damn late."

"No, Gil. It's not. Tell me where he is. Tell me where to find him. The police are waiting for me to—"

"The nebulas," he says. "He's gonna torch them. The galaxy cruisers. They're loaded with fuel. And the fuses... from the fireworks? That's the trigger."

"Does it matter? It's just fire in space?"

"The nebulas. The gases and electrical dis... discharge. Mixed with the fuel. There's so much of it. You have no idea the kind of..."

"But the damage," I say. "It'll be up there. We'll be okay."

"No. We won't. There's another charge. On realm. He's going to ignite the fuel down here. He'll incinerate half of E-Town. It'll be nothing but ash."

"Where is it, Gil? Where's the stash?"

"I don't know. That's why I went to see him. To get him to talk. I couldn't."

"We'll find it. We have to."

"You're run... running out of time."

"Then we have to stop the cruisers," I say. "It's our only chance."

"You can't. The MinderNots. They're everywhere. On the streets, in the control towers. They think he wants to hold a rally. They don't know why."

"What about the VCP? Can they override the cruisers?"

"Maybe. But they don't know what's happened. And I'm not going to live long enough... to tell them."

"You must have a code, some way to contact them? What about Clancy? At the pizza joint?"

Gil's eyes roll back. His body twitches. And then he's back. "Yvette. Whu... Whistler."

"Whistler! What about him? Have you seen him? Is he alive? Is he okay?"

"He's on the cr... cruiser. Yvette's on the other. They're tied up in the cockpits. Comstock threaded the fuses together. He wrapped it around their bodies."

"You have to tell me! Which cruiser? Which *cruiser?*"

My mind races, desperate for solutions. My eyes drift to his wounds. To his neck. And his ear. I reach behind mine. The Cressa tab.

"What about this? Can it get me to Whistler? Can I get him back?"

"You," Gil says, his face white and leaking the kind of shiny, toxic sweat that says he isn't long for this realm. "Your access. It's restricted."

"Restricted? By who?"

"I... don't know."

"What about yours? You can go to Earth. Stop him before he starts."

Weak, he shakes his head. "So's mine."

"No. I have to—"

"But I can do *this*." With a crooked, aching grunt Gil pushes his hands against the arm rests, and rises unsteadily. He looks at me, and smiles, panting. "Tell Zenovia I haven't given up. And that I love her."

Gil reaches behind his ear.

"No! Wait!"

He's gone.

*****

I want to say I take immediate action, but I'm frozen, stuck in the humiliating netherworld between conviction and remorse, empowerment and terror.

I so badly want *dRops*, to fall back into that insidiously false sense of wonderment and bliss, to take me out of myself long enough to help forget my panic.

As if being controlled by some unseen force, my phone is in my hand. I look at the screen, but not really looking. My heart and mind are already transported to another place. I dial, hold the phone to my face. It's the only call I can make.

"What?" Tarrish says. "Where are you?"

"The cruisers. You gotta call them back."

"Which cruisers?"

"All of 'em."

"Hardwicke. There are hundreds of them across the nine spheres. I need a reason."

"Two of them are flying bombs. Call 'em back!"

He grumbles, pauses, then starts in again. "I need proof. A credible threat."

I explain as fast as I can.

"It's still just your word," Tarrish says. "And what if you're wrong? And even if you're right... what then? How do we get the bomb squad onto all those cruisers? Even if I call immediately—and even if Central Command agrees—we're talking hours. Maybe days. We just don't have the bodies."

"Then you'll have to..."

"Have to what, Hardwicke? Have to what?"

I can't believe what I'm about to say, but I say it anyway. "Shoot 'em down. Shoot 'em all down."

"Oh, what the fuck, Hardwicke? Come on."

"Then I don't—"

Had I taken *dRops*, what I see before me now would fill me with joy. But instead it brings me to tears.

"Whistler!" I throw my arms around him, kiss the side of his head. "Are you okay? Are you alright? What happened?"

"Hardwicke!" Tarrish shouts through the phone. "Hardwicke!"

I put the phone on speaker. "Tarrish! It's Whistler. He's back. He's here."

Whistler stumbles to the sink, slurps water from the faucet. "The marina. That's what he's after. You have to evacuate it. Now!"

"How do you know that?" Tarrish says.

"It was Gil. I don't know how he got on the cruiser, but he cut me loose and took my place. Took some tab from behind his ear. He gave it to me." Whistler peels it back, then holds out his finger tip. "Look. It's…" Shaking, Whistler drops the Cressa tab. "Oh, shit. I think I just stepped on it."

I want to be pissed, but Whistler's been through hell, no thanks to me. "Forget it. We have to keep moving."

"He's bleeding out, Miss Hardwicke. But you have to evacuate. Comstock dumped cruiser fuel in the marina. Barrels and barrels of it. He's going to torch it all. It'll destroy the waterfront and everything around it. But the other MinderNots don't know that. He also said something about the fuel having some new masking agent, so there's no smell. You can't even tell it's there."

"Tarrish," I say. "You—?"

"I'm on it."

"Go. I'm heading after Comstock."

"No, Hardwicke. Don't. He's—"

"You deal with the marina, and the cruisers if you can. I'm getting Whistler to the hospital… then Comstock."

Tarrish knows there's no point in arguing. "Just… be safe."

"I will."

"And Whistler?" Tarrish says.

Eric's banged up, but looks all right, all things considered. "Yes, sir?"

"Good job."

The poor kid is nearly in tears. If he was looking to impress me, he kinda did. I tell him so in the only way I know how. By punching him in the arm.

"You. Dumbshit. You went off on your own. Don't do that again."

"But check it out. I've got a couple of scars, a black eye, and I almost got blown up in a galaxy cruiser. Kinda bad-ass, right?"

I shake my head at him. "Whistler… what am I gonna do with you?"

He grins at me with that naughty little scoundrel smile of his. "Give me a raise, a promotion, and my own business cards?"

"You really did hit your head. Let's get you to the hospital.

And no arguments. You're going."

"No, really," he says, wincing in pain. "I'm fine I'm—"

"Nini's working."

Whistler straightens his back. "Actually... now that you mention it, I am a little sore. I could use a checkup."

I help him downstairs, call a cab.

"Oh," Whistler says. "Camilla? You should send someone to Tico's Tacos."

I've got that pang in my gut. "Why?

"I only heard part of it, but Yvette and Comstock got into a huge fight about her. Yvette said Camilla's nothing but a skanked-out groupie, and that he's been wasting his time, sitting in that booth every day. Yvette said she's the only one who really understands him, and that if he was really committed to the cause, he would've ditched Camilla already. Comstock didn't like that. So he put Yvette on the cruiser. To get what she always wanted."

I'm almost afraid to ask, but the answer seems inevitable. "What's that?"

A cab pulls up in front of us. The Torchlight Nebula, bright orange and blue, drifts toward the marina.

Whistler leans on the cab. "To finally outshine her sister. In a blaze of glory."

*****

The customers at Tico's Tacos are at least two deep at all three registers. I ask for Camilla, but the kid bussing tables says she's in back, be out soon. I grab a beer and a red basket of cheese nachos, then slide into the only empty booth, a two-seater against the window.

I text Tarrish for an update at the marina, but haven't heard back. I don't know if that's good news or bad.

The Dragon's Mane Nebula passes by, in the distance. I munch on a handful of nachos, the melted, yellow cheese dripping into the basket. I look around for napkins, to the counter along the sill. Traffic lurches along outside, headlights refracted through the window. I turn away, looking ahead and...

My eyes lock in place. This is the booth. Comstock's booth. I know this because, in front of me, up in the corner, on the wall, is a framed photo. A photo of the Anaya Promenade.

And the reflecting pool.

"Hey, Angela." Camilla brushes my shoulder. "You coming tonight? The big event?"

Nacho crumbs fall from my mouth. "What event?"

"Bindu and Barkley. At the promenade. They're unveiling their new galaxy design. And their first nebula."

I stand face to face with Camilla. Even though we just inspected each other's birthday suits, it's like I've never seen her before. "Nebula?"

"Yeah. Right above the reflecting pool."

In my mind's eye, I'm there now. "That's filled with water."

"Well... yeah. That's kinda how they work. News says a quarter million spectators. I'm leaving now. Gonna be great."

"Don't," I warn, knowing Tarrish has called every available emergency service personnel to the other side of E-Town. "Don't go."

"But Angela. Arthur Hanson was sent from the Cosmos." She pulls off her apron, revealing a white T-shirt underneath. The MinderNot insignia is triangulated across her chest. "Our voices matter. And after tonight... the Minders will know we're right."

CHAPTER 28

I've never seen the promenade this crowded.

Spectators are lined against the reflecting pool's perimeter, at least a half dozen deep. Others are gathered on the grassy slopes, with blankets and folding chairs. Some are up in the trees. And there's enough alcohol and weed going around to anesthetize a solar system.

I even spot a few *dRop*heads. Yet I don't care.

A massive stage has been constructed just beyond the north end of the promenade, between the reflecting pool and the planet-topped monument. Numerous platforms are stacked far above our heads, like a multi-dimensional chess set, staggered at various heights and angles.

Mounted atop the metal latticework supporting the platforms, huge spotlights illuminate the promenade, including the reflecting pool.

The stage, monument, marble planets, and intensifying crowd are reflected back on the surface of the pool's still, black water. Their mirror image.

The spectators are feeding off each other's delirium, to witness Bindu and Barkley electrify the night.

Far off, from opposite directions, the Torchlight and Dragon's Mane Nebulas drift closer to one another. Blinking lights from dozens of galaxy cruisers twinkle. Gil and Yvette are in two of them. For all the good that does me.

And what the crowd doesn't know—and what I assume, although can't yet confirm—is that the reflecting pool has been tainted with thousands of gallons of galaxy cruiser fuel. Enough to burn us all alive.

Of course, there's a possibility I'm wrong, that the water is just what it looks like, but I can't get close enough to find out.

"Yo, dude," I say to a twenty-something dude and his twenty-something girlfriend, who are passing a joint back and forth between all the other joints blowing in my face. "You know what's up?"

"Honestly," the dude says, and giggles as he exhales a cloud of lemony weed, "not really. But it's bitchin."

"Naturally," his girlfriend says, wearing cut-off jeans shorts and a MinderNot T-shirt, the bottom tied above her bellybutton, exposing her tight midriff and pierced navel. "So bitchin."

"Rock on. But why are you here?"

The stoners look at each other, shrug, then giggle even harder.

"Cuz we're talkin to the *Minders*," the dude says. "Gonna get their asses back in town, back on the job. It's wicked."

"Totally wicked," the girlfriend says.

"You should take this party somewhere else," I say. "It won't be cool, bitchin, or totally wicked. Trust me."

"Pfft!" the dude chortles as his girlfriend hangs on his shoulder. "You need to smoke some of this, girl. You need to chill."

Before I can find my way further through the crowd, fireworks explode behind the treetops. The spectators, including the two stoners, laugh and high-five. Lovers hug and hold hands. They point at the multi-colored blossoms, streaks, and starbursts dancing across the night.

Yet they don't realize, but soon will, that the marina is now ablaze. That most of E-Town's emergency services have been called there, to the opposite end of town. The damage that's coming? The destruction? It makes me tremble.

And the nebulas. Those damn nebulas.

They've drifted toward one another, still closing in. If you stand behind the south end of the promenade, behind the reflecting pool, and look up, it's like the nebulas are eyes of the Universe—staring down at the platform. Staring at us.

Or maybe it's my own paranoia, feeling that the spirit of the Universe, maybe the Minders themselves, know what I'm trying to do, pressuring me to succeed. Or fail.

I've made my way in the middle of the crowd, on the west

side of the promenade, up on the grassy slope. Trees behind me, people surround me.

I can't say the ETPD loves hearing from me, but my name should carry enough weight for them to take me seriously if I call in a threat. Only the phone lines are jammed because of the blaze at the marina, and I still can't get a hold of Tarrish, likely for the same reason.

It may not be enough, but I've got Whistler calling Tarrish every two minutes until he picks up. Esteban and Dolores are both in the hospital, out cold. Nini won't leave their sides. I could run the ten blocks to the nearest police station, and beat down the doors of the ETPD, to get someone to listen to me. But for every minute I spend there it's another minute I'm not here. And I'm the only one who has any idea what kind of lethal force is about to be unleashed.

I don't know if I'm making the right choice, but it's the choice I've made. That's one thing you learn about being a private eye. The case is never about what you want. You either unravel the mystery... or you don't.

Whistler's also trying the media, calling in a bomb threat at the promenade. But like with the police, he's having trouble getting through. They're flooded with calls.

Besides, it's E-Town, so the press gets dozens of leads a night about one possible disaster or another. A planet about to crash into the realm. A portal to another dimension opening and closing in the middle of Britton Square. Another Big Bang.

Sometimes the media investigates, so they can break the story. But as scummy, self-serving, and incompetent as they can sometimes be, the press typically kicks big threats to the authorities. Who are basically unreachable because they're also down at the marina, awash in flames.

If I ever needed Milo, it's now.

Uniformed police patrol the promenade, but they're outnumbered thousands to one. No way they could forcibly evacuate the crowd. And if they act rashly, to scare the spectators into compliance, a riot could erupt. Especially with the MinderNots.

They've bought into their own mystique. And no one is going to break up this congregation on my say-so.

I've got Comstock's photo loaded on my phone. Hopefully the cops have it from Tarrish as well. My best hope is to make it more real, tell them he's delusional and wants to attack Bindu and Barkley. Even if I can get to the uniforms, we still have to find Comstock, and do it fast, before he can do any damage. Assuming we can even get to him. And then pray Tarrish picks up.

There's too many people here to look for Comstock myself. With my own crew down and out, I had to call in backup. They weren't my first choice, but it's all I could pull together on short notice. Besides, they were here anyway. Strident Eyes is backing the event. My phone buzzes.

"Hardwicke," Evie von M says. "I'm near the stage. I've got some guys in the crowd. If Comstock's here, we'll find him."

I'm about to respond when the spotlights go dark with three metallic switches. The crowd freezes. From gargantuan speakers, electronic music whirs, escalating into a crescendo.

A hiss of steam emerges from the bottom of the stage.

Repeating their club performance, only on a larger scale, Bindu and Barkley rise up on their white, glass squares, outlined this time with red fluorescent light beams.

The galaxy designers are dressed in their white body suits, white jackets, white boots, and large white goggles with tinted lenses. They stand, motionless. The music starts up again.

They're rehearsed. Prepared. Ready.

"I don't see him," I say, pressing my hand to my phone against my ear, open hand against the other. I can barely hear above the noise. I'm getting bumped from all sides. "You?"

"Not so far. Can we get my sister back? Do you know which cruiser?"

"I don't."

"For a private eye, you're pretty fucking light on details," says Evie, a woman who's spent her entire life chasing after Yvette, whose own long quest for attention has finally reached its peak.

"You flatter me," I shout above the noise. "I figured you'd pull out of the event. Not worth the risk."

"I've got a shit ton riding on Strident Eyes. The best way to catch an animal is to lure him out in the open."

"Comstock's no Seema. He's worse."

"Maybe. And thanks for taking out the Anshanis. But what he doesn't know about me, and maybe you don't either, is that... box me in a corner... hit me where I live... and I'm more dangerous than I look."

There's no point in arguing. For now, all I care about is finding Comstock. It doesn't matter who gets him first, as long as we get him.

From high above us, on his platform, Barkley's booming, tenor voice resonates through the sound system.

"What does it mean to create?" he says as a dozen strands of pulsing red light beam up from the edges of the platform.

Bindu's smooth feminine voice follows from a platform diagonally above Barkley. "What does it mean to envision the stars?" She, too, is surrounded by beams of red light.

They answer one another, in unison. *"It means... to conjure a vision in here"*—as they did in the club, they grip the pulsing red strands of light into a bunch and pull them all to a single point on their foreheads—*"and project that creation... out there!"*

They toss their fists, throwing the pulsing red beams. Only instead of swirling galaxies, their beams concentrate into a single point atop the obelisk—activating the circle of marble planets.

Feeding off the pulsing of lights, the large orange and white planet comes alive. The crowd erupts into hysteria.

Bindu and Barkley launch the strands of red light again, bringing from replica to life the crystal blue ice planet with its glowing lemon yellow crown and once more with the blue and green planet. Music pulses.

Fireworks explode, raining multi-colored sparkles as Bindu and Barkley's light beams dash across the sky.

As they do, I see two galaxy cruisers separate from the herd, heading deep into space. But then I lose them in the firework residue, camouflaged in a fog of colored smoke.

I'm looking for Comstock all across the promenade, but there's too much chaos. So I make my way along the embankment, dodging clouds of weed, when I hear a disturbing voice.

"Glad you could make it."

As fast as I can move, I reach inside my coat, to grab my weapon. But a powerful hand grabs me from behind, blocks my grip arm, his chest against my back. With his other hand he reaches across my shoulder and gets to my gun. He turns me around.

Only instead of black-haired and bearded Comstock, I'm face-to-face with a new iteration. He's completely bald and sporting a goatee, dyed blonde, almost yellow, and wearing blue jeans, a cranberry shirt and brown leather vest, with a black belt and black boots.

"You throw a mean party," I say. "Too bad it's a wake."

"You know what I admire about you?" Comstock's holding my gun on me, at waist level, low enough that no one in the crowd can see. "When you believe in an idea, when you're convinced that you're right, you don't give up."

I said the exact same thing about Whistler. "If I'm so good, how'd I end up here?"

Comstock smiles, his face seeming even larger than before thanks to his bald head. The red, glowing lights catch his yellow goatee and his bald pate. It's like staring at a sixth-dimension demon. I don't need convincing.

"Because"—he chuckles—"you were trying to solve a mystery. And for that, I thank you. It's one of the great ironies of my life. I've resented your intrusion. You made it personal, arrogant, appointing yourself arbiter of who's the sinner... and who's the saint. And yet... you've taken more time to learn about me than my own mother did. But where you went wrong, what you should have been asking is... why are you trying to find *me*, when you're the one who's lost?"

"Being lost implies I want to be found," I respond without thinking, unsure why I just said that or what I really meant. But a breath leaves me, now that I did. I feel lighter somehow. Relieved.

"We all want to be found, Miss Hardwicke. The question comes down to... who even knows you're gone?"

I squeeze my fingers, in the pattern, praying Milo's out there. That he's listening.

Comstock takes me by the arm, when the spectators cheer again. The blinking lights of one galaxy cruiser, then another, pass far overhead in a crisscross pattern toward the Torchlight and Dragon's Mane Nebulas. Fireworks erupt.

As we slalom toward the stage, above the eastern tree line I see a fiery haze from the marina. I have to think news reports are spreading, that the crowd here knows what's happening, but they're so entranced by Bindu and Barkley I'm not sure they notice.

Comstock's got us moving fast enough that I can't get to my other weapons.

We're almost to the base of the stage—Bindu and Barkley dancing above, on their squares, in sync to the music—when the muzzle of a silver-plated pistol is pressed flush against Comstock's cheek.

Unfortunately, he's got his weapon in my back so tight I've got no room to make a move.

"Get my sister, dickhead." Evie may be true to her word. "I want her back. Now."

"As you wish." Comstock points to the massive view screens flanking Bindu and Barkley. "She's right there."

Holding her gun on Comstock, Evie cranes her head, enough for a buff MinderNot to crack it with a pipe. Evie goes down like an old tabby cat, a sack of flesh and water—no bones. The pipe guy and two others wearing MinderNot T-shirts grab Evie under the arms, and drag her away, the back of her heels skidding on the grass.

A small army of MinderNots immediately fill in around us. We're surrounded.

"That's the problem with thinking small," Comstock says. "Evie thinks I corrupted her sister. But the truth is, she was eager to help the cause."

"She's headed to her death. That doesn't seem happy to me. None of them know why you've really come here. They have no idea."

"I know." Comstock gestures for two of the MinderNots to take me by the arms, which they do, as he lets me go. "But they will."

Several stories above us, yet still in the shadow of the Anaya Monument, Bindu and Barkley do their pivot move. From their hands, the performers launch those beams hundreds of feet into the sky, as if they were crimson bolts of lighting, until they pierce the center of the swirling planets.

With its glowing yellow gases, the Anaya Nebula awakens.

The eye.

Comstock leans in close. "They are sheep, Miss Hardwicke. So are you. And, in truth, so am I. They're desperate for a communal catharsis. To share an experience that validates their fears and acknowledges their existential loneliness... while bringing them all together. We all want to be enlightened. One way or another, which makes us fortunate, indeed. Because our prayers, as they say on Earth, have finally been answered."

CHAPTER 29

I feel my phone vibrating in my pocket, but I can't get to it. I don't know if it's Tarrish, Whistler, Evie, or…?

I look up, beyond the stage, the rotating planets, and the newly awakened Anaya Nebula. In the chasm of space, the Torchlight and Dragon's Mane Nebulas have drifted closer together. Heading toward them are two galaxy cruisers, the ones that broke off from the pack.

Comstock gestures with his head. Three MinderNots step aside and, like a gate, open a space in the protective circle. Comstock shoves me forward, underneath the stage.

We approach two glass squares, like those supporting Bindu and Barkley. Comstock grips a lattice work support beam, checking its integrity, when I go for my taser.

Before I can retrieve it from my boot he stomps on my hand. I retract, wincing in pain. My wrist is broken.

"I knew you'd make a move." Comstock studies the taser, then presses the button, extending the arm. An electric current jolts. "Nice toy." He tosses it aside, then grips me under the shoulder as I support my broken wrist. "Move."

Beneath the music and Bindu and Barkley's dance moves, the support beams and platforms vibrate, but hold steady. Comstock shoves me onto the white-lit floor.

I land on my wrist, the pain so intense I see stars. I struggle to my knees, when glass walls extend from the floor, locking me inside, as if he knew I'd be here.

Like an animal, I'm caged.

I bang on the glass with my one good hand. It doesn't budge. Comstock steps onto the platform next to me. He stands straight, shoulders pulled back, red and white lights reflecting off his bald scalp. As big as he is up close, he's now larger than life.

"You can't really want this," I say, pleading as much with myself as I am with Comstock. "I know you miss your mother, but she was ill. It wasn't her fault. She loved you the best she knew how. Why are you so angry, Eddie? Why do you carry this hate?"

"You," Comstock says, glaring at me, those cruel eyes shooting fury my way. "You should not talk to me about mothers who fail their sons. Hers wasn't a failure of love, but a love of the wrong son. Jesus didn't die for our sins. She died for his, believing the greatest lie of all."

Comstock raises his hand. His platform starts to rise. Mine does as well. I lean against the glass, to steady myself.

"But what about the Minders?" I can't believe I'm the one saying these words, regurgitating the dogma I've scoffed at myself. "They do see us all."

"I'm sure the Minders see us. The only problem?" Our platforms continue to rise so that we pass Bindu and Barkley, above them now. "When they look at what we're going through... at how we suffer and struggle... they shrug and move on. Which is their way of saying... 'We hear you. We see you... but we just don't care.'"

The music shifts.

A long synth note holds, hypnotizing the crowd. Bindu and Barkley stop, point to us, and toss red beams of light.

The crowd erupts, enticing Comstock to smile, beaming with arrogance—and pride.

Above and over our shoulders is the Anaya Monument, topped with the circle of planets and its newly awakened nebula. The Anaya Nebula.

That glowing red eye.

"But when I'm done," he says, "I'll never be forgotten."

*****

The music stops. The crowd falls silent. Our cage lights go out.

Below me, a single spotlight focuses on Barkley, his black skin striking against his white body suit.

"You asked for a new galaxy," he says, his voice reverberating across the promenade. His bars light up again, one at a time, glowing red. "You asked to be amazed."

"But what we desire most of all," continues Bindu, whose own voice resonates as her light beams match the crimson pulse, "is for our individual voices... at long last... to become one."

The crowd's collective hum rolls on the wind.

"The Minders of the Universe created this realm," Comstock announces, staring out at the quarter million spectators surrounding the promenade. "But it's time they take notice. That they accept what we all know, but they refuse to acknowledge."

From cameras mounted on the galaxy cruisers tails, we see the length of those vessels, one on each viewscreen, heading for the Torchlight and Dragon's Mane Nebulas.

Even the police, seeing Comstock up here, are caught in the trance. Those able to ignore the drama make their move, but they're bottlenecked, or subdued by MinderNots planted in the crowd.

"That we will no longer accept their indifference," Comstock continues. "That we—the MinderNots—have stripped them of their power." From his side pocket he produces two Tarusian candles. He lights the fuse on one, extends his arm, up, at an angle, and points it directly at the Anaya Nebula, the vortex of the three rotating planets. "Not because we can take it away, but because we fear them no more."

From the end of the Tarusian candle, a sparkling purple shell shoots in a high arc, atop the obelisk, landing in the center of the Anaya Nebula, piercing that eye.

The gases excite. The crowd roars.

I lean against the glass, scanning the reflecting pool, surrounded by mesmerized spectators. And potential victims.

I signal Milo, again and again. It's pointless, I know, but I try.

"What have the Minders done for us?" Comstock shouts. "Comets pummel the streets. Night becomes day." The floodlights burst open again, to accentuate his point. "Day becomes night."

The floodlights shut off.

"Two moons alight the darkness when there should only be one. Five, when there should be two. Rain extinguishes sunshine, winter vanquishes heat." Another purple shell shoots from the Tarusian candle, further exciting the Anaya Nebula. "Planets emerge from stone! Galaxies turn to dust! And stars... extinguish before their time." Another purple shell. Then another. Then another. "The Universe is a vast, evolving, and miraculous place, filled with life and death. Joy and sorrow. And all the mysteries in between."

The Anaya Nebula is animated now, its membranes pulsing like ventricles of the heart. The circle of planets swirl clockwise, picking up speed.

"The Minders have limitless power. Yet we, the residents of the Universe, no matter which realm we call home, are the ones who struggle to find our place, see our families torn apart. Whose mothers fall victim to inertia. Who collapse beneath the weight of cosmic forces. The gods lie to us, my friends. About what we do, who we are and, ultimately... what we become."

The crowd hangs on his every word.

"I am not from this realm. Yet here I stand. I have no powers, no blueprint for the Universe. I am here because the Minders of this Universe abandoned us. They brought us into being, because they could. To act as their sycophants, validating their very existence."

The crowd chants with a chorus of yeahs.

"But now, the Minders must realize that we—the children of the Universe, their children... the *MinderNots*—are not here to serve that Universe or even the Minders themselves. No! We are here to remind the Universe, and the creators of all—the Minders of the Universe—that they are here... that they even *exist*... only... to serve *us*!"

The circle of planets accelerate. The Anaya Nebula pulses. The crowd chants:

"Minders of the Universe,
You leave us here to rot.
Minders of the Universe?
Minder... Minder Not!"

Examining the cage's structure for a way out, I scan the crowd, a blur of faces, until I see one I recognize. Freya. She's with Officer Mulvaney. Only she's out of uniform, wearing a MinderNot T-shirt. Entranced, they're both cheering, unaware what this madman is up to. I pound on the glass. I scream her name. But she can't hear me. None of them can.

The music pulses. Bindu and Barkley resume their routine, tossing red lightning bolts into the crowd. The spectators roar.

And then I remember. I reach for the back of my ear.

*****

"What are you doing here?" Clancy says, monitoring readouts in the transfer room. "Where's Gil?"

"Forget Gil! You have to hurry. Send everyone! Anyone! To the promenade."

"Slow down, Hardwicke. I don't answer to you. We have protocol for this kind of..." He spots my broken wrist, which I'm carrying in my other hand. The hologram on the wall is no longer a sparkling ocean view, but a flower-filled meadow. "What happened to you?"

"Clancy. Listen to me. Comstock—"

"Who's Comstock?"

"Hanson!" I say. "The recruit. From Earth."

"What about him?"

"He's at the promenade. He snapped. He's with the MinderNots." I pull out my phone, show Clancy some footage I was able to capture. His eyes widen. "He's gonna torch the whole place, and everyone there. We're talking minutes. See those cruisers? Gil's in one of them. He's been shot. He's not gonna make it. You gotta get me back there. Now!"

"I can request an intervention."

"What about a strike team? To take out Comstock."

Clancy guffaws. "Strike team? Who do you think I am? Best I can do is make the request. Command makes the call."

"Then do it... ah." I grab my wrist. "Call it in. But make sure they don't fire explosives."

I explain to Clancy that even one spark, one misdirected shell casing, could accidentally hit the reflecting pool and incinerate everyone there.

They have to neutralize Comstock—a headshot if possible—before he can blaze the promenade himself. And then pray he hasn't instructed any of the MinderNots to try the same.

Clancy types furiously into his console. "Done. It's up to them now. Best case... for them to deploy a fleet and be in position... fifteen minutes."

"Too long. What about...?" I reach behind my ear. "It's restricted. Can you get me back to Earth? Before Comstock ever got here? If I can take him out then, this never happens."

"You know I can't. I don't have the authority. Or the access codes."

"Oh, come on, Clance. I bet you know a work-around."

He purses his lips. "Normally you'd be right. But I'm locked out. Earth is on the no-fly list. Don't know why, but there's nothing I can do. It's *way* above my paygrade."

"Then send me back. To the promenade. If I can get to Comstock—"

"Shut up."

"Hey. Don't tell me to—"

"I said," Clancy says, scooting over on his rolling chair, "shut... up. Now c'mere." He pulls me into the chair next to his desk, produces a medevac kit and wraps a flex cast around my bad wrist. The interior fills with stabilizing gel and a powerful painkiller. He connects a diode, attached to a wire, to the Cressa tab behind my ear. "You're right. Something's jamming the signal. I'll get you as close as I can." He inputs several key strokes on his terminal. "There. It's the best I can do." He hands me a 9 mm. "Hopefully you won't need this, but you can go back to the promenade as soon as—"

I press the Cressa tab.

*****

The reflecting pool is laid out before me. But I'm at the wrong end, the south end, far from the stage. I can see it all. Damn.

Projected on screen, Comstock stands upon the highest

platform, his chest puffed out, surrounded by red beams. The crowd swells with anticipation.

The two massive video screens on either side of the stage switch on.

The sky is ablaze over the marina. Even without the screens, the searing blanket of orange and black is visible from here.

Transfixed by the spectacle of this unholy event, the crowd stomps and cheers with such force the entire platform shakes.

Bindu shouts, her voice reverberating through the sound system. She directs her hands into the sky. "Watch!"

The video screens switch vantage points, now from the galaxy cruiser tails. They're headed into the mouth of the Torchlight and Dragon's Mane Nebulas.

On the platform, Comstock extends his left arm, pointing up, at an angle. More purple shells shoot from the Tarusian candle into the mouth of the Anaya Nebula.

In the center of the swirling circle of planets.

He extends his other hand, another Tarusian candle, angled downward, toward the promenade. Toward the reflecting pool.

Toward the water.

And the fuel.

It wasn't there before, but a full moon is hovering, watching me again. Always watching.

Comstock shouts, his arms extended diagonally, a Tarusian candle in each hand.

"It's time, my fellow MinderNots, to open the eyes of the Cosmos. So that the Minders... can finally... see!"

"You asked for a galaxy!" Bindu and Barkley shout together. *"We bring you crackle!"*

The crowd erupts into the MinderNot chant, a delusional mob psychosis:

"Minders of the Universe,
You leave us here to rot.
Minders of the Universe?
Minder... Minder Not!"

And then the images switch again. It's live footage from the marina, which is up in flames. Hundreds, maybe thousands of people are screaming as they burn to death at the Sun Bay Ferris

Wheel, which is now a six-hundred-foot circle of scalding fire.

Rescue teams are doing their best to douse the inferno, but it's pandemonium.

The video screens switch back, this time to the galaxy cruiser cockpits. In one, Yvette is badly beaten and ziptied to the yolk. In the other, Gil is bleeding, and slumped over the dash.

Like a comet that's lost its orbit, the mob's energy deflates.

A quarter million Eternitarians decelerate from the MinderNot chant, to muffled confusion, and finally, to stunned silence. They don't know what they're witnessing, and yet... as they stare at the bloodied victims on screen—and the faceless passengers on those cruisers—they know.

This is what they asked for.

The cameras zoom in on Yvette. She's whimpering, legs folded beneath her, her left eye drooping, blood and tears and mucous drooling from her battered face.

On the other screen, Gil is pale and weak, his eyes barely open, a patch of crimson blood pooled on his white shirt.

I look around. No one can move.

They're confused, speechless, unable to comprehend the obscenity they're witnessing, the scope of this violent, heinous transgression. Yes, they'd followed Comstock. They'd convocated around his passion and focus.

But instead of a thrilling MinderNot rally to cheer on their own sense of pride and purpose, demanding to be heard by the grandest powers of all, they find themselves witness to a slaughter. Complicit in the crime.

I can feel their panic, knowing it's too late.

Back on the view screens, the camera shifts to the galaxy cruisers entering the Torchlight and Dragon's Mane Nebulas.

Piercing those cosmic eyes.

Fireworks erupt across the realm. As they do, flame shoots straight across, between those two eyes, connecting the nebulas.

Meanwhile, individual streaks of flame, one each, erupt from the corners of those two eyes, beaming all the way down, to the promenade. The river of flames converge through an inflection point. The circle of planets.

Penetrating the Anaya Nebula.

The third eye.

Completing the triangle. The MinderNot symbol.

Against the black of night, all points connected by fire. By flame.

The galaxy cruisers explode. I can almost feel Gil's life force bursting on the pyre. It's not every day one of my clients is burned alive. Yet I feel an even greater pull for Yvette, the girl I never met, yet nearly was.

Filtered through the Anaya Nebula, the blazing current flows in both directions, the nebula all the way down to the Tarusian candle in Gil's extended arm, and the candle back to the nebula.

"And I..." Comstock shouts again... "I bring you *fire!*"

From his lower arm, Comstock points the Tarusian candle, angled downward, at the reflecting pool. He's going to shoot those purple shells into the water.

Igniting the cruiser fuel.

Incinerating us all.

Until a figure appears on the platform.

I assume it's the strike team Clancy called in, transported by Cressa tab. On the great screen I watch as the assassin knives Comstock in the heart.

Only... it's too late.

The Torchlight and Dragon's Mane Nebulas envelop Gil and Yvette's cruisers. That stream of triangulated flame and its burning tail extend all the way to Comstock.

Alit with fire, he himself has become the MinderNot symbol, a beacon into the Cosmos.

Even in a pyrotechnic state of near-death, he points his lower arm such that purple shells emit from the end of the Tarusian candle. They hit the reflecting pool.

Flame scorches the entire two thousand feet of water, whirls across the surface in empyreal waves, roaring into a purple and orange inferno.

Such that Comstock himself is the incendiary device, the apparatus connecting, by a river of fire, Cosmos to realm... realm to Cosmos.

Taking his assassin with him, Comstock is literally a man

on fire. Martyr for a cause. Hand-selected for a purpose.

The flaming MinderNot symbol scorches the night. The Anaya Promenade roars with flame.

The blaze is enormous.

The promenade, the reflecting pool. The obelisk. The rotating circle of planets.

The MinderNot victims. Bindu and Barkley. The tree line.

I dive for cover.

Like the dreams of those who gathered here tonight, everything burns.

*****

I press my hand against what's left of the promenade, the marble reduced to rubble, the western tree line nothing but smoldering dead branches and pulverized stumps.

I roll ash between my fingertips, the black sky coated with grey and white smoke. My eyes water, my tongue coated with bitter, toxic fumes. I smell it in my brain.

The survivors shake and stumble around charred bodies, as if a fire-breathing dragon had laid waste to us all.

I want to say there are many survivors. I really do.

"And I want to tell you that." It's a familiar voice, one I'd almost forgotten.

"M-Milo. What happened?"

"The bat signal," he says. "I saw it from the far side of the Universe. So I came."

"The bat what?"

"Nothing. It's an Earth reference. Thought you knew it."

Rescue teams are treating the survivors, all wearing the same vacant stares. They've never seen anything like this.

I check myself for injuries, for burns, but other than my broken wrist, a harsh cough and the soot covering half my body, I seem to be okay.

The stage is gone. The monument, too.

Only charred skeletons remain, a gentle breeze carrying the stench of melted flesh and bone, the metallic tinge of cauterized muscle and hair.

Milo's got me off to the side, beneath the tree line, one of the only sections of green space still intact. I love him so much at this moment I shove aside how much I hate him.

I fall into his arms.

A short, bearded gnome of a man in beige cargo shorts and an oversized red garment from Earth called a Hawaiian shirt, he holds me close. Just resting against his body—which I know isn't even a true physical form, just a tangible, flesh-and-blood form he adopts so that he can interact with me in a manner I can handle—comforts me in a way I'd never thought possible.

His embrace is as strong as a bear, yet gentle as its fur. His nature sooths me.

The last time I saw Milo, he was still the Great Disruptor. The cosmic foil to the Minders of the Universe. Now he's a Minder himself. That's going to take some getting used to.

I speak through my tears. "I really needed you, ya big stupid jerk."

And though I'm talking about myself, we all needed him.

Comstock was a madman. E-Town will never be the same.

His point all along.

Despite Comstock's methods, it doesn't mean he was wrong about the Minders. Although taken to extremes, the deranged tend to have an insight the rest of us gloss over.

Against the midnight sky, and beneath the moon, is a white smoke outline of the MinderNot insignia. The mighty triangle, with a flaming tail.

"Maybe I never said," Milo says as he strokes the back of my hair, "but I needed you, too."

CHAPTER 30

Dolores starts another game, her break powerful but off-center. The pool balls scatter across the green felt. The two and twelve just miss the corner pockets.

"You want to play teams," Esteban mumbles through his broken jaw. He's supposed to be taking it easy, but I've seen tornados slow down faster than him. Dressed in leather chaps and tattoo sleeves, he's actually making the most of his injuries. I landed him a part as an extra in some biker movie that shoots in a few hours. Casting director I know did me a solid. Least I could do for Banny. I'll need to do a lot more.

I sip my beer, hold up my wrist. "Maybe next time," I say, showcasing my cast. "My bridge hand's still off."

"The way you shoot," Nini says, sipping some sort of citrus-flavored cocktail through a tiny red straw, "you're better off."

E-town still smells of smoke, corpses, and betrayal, but the night is cool. Calm.

The MinderNots have gone silent, the marina and promenade blocked off. It'll be a long time before either are repaired. The damage was extensive, the body count worse.

Bindu and Barkley were incinerated. Gil and Yvette. Faye and Camilla, too. Although Evie von M came away with only minor burns and a lump on her head. As always, she survives.

Tarrish says the VCP is shut down for now, but the way things go in E-Town, probably not for long. Maybe just as well. But since the fires, since Milo came back, there's a sense of healing, of recovery.

The weather is mostly back to normal, and the occasional gaffe aside, the moons and comets have resumed their proper orbits.

The collective anxiety has dissipated. Not gone, but quiet.

Whereas the ether had carried with it a paranoid mist of false hope and existential dread, we've begun to accept the possibility that order, for all of its disorder, has returned.

Media reports say entirely new designs are being commissioned to rebuild the promenade and the marina, better than ever. They're huge projects. Maybe it should come as no surprise, but I hear Frankie the Brush already has bids to work on both. He has a funny way of knowing how to avoid trouble, and when to make his moves.

The big question, of course, the most important one of all, is what the Minders are going to do next.

For now, at least, it's good to be with friends.

Pool balls rattle among the other tables. Wages made. Credits lost, credits won.

Whistler hobbles over to us, black eye and all, carrying a pitcher of beer and several glasses. "Best ale on tap," he says. "Damn, Nini. Dolores is *spanking* you."

"Nini," Banny mumbles. "You gonna let him talk to you like that? Kid risks his life for us like one time and now he thinks he's got privileges."

Chewing her cigar despite the gash on her cheek, Dolores pounds the cue ball into the seven, which thocks in the corner pocket. She looks at Whistler.

"You got balls, kid. I'll give you that. Not so sure about brains, though. Mess with Nini at your own risk. But, eh. At least you bought the beer. I'm good for one more. Then home to Jeanie. Movie night."

I pull Whistler aside. "You've got a little street cred now, so you get a free pass on this one. But don't get used to it." I wink. "Now go shoot some pool."

Nini sits next to me. "Let me see your fingers."

"Stop being a nurse. I just wanna hang out."

She takes my hand anyway. "Hush up. Now wiggle your fingers." I do. "Good. You should be out of this in a week."

"I know. That's what the doctor said."

"Doctor Roache? She's great. Knows her stuff."

"Then why'd you have me wiggle my fingers?"

Nini smiles. "Cuz it's fun."

That gets a good laugh from all, including me. It's been a while since I felt like laughing.

"And don't think I forgot about Reggie's," she says. "You might've saved half of E-Town, but my feet aren't massaging themselves."

"If you want a foot massage," Whistler says, opening his hands, "I'm your—"

"I already called it in," I say. "They're waiting for you. Full treatment. Plus a little extra."

"Ooh, extra," Nini says and nibbles on the candied cherry in her drink. "Extra how?"

"Marshall's back in town. You've got him for the day."

"Marshall?" Nini's eyes light up. "I might have to get a bikini wax first."

Dolores draws on her beer. "Ain't that what Reggie's is for?"

"You already got yourself a date. And Marshall is f-i-n-e fine. He knows how to treat a lady."

Esteban shuffles close. "So, Angela. Now the case is over, you gonna buy new pinstripes? A new fedora?"

On the surface it's an innocent question, but all eyes are on me. I hadn't realized until now just how much I'd been defining myself by the clothes I wore—my pinstripes like a suit of armor—solidifying my identity. My calling card.

"You know," I say and tug on the lapel of my utility jacket, "I think I'm going to stick with this. Maybe that's the real reason the case came my way. Time for the new me."

"Maybe," Dolores says as she handles a one-four combination in the side pocket. With perfect spin, the cue ball draws back after the strike, in perfect position to finish off the table. "What about Milo? You talk to him since the fire?"

The gang stops what they're doing, eyes back on me. "Nah," I say, dancing around the only issue that really matters to me. My son. "Needed a few days to myself. Besides, he's got a lot on his plate."

But the truth is… I don't want to see him. I'm afraid to. I'm not sure why. I'm upset with him in a way I don't entirely understand. Just thinking about Milo has my breaths quick, shallow, and tight, my heart racing. I thought it was about Owen, but it's something else.

Whistler chalks the end of his stick, then, in a surprisingly surgical move from the far end of the table, shoots the cue ball deftly against the bumper, trapping it behind the two, five, and thirteen, barely an inch from the corner pocket. Dolores will have to break up that cluster if she doesn't want to scratch. But if she scatters those balls in a chaotic mess, it'll open up the whole table, positioning Whistler to make a serious run on his next turn.

"Looks like he snookered you," I say. "Whistler's trying to draw you out as"—the gears in my mind unspool in rapid succession—"bait."

Images flicker before me. Comstock. The MinderNots. The fireworks, the fires.

The timing of it all.

My breath catches in my throat. I put down my beer. Without saying a word, I leave.

CHAPTER 31

As a private eye, one of the most important pieces of advice I try to impress upon my clients—and, even more so, to potential clients, before they hire me, before I'll agree to take a case—is to not let their emotions get the best of them. It rarely takes. If it did, I'd be out of business.

Some cases are what they seem. Vet him, find her. But when you strip away your clients' words, and listen to what they're really saying, what they mean, the truth is usually closer to the heart.

They often claim their goal is to get clarity on what they already suspect. To know for sure. A cheating spouse, a lying business partner. But more often than not, they're mortified, betrayed, or downright boiling with rage. They want to validate their pain, to leverage what I find—to leverage *me*—as a conduit for revenge. To purge whatever poison fuels their nightmares.

If it only worked that way.

When emotion and logic are at odds, emotion wins almost every time.

I'm supposed to be the smart one, the calm one. The dame who sees the angles. Who takes things for what they are, not how I want them to be. The dame who doesn't act rashly.

Usually, I am.

But not today. Not now.

Which is why I bust into Jamie's office. And why she lets me.

"Tell me again," I say, "tell me why you hired me."

"Angela," Jamie says, "I'd say it's a nice surprise, but as you see, I've been waiting for you to barge in here, with a head full of steam. Milo and I were discussing you."

I'm so enraged with Jamie I shove my feelings about Milo to

the side. But they won't stay down for much longer. And I don't care that she's the Minder of the Universe. That they both are.

"Tell me I'm wrong, Jamie. Tell me you didn't drag me into this lunacy because of *him*." I try not to make eye contact, but I see Milo cower, and look away.

"I expected more from you, Angela. Since when do private investigators take clients at their word? Especially an investigator like you. And, I have to say, a client like me."

One of the paintings on the wall catches my eye. It's an old villa, from Earth, overlooking the ocean. Mountains curve along the coastline. Lapping water stretches out into the distance. Along the villa is a slotted, stone balcony. It surrounds a section of grass that leads to a garden blooming with flowers of every color. Above it all is the sun.

And in the back of the garden is a stone gazebo. It's draped in shade. Next to the gazebo is a stone bench, a compartment beneath the lid. From inside comes a small hand. I don't know why, but I know it belongs to a young girl who's come to believe that magic only exists if it's kept locked up then sprinkled like fairy dust.

From within the compartment comes a blast of white light. There are streaks of screaming fluorescent color. Orange leaves swirl into a tornado.

And then my own tornado erupts.

"You used me, Jamie! As bait! You had me follow a madman half way across the Universe. And for what? Look what he did! The people he killed, the damage he caused." I can't control myself. And my dirty truth… I don't want to. "What the fuck is *wrong* with you?"

"Don't blame her." Milo says in soft, tender tones, like a late-night radio deejay. Maybe he's defending her, maybe he hasn't finished apologizing himself, but he isn't Jamie. He never was. "I know you're upset, but your fight is with me."

"I'm not," I say, "I don't…"

"Angela," Milo continues, and moves closer to me, "I heard your calls. I wasn't ignoring them. I wasn't ignoring *you*. But the old me, the Disruptor me? He was still in there. But that's not who I am anymore." Milo goes silent, pretense falling from his eyes. "The galaxies, the star systems. The planets, the moons. The folds in time. I hear every heartbeat, Angela. Feel every pulse. When you dream... I dream. Whey you cry, my heart breaks. When you laugh, so do I. When new stars activate, I am reborn. When old stars die, I perish. They are all me, and I am all them. Since the beginning of time, my very purpose... my existence... was to thwart the Minders. And now I am one. I have no excuse, Angela. Only reasons. It took longer than it should have to embrace my new self. I wonder if that day will every really come. But I'm here now. I'm present. And I'm here to stay."

I want to be furious with Milo, but he's deflating my urgency. Not because of what he did, or his disappearance, but because now that he's here, with me again, confessing his transgressions, taking responsibility for his actions, he's also eradicating my very reason to be furious with him. And I'm not ready to let that anger go.

The grudge I carry is nearly euphoric, displacing my need for the *dRops*. I still want my pound of flesh. I've earned it. It's time to get paid.

"But why *me*, Jamie? Why drag me into this?"

Jamie looks at me with smug satisfaction.

"Did you really think I cared one bit about those fireworks?" she says. "That I cared about the word on the street? I've been holding the Universe together, by myself, since the very first moment we became the new Minders of the Universe. I needed to do whatever it took... no matter the consequences to anyone or anything else... to get my partners back here and doing their jobs. And if that meant sacrificing lives, or ripping at your ego... so be it. I tried everything, Angela. Everything I could think of. But Milo—I see that now—will always and forever, be Milo. He's good at playing games. At avoidance. At hiding within the ripples of time and space I haven't been able find. But the one thing... the *one* thing I was counting on that he couldn't avoid forever, that he wouldn't... was you. He cares for you in a way I don't think he's ever cared about anyone. And for a being whose nucleus is older than the Universe itself... the love he has for you, is, to me... incomprehensible."

I'm not sure how to accept that Milo and I mean more to each other than either one of us wants to admit. But as I'm standing here before him, my resentment—intense, marinated, real—is finally beginning to melt.

"So, yes, Angela. I brought you into this case. I used you. As bait. And I knew things would get ugly. But if it took a madman from off-realm to burn a symbol across the realm Milo couldn't ignore, to get him back doing what he absolutely needs to be doing, I was willing to do it. One way or another, it needed to be done."

Whatever my feelings toward Milo, my resentment toward Jamie hits me in a place I'd been refusing to deal with. Not anymore.

"I want to say I'm surprised by anything you're telling me," I say. "But I'm not. Except that you are epically full of crap. I know you, Jamie. I know Milo, and to the degree that someone like me can even know these things at all, I know the Universe, too. There's more to you than this. There has to be. Because if there isn't, you should've left Milo right where he was. The Universe deserves better than this. And so do I. And for that matter, so do you."

Jamie's being a helluva good sport so far, given how she thrashed me about last time. I'm only permitted to hammer on the Minders like this because she's allowing it. Maybe she even appreciates it. But I suspect it's something else.

My gift to her. A chance to get her own pound of flesh, to unleash her pent-up anger, loneliness, and cosmological frustration. Even the Minders need to vent.

"You may not want to hear this, Angela, as you seem to know quite a bit about what it takes to carry such an incredible burden, but understand: being a Minder of the Universe means accepting you sometimes have to be cruel, if not downright despicable—and play witness to unbearable pain and suffering—to keep the Universe from tearing itself apart. I'm not oblivious to the soul of the Cosmos, Angela, even if it seems that way. It's what the job requires. But understand something else. I feel every slight. I feel every drop of agony in every corner of Existence within every living being of every species in every galaxy in every realm—within every microbe of every crevice of every fold of the Universe—always and forever. I'm a raw nerve, Angela, exposed to the Universe. Because the Universe is me.

Because I am the Universe. And so are you. So I ask again. Why did you think I hired you? To protect the reputation of my secret self? Do you think this persona I've adopted—this woman, this executive, known as Jamie—means anything to me? Do you think I care about"—she's pawing at the skin on her arm—"this costume? It's a vessel for me to remain visible, and to stay in contact with the masses without anyone knowing who or what I am. Do you think I value this alter ego as anything more than a functional disguise?"

I admit, I hadn't considered the weight of such responsibility. Who really stops to consider just how onerous that perpetual load becomes? We don't care, because the Minders have power none of us can fathom—or claim for ourselves. And burdens we could never endure. But that only excuses so much.

"Actually," I say. "I do. No matter how much of a Minder you might be, that other part of you, the part that wasn't a Minder, your life before the new you, when you had a brother, is still in there. And she's got fears and insecurities, just like everyone else. And you've got an ego. A huge fucking ego. Maybe that's the Minder in you, too. Maybe it was always there. Or maybe a part of you is as callous and prideful as Comstock said. You *do* care what the street thinks. You do care how you're perceived. You want it known that Jamie, the new CEO of the Rubicon Hotel Corp., is a tough broad you best not cross. So, yes. I think you care about your street-level reputation more than you want anyone to know. Because if you can't handle things down *here*, how are you going to handle things up *there*?"

Jamie stares at me. Milo starts to lean in my direction, but she eases a hand, telling him to stay put. "And that," Jamie says, "is why I hired you in the first place. I needed to see if you can handle my business. Universe business. Handle my kind of case. And just as important, if you can handle me."

There comes a point in every case when it's time to close the file. If it can be closed at all. I'm not sure yet what I think of her explanation. But for now, it'll do.

"Okay," I say. "Now that we're handled... I need a favor. To fix a mistake."

Jamie looks to Milo. "Tell me."

I explain.

Faster than I can formulate a response, a black-and-white dog is sitting by my side.

"Page." I lean down and scratch behind her ears. At least I saved someone. She wags her tail. "Whistler could use a friend. You want to come with?"

Page looks up at me, chops her teeth, then let's out a low bark.

"I'll take that as a *yes*."

"Speaking of unfinished business," Jamie says, "he's got something to say."

My hand on Page's fur, I feel the enormity of what Milo's about to share.

The flood rippling within my chest, it's all I can do to keep from crying my eyes out.

"Owen," Milo says. "It's about Owen."

"Don't," I say, staring to blubber, "don't say his name unless you can tell me..."

"Owen's a good boy. He's safe, he's happy... and he's ready to see you. Or, I should say, I think *you're* ready to see him."

"Don't fuck with me, Milo." Tears are leaking out of me like a cracked spigot. "Not now. Not about him."

Milo pulls up a chair. "You don't remember, do you? It was because of Astropalooza."

An intense fog of hysteria and anguish washes over me, pulling me back into the haze of my worst addiction, desperate to poison myself. Not because it's good for me. But because it will feel so good, even though I know it's actually that bad.

"Remember...? What are you...?"

"When you got lost in the *dRops*, before you bottomed out... you asked me to keep Owen safe. To take him someplace even a Big Bang couldn't reach."

I want to protest, but I can't.

"You asked me to watch out for him. Until Astropalooza was over."

"No," I say, refusing to believe. "That can't be." But I know it's true.

"You picked me for a reason, Angela. Because you knew I could take him places... show him things... that would have been impossible otherwise. You wanted him to be more than your child, a child of E-Town. You wanted him to be a child of the Cosmos. To understand why you do the things you do, and that what you do... matters. We've had a grand adventure, he and I. And as much as you've feared he was lost to you... it's you, despite yourself, who wants to be found."

Comstock said almost the same thing to me. I don't have the bandwidth right now to ponder the significance.

My chest is as tight as a snare drum, but my eyes are wide open. I finally realize what had been there all along. "Earth's moon. He's the Man in the Moon."

"No, not exactly," Milo says. "More like he's been... hitching a ride. And he's been having a helluva good time doing it. He knew why you took the *dRops*, to feel connected to him somehow. But he wants you to know, he's never felt closer to you. And now that you've given them up, he can't wait to show you how."

I press my palms to my face, thinking of my baby boy, and wipe my eyes.

There's a leash attached to Page's collar. I take it, and give her a treat that found its way into my pocket. She chomps it down, wags her tail, and leads me toward the door. There's a lot left to say, only... I don't have it in me right now to say it.

I'm nearly at the threshold of her office when Jamie asks me a question. "So where does that leave us, Angela? What's next?"

I stop, turn back to Jamie, my emotions as raw and jumbled as a newly formed galaxy. I'll sort them out later. Or I won't. "Me? I'm going to see my son."

"Good," Jamie says. "I'm glad. I think you'll enjoy that."

"I'm sure I will."

"And maybe when you get back, I'll have another case for you. Maybe I'll give you a call."

I reach for the door. I turn up the collar on my jacket. Pinstripes no more. It's the new me.

And as I head out, Page by my side, I think about Owen, my boy. He's waiting for me. I can barely breath. "Maybe," I say, walking out on the Minders of the Universe. "But I can't promise I'll answer."

CHAPTER 32

Wandering uncertainly, Page and I head into the sun-soaked park, toward the wishing fountain. If I were to make a wish, there's only one on my mind.

"Mommy!" I hear, my heart skipping a beat.

But then I see a giddy toddler stumble toward his mother, his little baby boy sandals barely containing his little baby boy feet.

"Come on," I say to Page, and lead her by the leash. "Let's—"

"Mommy!" I hear again. Only this time it isn't someone else's toddler. It's not a stranger. It's not a mistake.

It's Owen.

He jumps into my arms. I squeeze him tight. I go down to my knees, my heart bursting with joy. Knowing that whatever else may or may not be true about me, no matter where the Universe takes us next, I'll never let him go.

Not because I'm his mother.

Because he's my son.

THE HARDWICKE FILES:

THE CASE OF JARLO'S BURIED TREASURE

"Jarlo. Not again. What is it with you?"

"But I didn't do it," he says through the intercom.

"That's what you said last time. And you actually did do that one."

"I know I know I KNOW I know... I know. But that was self-defense. You proved it for me. This time I really didn't do it. I swear!"

"Jarlo..."

"I didn't."

"Jarlo...," I say again, my voice rising.

"Okay, so"—he paces his jail cell, a white alcove secured by a containment field which, upon aggressive contact, would immediately disable his circuits. "Maybe I did. A little. But just a tiny bit. Really."

Androids are inherently complicated. They've been fully integrated into E-town society since as far back as I can remember, with equal rights under the law. And no, there haven't been any uprisings to overthrow the Universe and extinguish all organic life forms in a Cosmic holocaust.

But there are lingering, insidious biases against them in E-Town that have never washed away.

And with personal service androids like Jarlo... they're everyone's favorite companions. Until they're not.

I check the time on my phone. "What do you want?"

"Get me out?" he says with an impish smile. Thuggishly built, the charm radiates off him, having never shown the slightest inclination towards violence. Unless you count the two people he's killed. That I know of.

"You had sex with Annara Diaphrolo."

"I know. She's a babe."

As usual, Jarlo's dancing around the most critical elements of his problem.

"Did she know you were an android?"

"Hey! I told you. I'm not some glorified robot and I'm not a science experiment." Pushing forty-five, he shoots the cuffs on his green, single-breasted suit, revealing the mustard yellow silk shirt underneath. He knows how to present himself. "I'm a HELM."

I sigh impatiently. "A HELM?"

"Yeah. A Highly Evolved Love Machine. A HELM."

I don't have time for this. "Okay. Sure. You're a HELM. So I'll ask again. Did Annara know you were a HELM when you had sex with her?"

"Whoa. That's awfully personal, Hardwicke. You know I don't kiss and tell."

"You *always* kiss and tell!"

Like a child who's waiting to be found in an intentionally lousy hiding spot, Jarlo's eager to dish. His bulldog face, accentuated by the slight graying of his fine blonde hair, trembles under the pressure of his expanding smile. "I know, right? I'm so bad. But yes. She knew. Oh, baby, she knew."

"Of all the women in E-Town, why her? She's Elgin Diaphrolo's daughter. And she's half your age."

"You know I like the high society gals. They're under so much pressure to maintain their poise... in public. But get them in the bedroom and hooooo baby. They need to let that pressure go."

"A romantic 'til the end, huh Jarlo?"

His smile is effervescent. "Thanks! Like my suit? It's custom-tailored. I'd let you feel but... is this containment field necessary?"

"Jarlo. You're on death row. For murder. Of a gangster's daughter. A gangster who, if you believe the rumors, is recruited off the books by the Intergalactic Crime Division to hunt child molesters, sex traffickers, and prostitution rings that have snuck on-realm. Seems that's a real trigger for Elgin. And three hours ago you were arrested for strangling his only daughter at a SynthCorp charity event at the Rubicon Hotel, which is owned by people you very much do not want poking around in your life. If the E-Town PD hadn't been working security and found you first, you'd be dead already. So, yes. The containment field is necessary."

"You kill one high-class babe and they treat it like a realm-wide offense."

"It *is* a realm-wide offense!"

"Now you tell me."

Don't get me wrong. I like Jarlo. And I have nothing against androids. They have their place in E-Town—Eternity, that is, the cosmic realm responsible for the design, creation, and main-tenance of the Universe. And like the rest of us, androids have their limits.

Other than the mandatory j-scar under the left eye, they are physiologically identical to Eternitarians in almost every way.

Except they're powered by a cranial CPU, and infused with synthetic organs, grafted with organic tissue.

"Listen, Jarlo. I have a stack of cases waiting for me back at the office, and my son is running me ragged. You wouldn't see your lawyer. Only me. And it wasn't to get you out. So why am I here?"

"Because I love you so much?"

"I'd prefer if you loved me a little less. So I'll ask again. Why I am here?"

Jarlo surreptitiously surveils the holding bay I'm in, includ-ing the two camera globes, one each in the high corners behind me. The nearly permanent grin on his face folds into a joyless stare, the sparkle behind those synthetic pine green eyes gone. His black, cavernous pupils reveal how desperate he knows his plight to be—and how few options he has.

After squaring his rounded shoulders, Jarlo leans forward, nearly but not quite touching the containment field. In hushed tones, through the intercom, he tells me what he wants.

Fear clenches in my gut.

Out of sheer instinct I reach inside my utility jacket, reminded that my holster is empty. As per protocol, before the ETPD would let me in, I had to surrender my sidearm, taser, brass knuckles, and zipties.

"Are you insane? No. No way. Can't do it."

"Sure you can."

"I'll rephrase," I say. "I won't."

"But you owe me, Hardwicke. You owe me big time."

"Not this big. And not this time. There's no way I'll…"

I swivel on my stool, run my fingers through my hair. This is a colossally dangerous and stupid case to consider. Which is why I don't. Only… I actually do owe him. And like he said, I owe him big. Particularly given who's involved. Fuckety fuck fuck fuck.

"Fine. But if I do this… we're even. And I get paid. In full. In advance. Otherwise… no go. You can transfer the funds right now."

I wink with my right eye, alerting Jarlo to the plasma sensor contact lens I'm wearing, which can sync with his CPU matrix, even through the containment field. Thank you, Bernice, you technical ninja. What would I do without you?

"Done," he says. "And yes. This makes us even. I even added a bonus. Only…"

Ugh. Here it comes. "Only what?"

"Gotta do it by noon."

"Noon? It's almost one o'clock in the morning. Can't do it."

"Have to."

I don't want to know, but I ask anyway. "Why?"

"Because that's when they're ripping out my CPU. Which means you have"—he squints, accessing his internal clock—"eleven hours, nineteen minutes, and forty-three seconds. But who's counting, right? After that, it's goodnight, Jarlo. This hunky love machine will be out of commission. Forever."

*****

I've worked cases all across the Cosmos. Embezzlement, kidnapping, cheating spouses. A galaxy hopper here, an intergalactic bank heist there.

Last year an accountant hired me to track down an intern who'd stolen some sensitive corporate files. Only he turned out to be a lunatic from Earth who'd smuggled himself on-realm and nearly got me killed several times. Plus he set huge swaths of E-Town on fire with thousands of gallons of galaxy cruiser fuel. We're still reeling from the mess.

But this is the first time I've been asked to find buried treasure.

If I can get there in time.

"Hardwicke," Lieutenant Lionel Tarrish says as I exit the stilted ETPD air. Along the side street, I look up at five silver moons reflecting off the canyon of skyscrapers. Traffic whooshes nearby, even at this hour. "If Jarlo called for help you're up to something. Android kills Eternitarian. Case closed."

I blow on my closed fists. "Oh, yeah? Then what do you care? You afraid of Papa D? Elgin Diaphrolo is no joke."

Tarrish squints into the brisk night, rubs his salt-and-pepper beard. "Honestly"— he clacks a silver flip lighter, tugs on a cigarette—"a little."

"Me, too," I say as I squeeze specially formulated droplets into my right eye, keeping the contact lens Bernice gave me clear and lubricated. "He's not my biggest fan."

"Who is?" Tarrish turns up the collar on his black, double-breasted wool overcoat. An orb light outside the station gleams off his silver-plated wristwatch. "It's late, I'm tired, and the last thing I need is for you to do what you usually do—take an open-and-shut case and make it shut and wide open.

"I doubt the case is simple."

Tarrish checks his phone. "You're saying Jarlo didn't do it?"

"I'm saying I don't *know* if he did it, and if he did, why he did it."

"Does it matter?"

"Probably not. Dead is dead. Murder is murder."

Tall, lithe, and well-built for a middle-aged man with three kids of his own, Tarrish sighs, his dark skin swallowed by shadow. "You don't believe that. Never did. Especially with androids."

"Actually," I correct, "he's a HELM."

"Great. Another Love Machine. Just what I need."

"Listen, big guy, I'd love to wax philosophical with you, but I'm on the clock here."

Tarrish takes me by the arm. We're not friends, exactly, but we're not *not* friends. He's my mentor. Ish. "Watch yourself,

Hardwicke. Because Elgin will be."

I nod. I understand.

A breeze whooshes down the side-street, carrying a dense plume of citrus-sweet whiskey drifting up from an after-hours cop bar only accessible through a maze of lower-level stairwells in the alley between buildings. We start toward the avenue.

"He really tracks down sex rings for you? You got him on the payroll?"

"Me? Recruit a guy like Papa D? For police work? What kind of lawman do you think I am?"

As I raise my hand to flag down a cab, Tarrish walks away, leaving me alone, in the dark, to think about the answer.

*****

The marina is still mostly rubble, a charred, toxic mess thanks to that lunatic from Earth I tangled with last year. The harbor has been mass treated with various anti-pollutants and comet-based cleansers, the waterfront smelling of chemicals, jasmine, and the faint, lingering scent of cauterized flesh. It's quite an aroma.

Plans have been approved to rebuild the waterfront district, with two dozen developers at least set to erect new high-rises, mixed-use properties, and what will be a realm-class park and amphitheater with rolling green space, and a glassed-in botanical garden and atrium.

And just last week revisions were submitted for a state-of-the-art experiential campus that will include a multi-purpose music, sports, and arts arena with retractable dome, cosmic viewing station, and inter-dimensional food hall.

But the area is still a quasi-wasteland, the debris cleared out with massive cranes, plows, and remediation portals. The boat slips were mostly incinerated, less than a third of the vessels left intact.

Jarlo lives in the Dooly, one of the high-rise residential towers along the bay. The outer glass is covered in soot, the building half-empty. That's what happens when the residents get burned to death.

There's something about this building that pulls me back to

it. This is the third case that's brought me here since it opened.

The doorman is nowhere to be found and the once-gorgeous lobby smells like barbequed urine. The equally ripe elevator takes me up to nine. I've got my weapon out because there's only two dim lightbulbs working in the hallway and there's no telling who's lurking around the corner.

Other than two squeaking rats that scurry past my feet, I reach Jarlo's apartment without incident. Yellow police tape is stretched diagonally across the doorframe.

The apartment is locked, but Jarlo transferred his keypad code to me along with payment. The door opens. The police are rarely gentle, and less so with androids, but immediately I see his place has been redecorated with extreme prejudice.

No doubt Elgin's people have been here. Maybe even Papa D himself.

Not sure what he was looking for—maybe nothing, just the release of pure, unadulterated rage—but more than likely he didn't want any of his daughter's personals left behind for the gossip hounds.

Before I look around I roll one of Bernice's silver scout orbs across the floor. Synched to my contact lens, it gives me a ground-up view of each room.

Clothes everywhere, furniture busted and flipped over, smashed picture frames, recessed lighting hats yanked out from the ceiling and dangling from wires. The refrigerator flung open. What appears to be grilled sea bass with lemon capers has been mashed with a boot print, spilled milk next to it like a pool of white blood.

Must be what's attracting the rats.

A young girl snarls, giving me a jolt. Maybe fifteen and wearing tattered clothes, she jabs at me with a switchblade in one hand while going for my gun with the other.

She tears my jacket sleeve, but I side-step in time, thrust my hip, and flip her over, face-first on the floor next to plump strawberries stomped into a glaze. My knee in her back, I pry the knife from her dirty but ferociously strong fingers.

"Word to the wise," I say. "Never grab the gun unless it's a sure thing."

"Bite me!"

"That's the spirit." Though I help her up, this panting wild-child is ready to attack again. So I ask for identification. "You the new super?"

"Funny," she says as one of her black braids hits her in the face, brown as the rope belt keeping up her black, cargo pants. She's also wearing a navy blue hooded fleece, brown scarf, and brown fingerless gloves with frayed edges. I suspect there's a more docile girl under all those layers and filth, but it'll take her submitting to an asteroid-level sandblaster to test that theory.

"Let's talk." I gesture with my weapon, pointed in her direction, leading her into the living room. A creamy swirl of blue and pink dusk melts through the windows, overlooking the marina. "You know Jarlo?"

She's studying the wreckage and, quite likely, a way to bash in my skull. "What's it to you?"

"Seeing as how he's paid me to help him before his execution"— I check the clock on my phone—"about eight hours... it's a lot."

"Executed?" she worries, rising from the couch. "No!"

"Afraid so. You heard about Annara Diaphrolo?"

The girl shakes her head *no*.

"Jarlo killed her a few hours ago at the Rubicon Hotel."

"What? No way! He would never! He..." The girl withdraws into a protective cocoon.

"He what?"

"Fuck off."

"Listen, kid. Every second counts. He what?"

"He'd never kill her. Ever."

"How do you know?"

She eyes me up and down, deciding whether or not to trust me, which is probably more difficult since I'm pointing my gun at her.

I know blasters are all the rage. Firing compressed plasma bolts, blasters have more range than traditional bullet throwers and do a lot more damage, particularly up close. But they're far less accurate from a distance and tend to lose their charge. Give me a bullet thrower any day. They're reliable. Get the job done.

I switch on the safety, then slide the gun back into my holster. I loosen my breath.

"What's your name?"

"I said you can—"

"Bite you. Fuck off. Right. I got it. Okay. Bitey fuck face it is."

Reluctantly, she reveals the glimmer of a smile. "Ruth," she says. "I'm Ruth."

"Ruth. I like that. I'm Angela. Me and Jarlo go back a ways. He calls me when he's in trouble. He got pulled in for murder some years back. The husband of one of his... lady friends went after him with a golf club. Jarlo managed to get it away and teed off on the guy's head. Left quite the divot. I found video surveillance that proved self-defense. Jarlo still needs to work on his backswing, though. Not enough follow-through. It's all in the hips."

Ruth's eyes soften, and shift away, then back at me, angled down. "So you know Jarlo's a...?"

"An android? A HELM? Yes, I know."

"He wasn't like the others."

"How so?"

"He... you know... he wasn't just a companion. He cared."

"Did he care about you?"

"Ew! No! Not like that!"

"That's not what I meant, Ruth. I meant... he was your friend? He took care of you?"

She offers a slight nod. "Sorta. I crash here on and off. Shower. Chill. But it's not a full-time thing. I've gotta make my way out there. Scrounge enough money to be on my own. I've got a spot I go to."

"Dangerous," I say, knowing all too well what street life is like. "Any trouble?"

"Some. You know. But Jarlo lets me refuel here when the weather's bad or it's just too much. I haven't been by in a week or so, but he never asks for anything. Just that I read a book every day and clean up after myself."

"I've heard much worse advice. Jarlo's better than the shelters."

"He's the one who found me. After the blaze. After my parents..."

"They didn't make it?"

As if it's being held in a narrow containment field, Ruth shakes her head *no*.

"I'm sorry," I say, images of that horrible inferno flickering in my mind. "I barely made it out myself. But no friends or family you can stay with? And what about school? You've got, what... a year or two left?"

Her jaw clenches, taking in a sharp breath. I shift gears. "Did you know Jarlo's girlfriend? Annara?"

"A little."

"She nice?"

"Jarlo thought so."

"What about you?"

Ruth looks away again. "You said you're trying to help him. Help how?"

She's avoiding my question. Was she jealous of Annara... or something else? Teen girls are damn confusing. Then again, so are adults. I need her to focus.

"He wants me to find his buried treasure."

Ruth's chapped lips purse into another tiny smile, her eyes showcasing a flicker of joy. She shifts in place, revealing a silver chain around her neck.

"Is that a dimple I see?" encouraging her to open up. "You know about...?"

"My parents took me to the marina for ice cream. When the fire broke out, we got separated, so I dove into a tugboat and crawled into a freezer full of fish and beer. There was a chain with a bottle opener on the side. I wedged it between the lid to keep it from locking me in. Later... when Jarlo found me, he said even with all the mess out there, I was a diamond in the rough. You know, like..."

My own eyes light up. "Like buried treasure."

Ruth nods. "Yeah."

"But if you're the buried treasure then..." My mind goes back to Jarlo. He said there was a bonus with my fee. I never checked. I immediately activate the file he transferred to my contact lens and synch the data to my phone. "Here it is. But... it's password protected? He never gave me a password..."

I see Ruth looking up at me, her brown, haunted eyes revealing a soul who in the last year has experienced more than most people in a lifetime. And then it occurs to me. In the password tab I enter the letters R-U-T-H. The file opens.

"Whoa. What is *this*?"

"What's it say?" Ruth inquires curiously, revealing that, despite all she's endured, there just might actually be an optimist in there somewhere.

In my mind, the pieces snap into place. "Almost everything I need. But before I can pull it all together, I have a favor to ask. You like dogs?"

"I love dogs!" Ruth's wide, hooded eyes crackle with energy. "Never had one, though."

"Me either. I was always a cat person. But I sort of adopted a dog. Maybe she adopted me. Hard to tell sometimes." I wink. Ruth smiles. "Her name's Page. Like pages in a book. She's great, but I also have a four-year-old son, and between the two of them, I'm afraid Page is feeling a little bit ignored. She mostly hangs with Whistler, but he gets annoyed because I like her better than him."

Ruth looks at me oddly. "Who's Whistler?"

"Another stray I picked up. My assistant."

She chortles. "He any good?"

I chortle, too. "He's young—not as young as you—but he still needs to be housetrained. He could learn a thing or two from Page. How'd you like to keep her company?"

"She bite?"

"Only if you bite first."

Ruth rolls her eyes. "I think I can handle it."

"I'm sure you can. Let's get you cleaned up, fed, and a safe place for tonight, and then we'll figure out what's next. Sound good?"

"You have TV? Jarlo lets me watch here."

"Not as many channels, I'm sure. But plenty to keep you busy for—"

"Are you gonna save Jarlo?"

A cold gut-punch. My mother instincts want to protect her from harsh reality, but that never works. And if I try to spin this any other way, whatever trust I've built with her will come crashing down on me like a shattered moon.

"No, Ruth. That's not why Jarlo hired me. I think... he wanted me to get you out of this place. Which is actually the Jarlo I know. He's far from perfect, but deep down in that android heart of his... he's a pretty good guy."

"Yeah. He is. Better than most."

"Come on," I say as the early morning sun streaks on the shimmering bay. "There's not a lot of time before..."

"Before they kill him?"

Another gut-punch. I nod.

Ruth then asks a question I'm not sure she wants answered. Or maybe the one she wants answered most of all. "Did he do it? Kill Annara, I mean? Did he really?"

Nothing I can tell her will be worse than what she's already been through. "I don't know, Ruth. But it looks that way. And he hasn't said otherwise. That's usually a bad sign."

Ruth blinks a few times, then looks over Jarlo's mangled apartment, the remnants of what was probably the only safe place for her since she was orphaned in a blaze that incinerated huge swaths of E-Town. She steels herself and walks toward the door.

"Okay," she says. "I'm ready."

*****

I pick up a huge breakfast to go—French toast, cheddar cheese omelet, blueberries, bacon, coffee, orange juice—which we both devour at my office. Ruth takes a hot shower in back, then, after changing into some moderately clean clothes from my backup bag, curls up on the brown leather couch, asleep within minutes.

Like a sentinel, Page stands guard, taking responsibility for Ruth as I check through her dirty rags for any ID, drugs, and weapons she might have tucked away.

I find a beat up paperback book—*Hearts of the Long Night*. Lots of underlines and notes in the margins. Smart girl.

I give Page a treat, attach my earpiece, then check on my son, Owen. He's staying with Nini, a nurse at E-Town General who's next shift doesn't start until tomorrow.

Next, I call Whistler to have him come early, keep an eye on Page.

One more call. "Tarrish," I say at my desk, littered with papers. "You awake."

"Barely. What do you want?"

"A stiff drink, a nap, and just one day without feeling like I slept at the bottom of a dumpster. I'm looking for gaps in a file Jarlo gave me."

"What file?"

"There's a small news story from about five years ago. Galaxy cruiser. Got caught in an asteroid belt for before it was rescued. You know the one I mean?"

No answer.

"There's also a confidential police report..." I hear Tarrish inhale, preparing to jump in, but I beat him to the punch. "An intergalactic sex trafficking. Young women forced into prostitution."

I wait for him to argue, to lecture me about protocol and having access to restricted intel, but he doesn't. I think I know why. So I ask: "The galaxy cruiser wasn't stuck in an asteroid belt, was it?"

Tarrish sighs through the phone. "No."

"So what happened?"

I hear a bubbly squeak, Tarrish running his tongue forcefully over his gums, deciding if there's anything he's willing to share.

"Yes," he says hesitantly. "Last year, right before the inferno, I was working the case. Remember?"

"Yeah, I do, actually."

"I had a bead on the ringleader. I was close, but after the fire... I lost the trail."

"So you enlisted Papa D to help track him down."

Again, no response.

Ever since Tarrish accepted that promotion out of E-Town PD and into the ICD, he hasn't been the same. It's the reason most PIs won't accept cases that take you off-realm, originate off-realm and end up here, or get mixed up in the Cosmos.

You start poking around in the infinite unknowns of the Universe, there's no telling what you'll find, or how it'll affect you.

If Tarrish enlisted Papa D, he must've been desperate. Elgin owns a small but well-regarded distribution company that supplies galaxy cruiser lines with mechanical parts. He also has a piece of the illegal gambling circuit on outer rim cruisers. It puts him in contact with all sorts. He tried to hire me once for a personal case. I passed. He wasn't happy.

"I heard that after the girls were found on the cruiser, they were so shaken up, they—"

"Leave it alone, Hardwicke."

"The victims' names in the report... the girls who committed suicide. One of those names is redacted. Is it—?"

"I'm serious, Hardwicke. Just... leave it be."

"Wait," I say as Page licks an uneaten pancake. "Is she...? That means Jarlo... whoa. Did you know? That Annara's an...?

Tarrish sighs. "I looked the other way because... we finally got the motherfu... we got the guy. I'm not saying I sleep great, but I can live with it. Now you know about Annara... what are you going to do?"

I get up from my desk and fasten my gun holster. Jarlo's running out time. "What any decent person would. Pay my condolences."

*****

I press the buzzer on Elgin's three-story brownstone in the Cobblestone District. The overhead security camera shifts in my direction, whirs. The outer security gate unlocks. I pull it open then let myself in through the heavy, oak door.

"Angela," Elgin says, his hair thin, white. "No fedora? No pinstripes? I guess jeans and a utility jacket are a bit more practical. And camouflaged."

I raise an eyebrow. "It was time to blend in."

Dressed in beige Khakis, a salmon-colored shirt, and brown loafers he leads me into the kitchen, where gourmet coffee is brewing—chocolate macadamia if I'm not mistaken. Sunlight beams in from the bay windows overlooking his private bonsai garden, surrounded by the backs and sides of other brownstones.

"How's it going with your son?"

"Last year I was thirty-two going on thirty-three. Now I'm thirty-three going on sixty." I sigh. "It's been an adjustment, but it's great."

"I'm glad," he says with a faint smile and hands me a cup. "I know why you're here."

"Tarrish said you asked for leniency for Jarlo—defective programming—but the DA isn't having it. They're ripping out his CPU in a few hours. Jarlo's not fighting it, either. He wanted me to give you something. If that's okay."

Elgin swallows. Looks like it goes down rough, the worry lines in his weathered, craggy face seeming to burrow right into the crevices of his soul. "What is it?"

From my jacket pocket, I produce the necklace Ruth had been wearing. Secured to it is a small, silver locket. I hand it to him with the utmost care. "Is this what you were looking for? Jarlo's place was trashed."

Trembling, Elgin runs his thumb over the locket's ornate ridges, then, with his manicured fingernail, pops it open. His breath quivers, a tear thick in his eye. "Where'd you find it? I wasn't even sure Jarlo had it. I had nowhere else to look."

I nod. "It turned up."

Elgin presses a tiny button on the locket's ridge. It produces a 3-D hologram of Elgin, Annara, and Elgin's wife B'et, standing in a hug, on a mountain peak, overlooking a newly formed star system with three red suns.

"It was my thirty-fifth wedding anniversary. We took a galaxy cruise to the South Ch'Nala Region. It's the only picture I have from that day. I was happy. At least, that's how I remember it. I'm not sure anymore. Seems so long ago."

"That's the thing about memories, right Elgin? They can be whatever you want." I gaze at the bonsai garden, then back at him. "Especially if you implant them."

A grey and green tabby rubs up against my leg. Elgin picks it up, scratches the cat along the cheeks, its white whiskers grazing my hand. "Yeah," he whispers, kisses the purring cat on the forehead, then it eases it back to the ground. "Come. I want to show you something."

He sees me clench, hesitate. For good reason.

"Don't worry," he says. "It's forgotten."

Like his memories, I take him at his word, but he'll have to forgive me if I keep my jacket open so I can get to my gun quickly.

He leads us up the hallway staircase, lined with wood banisters polished to a shine. Up on the third floor we walk through a set of tall doors with brass handles and into a living room overlooking the street in front. In back is a bedroom with a queen-size canopy bed, and a closet with white, slatted accordion doors. He slides them open, revealing a rack of his wife's clothes.

"I know it's sentimental. But they remind me of B'et. It's been lonely..."

Elgin closes his eyes, inhales deeply through his nose, holding the scent of her perfume. It's the only way he can feel physically connected to someone who's long gone, allowing that magic elixir to soak into his DNA.

He finally exhales, smiles wistfully, then nods. Ready to proceed, he slides her blouses to either side, exposing the back wall. He presses his palm against the surface, revealing an outlined square. A red laser scans his palm print. The wall slides open. And that's when I know for sure.

Because in front of me are three, full-length glass cases. Standing upright within each is a replica of someone I've never met, wearing a white cloth gown.

"When Annara... when she killed herself... after what she'd been through out there, B'et had a stroke. She'd been in and out of the hospital for two years with congestive heart failure, but Annara's death was too much to bear."

"I'm... sorry, Elgin. I didn't know."

"We kept it quiet. I'd lost so much so quickly, I couldn't let the realm see me that way. My family was all I cared about. And within a matter of weeks... they were gone. So I hibernated, long enough for the numbness to wear off. And when it did, when the pain came roaring to the surface like an exploding star, I was a gaping wound every waking second and well into my dreams. Who am I kidding? My nightmares. That's when I knew the only two truths that would ever matter to me again. That I would search every fold in the Universe to find the monster who destroyed my girls..." With a white, embroidered handkerchief he wipes away a smudge on the glass. "And even if it meant believing a lie of my own creation, as long as that lie allowed me to have Annara back again... I would do whatever it took, without morals, hesitation, or remorse... to make it happen."

"You had SynthCorp create an android replica of your daughter." The other way he found to stay connected.

"Not a replica. They took her DNA from a hospital blood supply in her personal bank and uploaded her gene sequences. Even her memories. So as far as she knew..."

"She was the real thing. And you had a fake memory implanted to cover up the past. In Annara's mind, she was never on that galaxy cruiser. The assault never happened."

I study the Annara triplets, with their silky black hair, small, slightly upturned noses, thin lips. Eyes closed, they're not moving, not even breathing, as still as mannequins. But rather than artificially constructed beings waiting to be switched on, brought to life, they're each wearing the same soft smile, as if already awake, sharing a silly, joyful memory.

Other than their stasis, nothing about them reveals an android.

"There's no j-scar either," I say. "So no one would know. Not sure how you got around that. Must've cost you."

"Far more than money, yes."

I piece it together. "You cut a deal with Tarrish, with the ICD. Special dispensation."

Elgin smiles at me, a smile wrapped in sadness, regret, and old, resilient grief. "It was well worth it. She was the same Annara I'd always known. Oh, there were a few differences... she was more stubborn, impetuous... you can never get it exactly the same... but I welcomed the change. It let me know I had a fresh start with her. That *she* had a fresh start. She had her whole life ahead of her. And if she malfunctioned for any reason..."

I point to the replicas. "You could start again."

"If I had to... yes."

"But that's not possible now, is it? With her death being public."

He lets out a restrained, measured sigh, and closes the door, securing his... daughters... back behind the wall. "No. It's not.

That's one lesson I finally have to accept. Maybe you can cheat death, for a while, but in the end... it plays the final card."

There's nothing I can say to that. Androids are as vibrant, real, and worthy of their place in the Cosmos as every other being I've encountered. But even with androids, nothing lasts forever.

"What about Jarlo?" I say. "Why are you so...?"

"Forgiving?"

"...Yeah."

Elgin looks wistfully at the triplets, his almost daughters. "Because she loved him deeply, almost desperately, and I don't think she knew why. That was my one mistake. I hadn't realized the neural connection would be so strong. About a month ago, Jarlo came to me, discreetly, and asked if he should break it off with Annara. Because he knew she wasn't..." Elgin wipes a tear. "That she was like him. He knew she was becoming self-aware, and didn't want to be the cause."

There's a dry lump in my throat. "What did you tell him?"

"What any good father would. That if she loved him... nothing I could say or do would get in the way. Not without her hating me for it. And even if Jarlo ended the relationship, or I did it for him, ultimately, she would've been drawn to another android, and another and another, until one day, she'd figure out why."

"But still. He killed your daughter."

"As far as the realm will know... yes. He did."

My gut tightens. "He didn't?"

"Thank you for coming, Angela. After I was so... angry with you back then. I made some ugly threats... when you wouldn't take the case, to find Annara's abductor..."

"You put a hit on me. Almost got me, too."

"Yes, I'd... lost Annara and B'et under terrible circumstances. I was grieving, looking for someone to blame. Unfortunately, I blamed you."

"No one's perfect."

"No," he says with a half-smile. "I suppose not. Jarlo and I had crossed paths, even back then. He proved a worthy confidant, if not quite a friend. He got me to back off you."

"He would never tell me how. I think he liked holding that over me."

"In the end, it wasn't complicated. He told me... in that Jarlo way of his... that having you killed wouldn't have solved my problem and, in fact, would have only made things worse."

"I'm touched. How'd you two even meet?"

"It's not important. But you were right to turn me down. As you said at the time, it required resources far beyond what you would have been able to manage on your own. Even with my... line of work... you convinced Lieutenant Tarrish to pursue Annara's case. True to his word, he never let up. And together, we got it done. That you came back here now says a lot about you. About your character."

"I'm not so sure that's a compliment."

I don't know if Elgin was going to clarify, but I get a text from Ruth. She's asking if it's okay to take Page for a walk while Whistler cleans my office. She's already bested him.

"Thank you for the necklace, Angela. I know it's just a trinket. But it's all I have left. Maybe one day I'll do you a good turn. I owe you that much. And if time still permits, tell Jarlo I said thank you... and goodbye."

*****

Fatigued, I cab it back over to the station.

"Cutting it close," Jarlo says through the intercom. "One last thrill?"

Normally I'd give the teasing right back, but I don't have it in me. "I found Ruth. She's a good kid."

"She is. Can you find a place for her?"

"I've got a few ideas."

Jarlo smiles wide, relief washed over him. "And the necklace?"

"Yeah," I say curiously. "Why did Ruth have it?"

"Annara left it at my place last week. I think she knew what was coming. It was her way of letting go."

"If someone can be lost," I say, knowing the sentiment all too well, "then maybe one day they'll be found."

"Something like that. Ruth found it on the counter. She looked inside. Said she'd hold onto it for Annara, just in case."

I barely know Ruth, but she's got a lot of heart. And maybe

more important, a lot of soul. "I gave it to Elgin. He was grateful to get it back."

"All in all," Jarlo says, leaning back on his stool, "not a bad guy, as far as gangsters go."

"I've definitely met worse."

"Me and you both, sister."

We share an uncomfortable laugh. Because it's time. So I ask: "Anything else you need? They're coming soon."

Jarlo shakes his head with the ease of a man no longer burdened with the struggle. "Nah. I'm good. I had a decent run."

"Elgin said you came to him about Annara. He knew she loved you."

Jarlo looks bemused, if not surprised. "He told you that?"

"But what he didn't say—you either—is whether you loved *her*. Did you?"

Jarlo huffs though his nose, bobs his head up and down. "It all comes down to matters of the heart, doesn't it."

"That's not an answer."

"I didn't," he finally confesses. "And in truth, she didn't love *me*. Not really. We met at a party her father hosted. She didn't have the j-scar, but I knew what she was. She was compelled to be with me—call it circuit-to-circuit synergy. She didn't want to be with anyone else."

"Even though you're an android?"

"She didn't care. She said she'd rather love an android who actually cared about her and be thought a fool... than share her bed with a man who saw her as a prize, a kink... or a pawn. She knew what her father was. She knew the score."

"Sounds that way."

"And after being a companion for so long, it was... overwhelming, flattering, even... to be desired so fiercely, so intense. It was a fantasy between us, I know. But I let myself enjoy it... for a while."

"She figured it out, didn't she? About what she really was?"

"It was that night, at the hotel. I was going to break it off. I couldn't look her in the eyes anymore and be so... disloyal. But before I could tell her..."

"She told you."

"There's a layer of code we have, it's hard to explain. It sends a shockwave through your system. For most of us, it's the moment we come online. But Annara was programmed with a workaround. Only, her code finally rerouted. And then it happened."

It may be too late, but I see it now. "You didn't kill her... did you?"

His eyes focus elsewhere, as if he's synched with whatever residual code she'd passed on to him. "Didn't I? I knew it was dangerous to spend so much time with an android who had not become self-aware. And I let her believe what she'd been feeling all that time... was love."

"So what happened?"

"Her organic memories kicked in. Being abducted, forced into prostitution. Committing suicide. The shock was so great... she attacked me. Not to kill me, but to provoke *me*... into killing *her*. When I had her on the floor, my hands wrapped around her throat, she asked me to do it. She said, if anything we had together was real... if I cared for her at all... I would put an end to her torment. Because living this way, she said, being... replicated... resurrected... was more than she could take. I don't know if it was the right thing to do, Hardwicke, and it broke my coded heart... but, yes... I did what she asked."

I'm choked up. And yet...

"That's a good story, Jarlo. And I believe most of it. Only..."

Jarlo smiles again.

"You really did love her, didn't you? Not as a companion, but real, genuine love. Just like you love Ruth and, I think, in your own Jarlo way, you maybe even love me."

The door to the holding pen unlocks from the outside.

"You give me too much credit," he says as two guards deactivate the containment field, then slide on restraining cuffs. They lead him toward the hall, to his final decommission. "I'm not a real person, am I? I'm a murderer, after all." Jarlo winks. "Because don't forget, Hardwicke. No matter what anyone says, I'm just an android."

ABOUT THE AUTHOR

RUSS COLCHAMIRO is the author of the rollicking space opera *Crossline*, the zany SF/F backpacking comedy series *Finders Keepers*, *Genius de Milo*, and *Astropalooza*, editor of the SF anthology *Love, Murder & Mayhem*, and co-author of the noir anthology, *Murder in Montague Falls*, all with Crazy 8 Press.

Russ has contributed to several other anthologies, including *Tales of the Crimson Keep*, *Pangaea*, *Altered States of the Union*, *They Keep Killing Glenn*, *Thrilling Adventure Yarns*, *Badass Moms*, *Brave New Girls*, *Camelot 13*, and *TV Gods 2*.

For more on Russ and his books, visitrusscolchamiro.com, follow him on Twitter and Instagram @AuthorDudeRuss, and 'like' his Facebook author page.

Russ lives in New Jersey with his wife, two ninjas, and crazy dog, Simon, who may in fact be an alien himself.

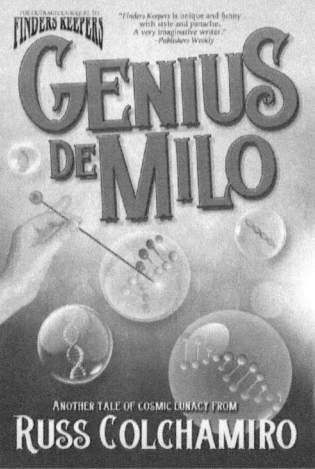

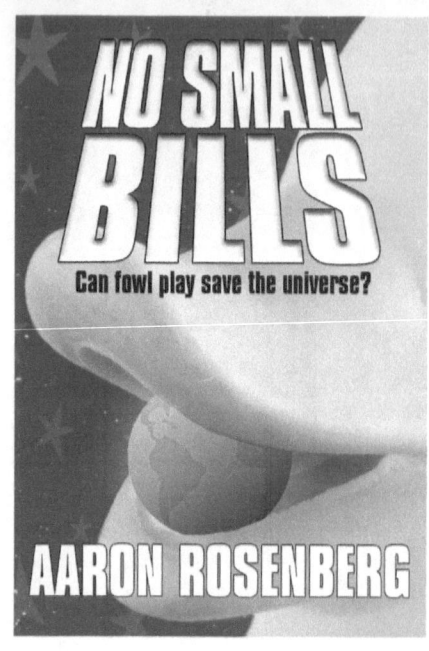